VIOLENCE & ROSES

JUSTIN BOURNE BORING

LITERARY DREAMS PUBLISHING

Contents

PRESENT DAY

My name is Mina, just Mina. I'm over two hundred years old, so my days of enduring narcissistic, lying, cheating assholes are over. Did I overreact by destroying an entire township in Jersey? Maybe, but sometimes you have to weigh consequences against comeuppance and scorch some earth. Sue me. I occasionally get a little stormy when someone rubs me the wrong way, but cheat on me, and you're gonna catch my claws. Fortunately for others, that did not happen often. My heart wasn't as black as my long straight hair, and my patience wasn't as pale as my alabaster skin, but I could be hard and unforgiving like my deep hazel eyes when it came to infidelity. Meh, I'm working on it.

Naturally, my recent shenanigans meant *they* would be coming for me, but it's okay; the just desserts were worth the calories. Besides, I'm finally ready to face *them*; it was long past due anyway—but that's a story for a little later.

In any case, I'm not the least bit ashamed to say I was deeply in love with a miserable phony prick for four years (a blink of an eye for me) or that I had recently agreed to marry said miserable phony prick a few days ago. When people are profoundly disingenuous about who they are, one can't be blamed for trusting them. I wear my heart on my sleeve; being powerful and ageless allows me to be vulnerable in ways others can not. However, the downside is that you tend to go to extremes when someone fucks you over.

Morristown, New Jersey? Collateral damage. Honestly, it was worth it. There's little left in the world that commands my full and total rage, and unfaithfulness is one of them. Not to mention, in all my years, I've known only one thing sweeter than love, and that's revenge.

When I received the call from Auri, my bestie of over a hundred years, and heard the frantic tone in her voice, I knew the shit was going down.

I answered my phone cheerfully, "Hello?"

"Mina? Hey, it's Auri," she blurted out.

"Hey, Auri. What's up? You sound... flustered." I wasn't used to hearing my normally even-tempered best friend so anxious.

"Flustered? Oh no, I'm pretty fucking far from flustered."

"What is it? Are you okay?"

"I'm across the street from that little dive bar here in Morristown, Goombas, and I'm staring at Roland... with his tongue crammed down some bimbo's throat." She whisper-screamed through the phone.

I became solemn and quiet. "You're serious?"

"I'm serious, Mina. Here..."

In an instant, my text message alert chimed. I opened it up, and there was a pic of Roland, my fiancé, my first true love in over 80 years, with his plump, pink tongue lapping some sluts cocksucker.

"Auri?"

"Yeah."

"Get out of there right now." My voice went deadly calm.

"Wha-" Auri scarcely had time to react.

"Get. Out. Of. There. *NOW*," I screamed.

"Okay, okay. But Mina, don't do anything rash -"

I hung up the phone and licked my drying lips. Motherfucker. Looks like honeybear is going to have to rain down some sulfur.

I flung open my front door and strolled out onto the sidewalk in nothing more than a sheer blouse and skirt. All six feet six inches of me (significantly short by Pentavi standards) was vibrating with angry anticipation. I breathed in the fragrant spring air, but it did little to quiet my wrath. Goombas was only about a mile away, and it was a beautiful night, so I decided to walk there. Maybe it would give me a chance to cool down a bit. Maybe not.

As I sauntered down the street with my curvy, muscular hips stepping in time, I began heating up instead of cooling down. My eyes smoldered and my body temperature rose dramatically. I used my well-toned, She-Hulk-sized frame to shoulder rudely through a group of people hanging out and talking on the sidewalk. They began to protest until they saw my burning eyes and felt the heat radiating off my body; then, they quickly backed away and took off like I was radioactive.

I left scorched footprints on the sidewalk with every bare step I took as the clothes I was wearing burned away from my body. The asphalt road next to me began to ripple and run like a black river as my hot, angry fury intensified. Cars driving past hit the asphalt pool and became stuck like dinosaurs in a tar pit, their wheels spinning before finally popping. The exterior paint on their cars bubbled, the heat threatening to cook the people inside alive. Trees all around me suddenly burst into flame, while the buildings glowed red hot. The windows started melting, and the bricks started exploding.

Pretty soon, the landscape behind me was a roaring fire about two thousand feet wide and growing. People were running and screaming from my epicenter as I strolled down the street like a violent act of nature. Buildings caught in my growing orbit began to wilt and run like warm butter. Cars were exploding and propelling embers into the sky that resembled a thousand devils' eyes as they rained down. This was only a small atom of my power.

As I approached Goombas, I saw Roland and his whore a few hundred feet down the road, fleeing the flames. He caught sight of me for a moment, and a terrible realization washed over him. They both made a mad dash towards a large church down the road while I slowly followed.

They began to stumble and waver within the field of my intense, inescapable heat. Finally, they fell to their knees and crawled toward the church doors in vain. They were on the verge of passing out, but Roland had the audacity to look pleadingly at me with those lying eyes.

That tore it. I unleashed every ounce of my power and focused it directly on them. Without warning, a fireball the size of an extinction level asteroid suddenly shot straight towards them, leaving a mile wide molten trench in its wake.

The two of them, dumb-struck, gawked in amazement as the white-hot comet instantly incinerated them, along with the church and a three-mile radius of Morristown, New Jersey.

The finale was an explosion the size of a small nuclear warhead that pushed a yellow and orange mushroom cloud towards the sky like a massive tombstone.

I thought of a fitting epitaph, "Here lies Roland. Roland lies, so Roland dies." I snickered and began to calm down a bit. I looked around and marveled at the refreshing destruction. Hell hath no fury indeed. I continued to look around and noticed I was stark naked. "Damn, I need a Macy's."

I could hear all manner of sirens and helicopters converging on the area, so I ducked away swiftly into the swirling smoke and falling ash.

The Story for a Little Later

I live - sorry, *lived*, in skanky suburban Morristown, New Jersey, for the better part of 20 years. After two hundred and thirty-ish years, you would think I'd be a billionaire living in a cliff side mansion somewhere on the coast of Italy; or perhaps some kind of highfalutin CEO in control of a major corporation, but nope, I'm just Mina—Mina, from the township formerly known as Morristown.

In any case, it has not been in my best interest to have a high profile in the past, no matter the circumstances, but I was looking to make a change. Come out. My...*indiscretion* from the other night was going to draw some *consequences*, but I anticipated that. In fact, I took my ex-fiancé's infidelity as a sign that it was finally time for me to face my *eccentric* family ancestry and their clans. I had recently grown curiously restless with the thought of confronting them. I was unbelievably tired of hiding, and I felt pretty certain my power had reached its apex, so I was spoiling for a fight something awful. I couldn't explain the feeling inside my gut, telling me I could finally take them on, but it was irresistible. Roland got what he deserved for sure, but it was also a test run of my power, and I was convinced I was ready, ready for retribution.

I was Yasmani Ro, which meant I was the hated, mongrel bitch daughter of outlaw lovers from two ancient warring clans known as the Pentavi, an all female shape-shifting clan, and the Sinteverete, an all male warlock clan.

Being the only despised Yasmani Ro in the last hundreds of thousands of years meant both clans had been tenaciously looking to capture or exterminate me—as they had my parents—since the day I was born.

A little backstory: Thousands of years before the first organism crawled out of the primordial soup, the Pentavi and Sinteverete lived peacefully together as one; they were the Zol. The Earth realm was theirs until fire rained down from the heavens, bringing new life with it. The destruction from their arrival and the evolution of this new life threatened the Zol and forced them into a vast, mystical realm, which they called Val Tebrae, accessible only through the conjuring of portals.

The Pentavi and Sinteverete lived together in Val Tebrae, angry and jealous of life in the Earth realm, which they perceived as having been taken from them. Their hatred of life on Earth grew and festered, poisoning their minds until mutual hatred was all they had. Naturally, it wasn't enough to keep them from eventually turning on each other.

The fuse was lit after a very talented young Sinteverete warlock was instructed by the Elders to create a spell for agelessness called The Eonian. The Eonian, when cast by a Pentavi or Sinteverete clan member, allowed them to live forever and choose their age at will, but the spell was not synonymous with immortality. Members of the Pentavi and Sinteverete under the influence of The Eonian could still be killed, but only in battle. This provision appealed to the Pentavi and Sinteverete Elder's burgeoning lust for war and power.

The toxic spell further exacerbated a gender divide between the clans and would soon lead to their uncoupling. Once the Pentavi and

Sinteverete no longer needed one another to perpetuate the blood-lines, the chasm widened between the males and females.

The Pentavi and Sinteverete stopped training with one another, weakening their abilities and ensuring no one gender could ever wield both clans' powers. Disputes degenerated into bloodletting, petty squabbles became war, and greed became God.

The Pentavi and Sinteverete people could no longer live together under one clan, so they split based on gender, known as the Great Divide, and criminalized having any more Yasmani Ro children. They no longer had to share anything with each other or future generations, so the clan Elders wanted everything for themselves. At the provoca-tion of the Elders, the clans fought with one another for millions of years until a tense treaty was drafted. Both clans created laws in order to maintain the benefits, as well as their segregation. They were now forever in pursuit of domination over one another, the Earth, and all the other realms.

There were miles of rules and regulations behind this weak treaty between the Pentavi and Sinteverete clans, but it was their laws sur-rounding coupling and procreation that were the most binding. It was forbidden and punishable by the pain of torture and death for mem-bers of the Pentavi and Sinteverete clans to bear any more Yasmani Ro children.

The Pentavi and Sinteverete clans, along with their Elders, were all under the Eonian, like myself (thanks to my parents), but they possessed vastly different abilities. The Pentavi, for example, have superhuman strength and intelligence, can cast mid-level spells and shape-shift into huge, regal feline creatures resembling jaguars, called yaggowar. The Sinteverete are powerful warlocks who can cast ex-tremely high-level spells, have incredible strength and physical abilities, and are hyper-intelligent. Since my parents trained me in the ways of both the Pentavi and Sinteverete, I possess all their abilities. I never stopped training and doggedly honed every one of my skills. This gave me an incredible advantage over either side.

My parents met when war broke out on the Pentavi lands before moving to the blood-soaked battlefield of a war realm known as Reclon. There were hundreds of these war realms, but Reclon was the worst. It was lousy with monstrous beasts, some so big they could be mistaken for mountains. Massive tornadoes of toxic ash and acidic vapor swirled constantly, while oily black rain poured down, but those were the good days. When the seven suns came out, blood turned to vapor the moment it hit the air, and the heat could cook you like a sausage if you didn't constantly manage your protection spells. Savage tribes of mindless rouges fed off the coagulated blood and fetid flesh of fallen warriors, while vicious, poisonous, carnivorous plants constantly lay in wait for any and all unsuspecting victims. Caustic oceans and acid rivers cut through the jagged, rocky terrain like toxic arteries; it was a hellscape of unimaginable cruelty.

My mother, Layluna, seemed to cherish the time she spent with the Pentavi, reflecting proudly on her training and service to the clan and her sisters. She was very young when the Great Divide split the genders but grew up and chose to remain at an adult age indefinitely, as most did. She largely supported their departure from Zol and condemned the Sinteverete for their relentless pursuit of control over the Pentavi women. In the end, she would ultimately realize the Pentavi Elders were no better than the Sinteverete Elders in their selfish quest for power.

My mother had dark green eyes, just like me, set within the porcelain skin of her face like emeralds, as well as a head full of long, abyss-black hair. She was a bold, brilliant, free-thinking spirit-of-fire, and I loved her dearly. She always wore the traditional Pentavi

Ceridome wraps until she passed them down to me. The Ceridome wraps were long, black silk strips decorated with elegant blood-red symbols and edged raggedly in gold to mark her rank. Almost like a mummy, the wraps crisscrossed chaotically over much of her body, except her head, hands and feet. The enchanted wraps accommodated yaggowar transformations with style and flair. Additionally, the straps would sheath and carry their weapons after yaggowar transformations. Being touched by magic, they were as hard as light armor but as flexible and breathable as cotton. Each Pentavi woman enchanted their wraps with different spells, making them a lethal weapon when needed. Equally as important, they carried the wearer's life story, usually one of warning. This was the uniform of the Pentavi and was embellished or decorated per the style and desire of the woman wearing them. Layluna was considered a bit of a rebel because she never wore armor, only her Ceridome wraps—nothing else. She never wore anything within her long, flowing, midnight-black hair either, but she sometimes wore a large, round, black, flat amiboshi hat when there was bad weather. I, too, wear her Ceridome wraps, but far more discreetly; I wasn't trying to advertise it after all.

My father, Vasser the Voracious, was head of the Nevuscar, or The Undying, a very small, very formidable sect of seven Sinteverete warriors who are almost as old as the Elders. They are the most powerful Sinteverete warriors and are truly immortal. While they cannot be killed traditionally or in battle, they are susceptible to incarceration and certain magic.

They possess a hyper-healing ability with one catch—they can only heal through the formation of scar tissue, so they do not retain their stunning good looks. When you see a Nevuscar, you know it.

My father, however, was impossibly handsome, possessed a classy gentlemanly disposition and was very stoic. He was naturally pale and ghostly like the rest of us, but was stippled with small gray freckles that made him very unique. He always wore his Absence of Light cloak, a cloak so black it was like staring into the Devil's heart. It was as powerful as a black hole, and fit like a tight coat, buttoned up the front by three rows of two side-by-side silver metallic coins. The massive hood enveloped his head and shoulders like a death shroud; only his two blood-red eyes could be seen floating within its lurking shadows. Always by his side was Sepultura, his cursed Blade of Black, one of the most powerful blades in all the realms. It had more trapped souls within its steel than any other of its kind.

The most important difference between Vasser and the other six Nevuscar was related to their rank and the reason Vasser was the leader; he had only one six-inch-scar that curved from the right corner of his mouth to the crux of his eye. Only my mother knew how he got the scar, but she never told me. Each of the other six Nevuscar knew their rank because they knew exactly how many scars they had, ranging from a couple hundred to several hundred thousand. Any Nevuscar could tell you the skin story behind each and every one of their scars.

My father was a very rare breed. He was once married to a Pentavi woman before the Great Divide, but she was killed in the ensuing wars. The Elders had long ago bred him to become a Nevuscar, which was only possible using special magic on an unborn Yasmani Ro child. He always fulfilled his obligations to the Sinteverete Elders but was a wild card. After the Great Divide, there were no more Yasmani Ro children; therefore, there were no more Nevuscar.

Now for my story...

"I'm pregnant," Layluna blurted out.

Vasser wore a look of complete shock. "How can you know?"

"Trust me, a lady knows," Layluna promised confidently.

"I'm going to be a father?" Vasser gasped, the entirety of the situation dawning on him.

"Looks that way, daddy," Layluna smiled and looked up into his astonished eyes.

"I've never been happier in my entire life," Vasser yelled, coming to life. "This is...a big change. I guess we can't go off trying to unite the clans and collecting the heads of our Elders now. What are we going to do?"

"Well, the way I see it, all bets are off. We have a child to think about now. It flips our path on its head." Layluna paced back and forth. "While I can't stand the thought of my sisters fighting and dying in Reclon, or the Elders getting away with their genocide, we have to redraw our destiny."

"What are you suggesting?" Vasser asked pleadingly.

"We can hide out in the Mandala realm. Time passes six times slower there than it does here or in the Reclon realm. We can train her, educate her, armor her against our oppressors. Then, we can fight by her side."

"Her?" Vasser asked.

Layluna smiled, "Her."

"How can you know?" Vasser demanded.

"I can sense her Alma—her soul smoke. What do you think of Mina as a name?" she asked tentatively.

Vasser sat down hard on a rock and put his head in his hands. "I think it's a beautiful name. I also think this is the most terrified I've ever been in my life," he chuckled.

"Good," Layluna said, smiling. "That means you will do it right."

Vasser and Layluna stood tensely on the edge of a swirling black portal to the Mandala realm.

"This is it," Vasser told Layluna, his arm around her, holding her tightly. "It's important you know I will never stop fighting to make sure you and Mina are safe."

"Same," Layluna said poignantly. "I think I love that about you."

"I think I love you," Vasser said nonchalantly.

"I think I love you too," Layluna said, putting her hands on his face and turning him toward her. "I know..."

"I know too." They shared a rare and tender kiss that filled them both with hope and promise. "Don't go hiding the marriage stone just yet," Vasser joked.

Layluna held up the blue worry stone and grinned ear-to-ear. "That's precisely what I intend to do." With that, she lept through the portal into the Mandala realm.

Vasser called out to her, laughing, "I'll give you a full minute to hide it."

Suddenly, her hand reached out of the portal, grabbed him by his collar and yanked him through.

When Vasser emerged on the other side, he was struck by how lovely the realm was; the only issue was everything, and I mean everything, was a different shade of blue. Layluna laughed, "Good luck."

Vasser grinned and began to whisper chant, but Layluna silenced him with a kiss. "No cheating, suitor."

Vasser let out a great sigh and began searching, "I don't get one hint?"

"It's within a hundred feet radius," she laughed.

Vasser stiffened, turned and wrapped his arms around her. As he kissed her passionately, he reached inside her wraps and touched the worry stone. "I knew you would never take this off."

"Then you know me." It was Layluna's turn to kiss Vasser passionately.

"And you me." They held each other and watched the blue dwarf sun set behind the myriad shades of blue that comprised the landscape.

The Undeniable Truth

One warm summer morning, when Mina was still just a wide-eyed, wonder filled little girl around the age of six, she learned a harsh, but very important lesson. She was desperately trying to help Layluna deliver their beloved mare's foal, but the little blue and gray colt was in dire straits. The foaling had not gone well, the mare was experiencing dystocia, and the baby was improperly positioned for birth. Both the mother and baby's lives hung in the balance as Layluna quickly realized they were going to have to make a very tough decision: either they were going to have to sacrifice the mare in order to save the foal, or they would have to forfeit the foal to save the mare. Naturally, Mina was bound and determined to save them both, but Layluna knew in her experience of raising horses it was impossible. They would have to either save one or the other. "I'm sorry, bunny, but we need to choose which one we save."

Tearful and despondent, Mina clearly could not make up her mind. She had grown up with the mare, Freya, but had been so excited about the birth of her foal, she simply could not bring herself to make the impossible choice. "I can't do it, mommy. I can't pick."

"I know it seems unimaginable, but we have to make a decision, and it has to be made now or they will both die." Layluna's heart broke for her daughter, but knew she needed to learn the hard lesson.

Tears continued to stream down Mina's cheeks as she buckled under the incredible pressure. "I can't, I can't, I can't..." She screamed in mounting hysteria, so Layluna pulled her away and held her tight.

"I know this isn't fair or easy, but this is what life is for most of us," Layluna told her weeping child. "We have to be ready to make hard, split-second decisions in the heat of the moment. They won't always be right, and they won't always give us the results we want, but right or wrong, we have to make those choices and stand by them. We do the best we can and live our lives without regret. Do you understand, Mina? If we don't do something right now, they will both die."

"Which one should I choose?" Mina begged Layluna for an answer, but ultimately knew only she could make the call.

"I can't tell you that, bunny," Layluna said through her own burgeoning tears. "Freya is your mare, and I can't be the one to tell you what to do. I can tell you this, as a mother, I would have gladly given my life to save you. I truly believe any mother would tell you the same."

This seemed to resonate with Mina, who bit her quivering lip to the point of drawing blood, and told her mother, "Save the foal."

Layluna acted immediately and brought Beauty out from the sheath on her hip. She took in a deep, ragged breath and began an emergency cesarean on the mare. "Grab hold of the colt's neck and front leg, Mina," Layluna instructed. "When I tell you, pull as hard as you possibly can." Mina positioned herself and grabbed hold of the foal as her mother split Freya's belly up the center in order to free the tangled colt within. "NOW," Layluna screamed, and Mina, sobbing, hauled the troubled foal out with all her might. The umbilical cord broke, and Layluna went to work cleaning the colt as soon as it was clear of Freya. Mina rushed to cradle Freya's head in her arms and reassured her softly that she loved her dearly as the life left her eyes. Crushed, Mina wept from deep within her gut and refused to let go of Freya's head. Layluna was able to get the foal up and standing right away, so she led it over to the barn and put it inside.

Upon returning, Layluna saw Mina still sitting there with Freya. She gently placed her hand on her head, stroked it a few times and gave her time to process. After a few hours, Layluna came back out with a blue, bear skin fur and draped it over her shivering daughter's shoulders. "It's getting cold out here. Can I convince you to come inside?" Mina did not answer, rather she hugged Freya's thick neck and continued to whimper. Layluna had her answer.

The next morning, Mina was still out by the barn holding Freya. Layluna quietly came down and let the colt out to run free and frolic in the early morning fog. Then she brought Mina some water and pressed oats, but she refused both. "Eventually you will have to move past this Mina and lay her to rest."

"How can I? I chose for her to die," Mina finally said.

"You chose for her colt to live. That means he will live to grow up into a stallion and bring his mother's and father's essence into future generations. I'm very proud of you." Layluna had never felt such pride. "Now, you've made the choice, and it's time you stand by it. I think you should help me bury Freya." Layluna was comforting, but firm.

"I killed her. How can I ever forgive myself?" Mina screamed inconsolably.

Layluna wrapped her arms around her and hugged her tightly. "Let me see your hand; there's something I want to show you," she whispered into her ear. Mina allowed Layluna to take her hands and placed them softly on Freya's head. "There's a simple, but very powerful little spell I learned back when I was a child, and I want to teach it to you now. You can only cast it three times in your lifetime, and this will be my third; but I can't imagine a more appropriate instance to use it. It's called the undeniable truth, and that's exactly what it will show you."

Mina wiped the tears from her red and raw eyes, then tilted her head towards her mother. "What can the truth show me?" Mina sniffled. "The truth is, I killed her to save her colt."

"The truth is not always a straight line, bunny." Layluna squeezed Mina tightly. "There are many facets to the truth, but context and understanding can oftentimes be elusive." She kissed the top of her head. "Here, let me show you. Close your eyes..." Mina closed her eyes along with Layluna. "Now picture Freya."

"Okay, I am..." Mina wrinkled her brow in concentration.

"Keep your hands on her head and think really hard about what you want to know. Any questions you want answered, or memories you want explored..." Layluna said gently.

"I want to know—" but Layluna silenced her.

"Shhhh, think about the question and memories; internalize them..."

Mina did as she was told, and Layluna began quietly chanting words repeatedly that were forever etched in her mind. Their hands began to glow, and Freya's eyes shot open with twin beams of light that began projecting images on the fog. They were Freya's memories with the stallion, Woe, who fathered the colt; and it was memories of Mina with them. The images struck her heart deeply, because she remembered seeing them from her own perspective. After a moment, Mina saw herself playing with the two horses in the summer moonlight, feeding them apples and pears and grooming them lovingly.

Then it wasn't just the images compelling Mina, it was the feelings and affection associated with them that suddenly flooded her senses. The love she felt for Freya and Woe, and the love they felt for her filled her with such an overwhelming sense of joy, she thought she might float away.

Then things darkened, and she saw Woe, cold and still on his side in the opposite stall to Freyas. Mina remembered how she felt when Layluna told her he had died, but it was absolutely soul crushing to feel that coupled with Freya's sadness and loss as well. Tears streamed down Mina's cheeks as her heart fluttered and wavered from the melancholy of the memory.

The story took another turn, and she was seeing Freya's memories from the night before; the pain she felt, the fear for herself and her colt, and the sadness...it all hit Mina at once and she cried out. She tried to pull her hands off the mare's head, but Layluna kept careful pressure on them so she could not. The sadness Freya felt was directed entirely at the weighty decision Mina had to make, and the mare desperately wanted to spare her that pain. This was like a massive load being lifted from her chest, but it was Freya's certainty that she wanted Mina to save the foal—at the cost of her own life—that unburdened her heart profoundly. Freya's dying wish was that Mina save her foal, and that's exactly what she had done. Mina collapsed in her mother's arms.

Layluna was also privy to the images, sensations and emotions, which gave her incredible insight into her daughter's poignant lesson. They released their hands and Freya's eyes went dark again, the two hugging each other tightly in the deafening silence. Layluna held Mina for a very long time, carefully choosing her moment to speak. "A mother wants nothing more than their children to be safe and loved. It's all I ever wanted for you, and it's all Freya ever wanted for her colt. You gave that to her."

Mina turned and hugged her mother fiercely, crying tears of joy. "Thank you, Mommy. Thank you..."

"Of course, bunny. I would do anything for you." Layluna kissed the top of her head again. "It's how I knew Freya's undeniable truth."

Out of nowhere, Mina suddenly felt a cold, wet nose nudging her hand. It was Freya's colt, tentatively probing her for need, while simultaneously showing her his trust and love. Mina scooped up his head in her hands and kissed him right on the lips, before almost hugging his head off. "Oh, you sweet boy."

The colt then nudged his mother's muzzle pitifully, but Mina was there to reassure him, "Your mother gave her life for you, and I will make sure that's not for nothing. You are safe and loved." The colt began to nudge Mina again, prompting another forceful hug from the girl.

"What will you name him, bunny?"

"His name will be Heartache," Mina said confidently.

"I think that's an absolutely beautiful name." Layluna hugged her sweet child, knowing if any of the clans came looking for trouble, they would find it in her and Vasser.

Eighteen years passed in Val Tebrae and Reclon, where a hundred and eight had passed in the Mandala realm. The war between the clans raged on in Reclon, while in Mandala, Mina had become a fierce warrior, blessed with the advantage of both Pentavi and Sinteverete training. Choosing to remain a gorgeous thirty years of age, with long, straight jet-black hair and piercing emerald eyes, Mina flourished and shared a loving, wonderful and fulfilling life there with her parents. However, always looming was the reality that they might be discovered, or at the very least they would soon have to face the Elders again, and try to put an end to the war.

Vasser and Layluna cast the Eonian over Mina on her third birthday, and on her eighteenth, informed her of their complicated plans to unite the clans and kill the remaining eleven Elders. They explained where Vasser and Layluna's trophy case containing the three collected heads of Layluna's Elders was located; deep in the dark lands of Val Tebrae, within a magnificent slab of pale Pentavi granite, marked with a simple rune. Layluna had Vasser repair Beauty's shattered granite blade and handed her down to Mina shortly after explaining her destiny. Mina took to Beauty like a bird to song and mastered her in no time at all. Beauty's new blade still had the fatter, half spear-tipped end, and narrow neck carved from white Pentavi granite, but with serrations on the top side and poignant symbols etched into the surface. Beauty retained her original handle, which fit into Mina's grasp like a lover's hand.

Layluna was a proud, loving mother who beamed with pride every time Mina walked into view. She taught her absolutely everything she knew, and Mina was like a thirsty sponge, absorbing every detail.

Vasser was also a wonderful, patient and kind father. He loved Mina more than anything in the realms and it showed. He would spend hours upon hours training her, educating her, and teaching her about the Sinteverete—good and bad.

Mina couldn't ask for more attentive, dedicated and loving parents. She flourished with them in the Mandala realm.

Many years later...

Mina was in the garden with Layluna, toiling in the surprising heat of the neighboring blue dwarf sun, when a snowflake lazily landed on her nose. "What's this? A snowflake in summer?" Mina proclaimed. Then it hit her like a bolt from the blue. "Nevuscar," she screamed. Layluna snapped her attention towards the sky, and there, swirling above them, was the growing Nevuscar portal. Snow began pouring out of the massive black hole, freezing their crops, as well as their hearts.

"Well, well, well, there's my favorite pussycat," a familiar voice called out from between the blue corn. Bael, Vasser's former second in command of the Nevuscar—now last in command—emerged from the center row naked and covered in thick, corded scars, with a coarse coppery mohawk growing through the asphalt of his head as best it could. The only thing he was wearing was what looked like a sleek, maroon plate of etched armor around the back of his head that covered his ears. His filthy presence wilted the crop of corn with his toxic aura. "And look here. A Yasmani Ro." He wagged his finger at Layluna, scolding her. "That's a no no."

Layluna, wearing only a long, black, modest robe garment, stood slowly from her aqua colored radishes, with a storm brewing in her heart. "Bael."

"In the flesh," he proclaimed.

"So to speak," Layluna corrected him. "I see my husband left you as handsome on the outside as you are on the inside."

Six tall, imposing Nevuscar warriors suddenly emerged from the remaining six rows of corn. Layluna recognized four of them, but the other two, completely void of scars, were unknown to her.

"I see you've replenished your ranks with a new breed." Layluna colloquially said, vying for any intel she could coax out of them.

One of the two new, unblemished Nevuscar fighters standing an imposing ten-feet-tall, and wide as a barn, stepped forward in front of Bael. "You are correct. I am Mayax The Malevolent. I am now Lord and leader of the Nevuscar." Mayax was disarmingly handsome. His long, flowing black hair framed an angular face before joining his long, burly braided beard down below. His eyes burned black with no pupil, like a shark's eyes. However, instead of an Absence of Light cloak, he wore a sleek, intimidatingly wicked black helmet, with spiraled horns reaching to the heavens. The other Nevuscar were also wearing helmets, although theirs were maroon. Now Bael's headpiece made more sense to Layluna. Mayax wore no cape or cloak, but he wore thorny, form fitting armor, carved from the impenetrable black shell of a Reclon titan. The other five Nevuscar boasted similar maroon colored insect armor instead of the traditional leathers that Vasser still wore.

Layluna was without her Ceridome wraps, or any weapons, for that matter. All she had was a spade, which she clutched as though it were a broadsword.

Mina tore off her dirty burlap poncho to reveal she was wearing Layluna's Ceridome wraps underneath, and sheathed within them, as always, was Beauty and her new blade. Mina pulled her out, showing off the wicked white granite knife.

"That's quite a blade," Mayax admitted flatly.

"Beauty is a blade," Mina replied stoically.

Layluna chuckled in spite of herself.

"Indeed, it is," Mayax admitted with zeal. "There's just something so irresistible about an outlaw woman on the run. What is your name?"

"Mina," she said curtly, trying to stall for time, "And I guess you are what my father warned us about, the unnatural, abomination conjured without a womb by both of our conspiratory Elders?"

"Conspiratory? That's a laugh. We are crushing the last few hundred of your Pentavi sisters in the Reclon realm as we speak, so what need would our Elders have to conspire with yours? In any case, you can stop trying to stall us," Mayax grumbled. "Vasser has arrived."

Vasser walked briskly up from behind Layluna and Mina in his traditional Sinteverete uniform, with Sepultura out and at the ready. "Took you guys long enough to find us."

"We found you; that is all that matters," Mayax stated coldly.

Vasser began to whisper chant, but Mayax smiled and tapped the side of his helmet. "New toys for a new breed." Vasser immediately charged Mayax with the tip of Sepultura leading the way, but Mayax didn't flinch an inch. Vasser suddenly froze in mid-charge, Sepultura millimeters from Mayax's eye. "We have accomplished much in the last eighteen years," Mayax taunted. He reached into Vasser's leathers, fished out the white and red swirling round pendant that contained the tortured remains of Vasser's former last in command, The Wrecking Ball, and unceremoniously yanked it off his neck.

Vasser spoke through clenched teeth, "See you soon."

"Promises, promises." With a blink of his eye, Mayax turned Vasser into a pillar of salt. Layluna wailed out mournfully, clutching her marriage stone before joining him in a twin pillar of salt.

"NOOOO," Mina screamed, but she knew better than to charge the Nevuscar leader, or his cronies. "Undo it." She quietly demanded threateningly.

Mayax maintained his smug smile and shook his head. "And what will you do if I don't, little girl? What can you possibly do? This is not a circumstance that facilitates your calling for demands."

Mayax nodded and motioned to the other six Nevuscar. They put their hands together, almost as if to pray, and a gargantuan slab of rare white Pentavi granite levitated above the corn, and over to their position. The tall monolith slowly touched down, crushing the blue squash and pumpkins in their garden.

Mina looked on, confused and frantic. "What the hell are you going to do with that?"

Mayax simply ignored her, looked to the slab of Pentavi granite, and a large door opened up in it. He turned his head towards the two pillars of salt that were Mina's loving parents not two minutes before and levitated them inside the granite with his mind.

"Don't do it, mage." Mina promised death and destruction with her eyes. "Don't fucking do it."

Mayax continued to smile pleasantly as the Pentavi granite sealed, imprisoning her parents. A strange rune of embracing figures etched itself into the slick surface.

"There, I've done it. What will you do now?" Mayax's smile widened to a toothy grin.

Mina stood there like a statue for a very long time with nothing to say.

"Well?" Mayax asked again, but Mina remained there; motionless. Mayax squinted and chuckled. "Looks like Mina has moxy." He strolled up to her and tapped the tip of her nose with his first finger, dispersing her cast off skin like an ash cloud into the wind. "She's clever, this one. Apparently, they've done some upgrades as well; never seen that little trick. Find her." The other six Nevuscar levitated up into the air and went in six different directions. Mayax chuckled as he attached Vasser's Wrecking Ball prison pendant to his belt.

Mina watched them from a far-off ridgeline. "They're still alive; that's all that matters." She then whisper chanted, snapped her fingers, and disappeared.

1870 During the Meiji Period in old Japan...

Later the next day in the Earth realm. "Hey. You. Giant woman. What the Hell are you doing in my garden?"

Mina sprang awake as a strange little old man poked her with a stick, while hollering at her in a foreign tongue. He was wearing strange sandals with tall wooden slats, a round straw hat with a pointed top, and dirty, tattered robes that looked like they needed a wash. It reminded Mina of when she used to garden with her mother and father. "Who are you?" The old man yelled again. She couldn't understand a word he said but held up her hands as if to say she meant no harm. The old man stared at her long, straight black hair, pale alabaster skin, and large round green eyes. "You are clearly not from around here. Western? Ugh, you probably don't speak a word of Japanese."

Mina tried to speak and used very docile, calm tones to try to communicate to him that she meant no harm. "Mina," she said, tapping her chest.

"I don't give a damn who you are; get your gigantic ass the hell outta my garden." He continued to clamor in a strange language.

Mina shrugged her shoulders and shook her head. The old man sighed a great sigh and motioned for her to follow him inside his home. What choice did either of them have? She followed the tiny old man into his gorgeous, intricately carved wooden house, with framed paper doors and straw mats. Mysterious runes painted on long paper scrolls hung smartly from the walls inside. She stole a glance over her shoulder back at the garden and marveled at how beautiful it was. There were preciously trimmed little trees in stone pots, and lovely flowers everywhere. Large trees with amazing pink blossoms lined the garden's perimeter and stone statues of strange men stood throughout. There was so much color Mina couldn't believe it. She had spent over a hundred years with only a thousand different shades of blue in the Mandala realm, so this was a sensory overload. In any case, she reeled in her fascination.

Once inside, the little old man poured her a cup of tea from a delicate tea pot while setting his hat down on the table. He poured himself a cup, bowed and drank. She bowed her head as well and drank with him. The tea was absolutely delicious.

She suddenly gulped it down greedily, but the little old man protested with a grunt and lightly smacked her hand. He shook his head no and demonstrated how to sip it slowly and politely. Mina rolled her eyes, which proffered her another smack from the little old man. She relented, smiled and showed she could properly sip tea. To this he smiled a great big, gummy grin and clapped the table with his hand. He then clapped his chest and said, "Geezer."

"Geezer," Mina repeated carefully.

Geezer shook his head happily up and down, while continuing to pat his chest. Mina smiled and thanked him.

After tea, Geezer motioned for Mina to follow him outside. A magnificent sunset stole Mina's breath away, and she gawked at it for what seemed like an eternity. She finally snapped out of it and saw Geezer standing there patiently waiting for her to finish taking it all in. When he was certain she was with him again, he led her down a path through the garden, and towards a clearing. Once they got there, he selected a strangely simple but beautiful forged sword from a modest armament. He tapped the sheath that contained Beauty within her Ceridome wraps and smiled that silly smile. She looked at him with a wrinkled brow and shrugged her shoulders, "What, you want to fight?" she asked, punching the air with her hands.

He quickly shook his head vigorously up and down.

She laughed and condescended down to him. "Wow. Listen little fella, I'd hate to injure you accidentally by playing too rough..." But before she could finish her sentence, he moved like a phantom, had her on her ass, and bent her wrist impossibly backwards. "Hey," she protested. He let her go and helped her up with a smile. She brushed herself off and tried to sucker punch the old timer, but he was already ten moves ahead of her. There she was again, staring up at the sky on her ass. He leaned in over her and helped her back up with that same smile. Geezer grabbed hold of her waist and walked her to the center of the clearing. He motioned for her to stay there and positioned himself in front of her. He bowed to her, and she reciprocated. Geezer raised his sword, let out an impressive battle cry and charged her. She was out with Beauty now, her old friend giving her the focus she needed. As if moving in slow motion, Mina hooked Geezers blade in Beauty's serrations, and snapped it like a twig before putting the salty samurai on his own ass. She leaned over him, extended her hand and helped him up with a smile. Once he was up and stable, he looked at his broken sword and nodded slowly with his grin widening across his weathered face.

"Sorry about that," Mina apologized, but Geezer waived it off and selected another strange weapon of war. "You know, for a little old guy, you're sure full of piss and vinegar."

To this, he nodded his head again slowly and smiled his silly smile.

Later that night, Mina laid on a straw mat in Geezer's main living space and cried for her parents. She was quiet about it, but Geezer could see her through a gap in the paper door of his loft. He knew she had sustained a great loss and was a stranger out of place.

The next morning, as the sun came up, Mina opened her eyes and saw Geezer staring down at her, smiling. "Whoa," she said, startled. He patted her on the shoulder and led her to the garden. There, he put a little piece of rice paper in her hand. She unfolded it and saw a simple but beautiful brush drawing of a young girl. Geezer patted the drawing and then patted his heart. He then pointed over to a gravestone in the center of the garden. It must have been his wife, or daughter; his daughter, she wagered. As realization spread across her face, Geezer knew she understood and grabbed her hands in his. He pulled her down to a kneeling position so they could be face-to-face. He patted her heart, then he patted his own heart again and hugged her. Unable to contain it, Mina let loose her floodgates of sorrow and burst into tears while Geezer held her tight and patted her back. He shushed her and stroked her hair while she let it all out.

When Mina had dried her last tear, Geezer let her go. She stood up, and he smiled at her. She smiled back at him. He grabbed her hand and led her back inside to a bowl of rice and a dumpling. He pointed to the bowl of rice and said, "gohan." She didn't repeat it, so he stuck his finger in the rice and said, "gohan."

"Oh, rice. Rice is gohan." She clapped.

He nodded his head, pleased with her. Then he tapped the bowl and said, "Cho."

This time she repeated, "Cho. Bowl is cho."

He nodded his head again and gave a reassuring grunt. Then he tapped himself, to which she replied, "Geezer."

He nodded and smiled again. She really liked this guy.

CHAPTER 1
BORN OF FIRE AND ICE

"Tell me about the day you were born," Geezer asked, precariously perched on a thick, taut rope tied between two barren trees across the face of a plunging, massive frost-encrusted waterfall. The sun was peeking behind the mountains, painting the sky in magnificent oranges and purples, but cast everything below it in a cold, monochromatic shadow. Geezer was wearing one of his out of style, dusty kimonos, had grown a long, shaggy goatee, and was showing off how great his balance was on the rope with his high, slat sandals. The air was crisp, on its way towards winter. There were only a few scant brown leaves still left clinging to the gnarly limbs of the cherry trees, and the sky smelled of the season's first snow.

Mina was still scantily clad in only her Ceridome wraps but didn't boast even one goose bump, despite how cold it was. She was five feet in front of Geezer, on the same rope above the abyss, clinging to it impressively with her pale, bare feet. "Seriously? Come on." Mina complained loudly in Japanese. She had all but perfected the language in just under a few months and had been speaking it fluently for the last 18.

Geezer used his "discipline stick," which was really just a long, thin rod of petrified bamboo, to smack her in the head as he often was wont to do. "GIT. Nanananana, answer."

Mina sighed deeply, trying simultaneously to maintain her balance on the rope and remember the story her mother and father had told her in great detail a million times. "Well, I was born in the Mandala realm, a beautiful realm that boasted a billion shades of boring blue," she began saying sarcastically at first, but became sadly nostalgic as she went on. "It was a cold and bitter winter...My father was struggling to find enough food to keep my mother strong. She was at the end of her pregnancy with me, and he shrank to half his weight keeping her fed. She kept insisting he eat, but he refused. He is immortal, but he still feels the pain of starvation just as much as he feels the pain of lost love, or parted flesh." She choked up with tears at the memory and almost lost her balance.

"Focus. Go on..." Geezer threatened politely with the discipline stick but was now more interested in hearing the rest of her story than he was in teaching her the lesson.

Mina, swaying a bit with her tall frame, found her balance again. "My mother always said father was his strongest when he was at his weakest; his spirit always burning the brightest when things were their bleakest." The words leaving her lips like poetry now. "Vulnerability was his strength." She lingered on the word strength for a long pause before going on, "Naturally, my mother went into labor when the snow began to fall, and they were at the apex of their hardship and famine." Unbelievably, it started to snow on Mina and Geezer in perfect time with the story. Mina had a strange feeling, an electric connection to the snow as it accumulated on her bare skin. "My father fought a brutal blizzard and a failing shelter during a difficult childbirth, all so he could safely bring me into the world without killing my mother." The tears were coming now, but quickly turned to ice in the harsh, snowy winds blowing in from the waterfall. "My mother and father always insist the next part of the story is entirely true, but I suspect they were embellishing things for my benefit." Geezer was completely enthralled in the story at this point, so she continued, "According to them, there was a lunar, blue dwarf star eclipse that day, and at the very moment the moon moved in front of the dwarf star, I was born. The air turned to ice, and the ground beneath their feet shook disastrously in a violent ground quake. This galactic force of nature caused a nearby gargantuan, but long-dormant volcano to suddenly erupt and spew fire miles into the atmosphere, directly over our heads. It forced hot embers and ash down on our shoulders with the fiercely blowing snow, but my weak and weary father fought valiantly to keep his protection sphere around the three of us. Unfortunately, he could only hold it for so long and his power faded fast. The protection sphere began to close in on us and threatened to let in the embers and snow. Suddenly—and this is from my parents, obviously I don't remember a thing," she lied. "I reached through my father's failing sphere of light and held a white hot ember in my bare hand like a firefly, giggling and cooing like a baby does. After that, I helped my father maintain his protection sphere through the worst of the threat and helped save all our lives. They were amazed and convinced I was remarkable and unique. They always said it was the day frost burned and flames froze; that I was special because I was born of fire and Ice."

Geezer almost lost his footing because he was so wrapped up in the story, but he quickly regained his balance and acted as though he never lost it for a second. "That is balladry, child. Absolutely the most amazing and engrossing story I have ever heard. In. My. Life. Looking at you, I can believe you are from a different realm, and born of fire and ice. Truly." Geezer was adorably excited, giving Mina a much needed morale boost, but it didn't last long, "However, I have to tell you—as amazing as that story is - at this very moment...I don't care."

Mina's broad smile faltered. "You don't care?"

"No. We are training. At this very moment, I am your adversary and I mustn't have any feelings for you. My single one concern is defeating you. Regardless of the emotion and feelings you may have for someone, whatever your history or present situation is with them, you must look past it all to the end of the fight. To your victory. Do you understand?"

Mina shook her head, hearing the lesson and fought feeling hurt, "I do. I do understand."

"Excellent. Would you like to hear about the day I met my wife?" Geezer asked, genuinely excited to tell her.

"Nope," Mina said flatly.

"Excellent, and why?" Geezer probed.

"Because I don't really care," she said in perfect Japanese.

"Ahhhhh, but you do," Geezer said confidently. "Try again."

"I. Don't. Really. Care." Mina offered in a frustrated tone.

"Now, that's more like it." Geezer was pleased. "One more time."

"I don't really care." Mina was finally there, she didn't care. Not one bit. Not even a little.

"Excellent," Geezer said. "When you stop worrying about your enemy, whatever they did to you, and what they think of your performance, you are truly free to perform. Balance is not only external, but largely internal as well. Now, come at me with everything you have." Geezer beckoned Mina politely with his right hand.

She had all the dexterity and skill of a jaguar, but despite her many years of rigorous training with her parents, or how nimble and graceful she was on the rope, Geezer always got the better of her. Mina had several welts across the glacial skin of her face; not enough to break the skin, but just enough to leave a lesson.

She huffed and attacked the old samurai again with gusto, using all the tricks in her arsenal, but she still wasn't able to lay a single hand on him. Geezer was like a phantom; effortlessly vanishing from standing on the icy rope, to aerial attacks and using misdirection like a magician. As was becoming all too common, he playfully slapped her head again with the rod of bamboo. Geezer smiled that toothless smile of his, "You may be beyond caring what others think, my dear, but you're still trying to impress *me*. Don't impress me—hit me. Again."

This time Mina casually strolled up to him, a mere inches between them. Geezer looked at her shrewdly, waiting for the attack, but Mina simply, slowly, raised her right hand and flicked him on the nose. He began laughing heartily and almost fell off the rope. "See. It doesn't matter how skilled or graceful the hit is, only that you land it. Style, flair, flamboyance—all for fat-head amateurs. Do *WHATEVER* you have to do in order to beguile, confuse, misdirect, and take out your enemy."

"Interesting. I never thought of acting...foolish in order to get the drop on someone. Very clever." Mina was already pondering the what if's. "And that's worked for you?"

Geezer looked at her now with serious eyes, "I once showed my balls to three fighters of the shogunate who outmatched me in every way; but I killed them with my sword while they were laughing their asses off. There is no shame in victory, and no protocol for achieving it. To be alive is always better; not to mention, whoever wins tells the tale."

"Damn, you are wise," Mina proclaimed.

"Of course I am," Geezer said nonchalantly while trying to hide his blushing cheeks. "Excellent work today, Mina. Let's eat."

After dinner, Mina, wearing the unassuming black kimono given to her by Geezer, brought all the dishes out to the ice-cold stream to clean and fetch more water for the morning. Geezer had been so kind to her over the last 21 months and had given her a facet of spiritual training she never knew she needed. Additionally, he had helped her sharpen her learned skills in unimaginable ways. What a peculiar, sweet old man. He spent hours trimming bonsai trees while he politely informed her that everything she was doing in her training was wrong. He never got frustrated or curt with her, though; he always took his time to explain and educate her until she had perfected the lesson.

In addition to her training, Geezer constantly reminded her to light a candle for her mother and father, who sacrificed themselves so she could live. Mina had primarily been taught by her parents that humans were an unpredictable, emotional species with more problems than they were worth, but this human was proving a compelling contrast to all that. She really liked him and told him as much. He was always quick to remind her that not everyone was as understanding and patient as he was; in fact, most humans were quite the opposite, mirroring many of the warnings her parents had given her. In Geezer's humble opinion, it was still worth figuring out who the good people were. His only lesson here was to try and figure it out quickly.

Mina took off her sandals, went inside Geezer's house and knelt at a picture Geezer had drawn in ink of her parents, from a description she had given him. She lit a candle to remember them and stared at the sketch for a very long time; promising revenge with her eyes. "I will not rest until you are free, and we have the heads of the Elders and the clans are united."

Suddenly, there was a hand on her shoulder. Mina looked up to see Geezer smiling down at her. He patted her shoulder lovingly and nodded. "From what you've told me, they were proud and loved you very much."

"They did indeed. I was fortunate enough to share a great deal of time with them before... Anyway, one day we will be reunited." Mina allowed one lone tear to track down her face. "When I am ready, I will seek them out, and their jailers."

"Ahhhhh, revenge. I love revenge." Geezer was strangely excited.

"Aren't you going to tell me revenge is a path that leads to destruction and undoing?" Mina was genuinely surprised.

"Of course not. There is no clearer truer path than revenge. It requires incredible patience, focus, determination, and skill. Not to mention, the satisfaction is second to none." Geezer plopped down on the floor next to her. "I've made it a point not to pry into the matter of your parents too much over the last 21 months—after you *FINALLY* learned Japanese," he said chuckling sarcastically, "and I've been happy to wait until you were ready, but now I think it's time you tell me everything—and don't leave out a single detail. I need to know all I can in order to help you get your parents and craft their jailers' perfect doom." Geezer sat, legs crossed, and rubbed his hands together excitedly.

Mina tugged on the kimono's wide collar and laid every atom of her story out for Geezer. He gobbled up the details like a greedy grandfather; even stealing a glance out to the garden and the tombstone during a few of the particularly juicy parts. She sensed Geezer hadn't been ready to talk about his past until now, but she knew he would reciprocate, since she was putting everything on the table. Was it his daughter in that immaculately kept grave?

When she finished, Geezer stared at her for a very long moment, before finally breaking the silence with a question, "So, this Alma and yaggowar business—show me."

Mina nodded, "Happy to, but not in here. Let's move out to the garden."

"Splendid," he said. "I'll be honest; I'm pretty eager to see this."

They moved out to the barren, frosty garden and Mina chose a spot that was wide open and more accommodating. Geezer looked on, transfixed as Mina pulled off the kimono over her Ceridome wraps, exhaled her Alma and transformed into a sleek, regal, solid-black yaggowar. Her Ceridome wraps stretched elegantly across her majestic, feline body and sheathed Beauty at her hip. She had long, fierce teeth like a saber-toothed tiger pointing downward to Hell, much like her mother, and was larger than most yaggowar at 13-feet-tall, 10-feet-wide, and 25-feet-long.

Geezer was amazed and energized. "My goodness. That is quite an ability. Very impressive. You are indeed a formidable warrior in so many respects."

Mina purred before transforming back to her female form, her wraps coalescing around her. She pulled on her kimono against the cold air.

Geezer spoke seriously now, "Mina, with all your training and abilities, there is nothing you can't accomplish here in the Earth realm. The possibilities are endless, but I encourage you to choose a path of honor and nobility. This is not to say you shouldn't fulfill your quest for liberation, unity and retribution; just be focused about it and I will help you in any way I can. You remind me...of my daughter." Geezer looked over to the gravestone and held back tears.

Mina stifled her own tears, putting it all together now. "That means a great deal to me."

Geezer exhaled briskly, returned the silly smile to his lips and wiped several tears away, "Her name was Ichika, which means a thousand flowers."

"That's such a lovely name," Mina said in a humble tone.

Geezer reflected, "I was so proud of her. Everyone always wanted boys. Boys, boys, boys, but she had more strength and intelligence within her than any man I've ever known."

Mina tentatively dared a personal question, "What happened, if you don't mind my asking?"

Geezer reached up and patted Mina on the shoulder, "It's okay, you've told me all the painful details of your life; it's only fair I tell you mine. After almost two years of talking about anything other than our pain, I think it's time we both have that lesson. My...wife died in childbirth," he began with fresh tears threatening, "so I took Ichika here to the Ryukyu Kingdom, built this house, then raised and trained her myself. Here in the Ryukyu Kingdom, women were encouraged to learn dance, be quiet servants to their husbands, and leave the martial arts to men. However, I never truly subscribed to that mentality. My thought was, women needed training *because* of men." Geezer seemed blissfully lost in the memory, his eyes focused solely on her gravestone. "There was only Ichika and I for a long time. During that period, I taught her everything I knew, and she flourished. She was the best student I had ever come across, and incredibly beautiful. One morning while she was fishing, a small group of shogunate warriors happened upon her." He took a moment to compose himself as his tone became solemn and sad. "Naturally, they tried to have their way with her, but she defeated them all in a vicious fight." Geezer emphasized the word 'fight' with his hands. "Her incredible prowess caught the eye of their shogunate general, who proceeded to court her relentlessly. After he tried to force himself on her, she clawed out his right eye. Later that same day...he...had her executed by the shogunate." Geezer didn't cry, rather he darkened like a storm cloud. "I've been planning my revenge and waiting for the perfect time to strike for so long, I got old. Now I fear I've missed my opportunity; but you—you have all the time in the world to fulfill your mission." His mood easing, "I will make sure you are ready."

Mina thought for a moment, "I could help you. Seriously, I could drag that bastard right down here and place him at your feet."

Geezer pondered for a moment, then shook his head, "No, no, no. You have your own path ahead of you. Besides, after the fall of Edo and the end of the Tokugawa shogunate, I wouldn't even know where to find him. Better you should focus on your journey than mine."

"But I want to help you like you've helped me." Mina felt frustrated that he wouldn't let her give back.

"I would much rather you live to see your journey through to fruition than die trying to fulfill mine. I will be reunited with my family soon enough; you focus on reuniting with yours." Geezer said, smiling sadly. "I appreciate the sentiment."

"You've been so kind and helpful to me; is there nothing I can do to repay you?" Mina asked, flustered.

"Live, dear. Just live." That said, Geezer left Mina's side and mournfully went back into the house. Mina understood.

It was roughly three weeks later when Mina awoke to loud, angry voices in the snow-covered garden. She sprang up, stalked out the back and around the house for a better look. There was Geezer with his sword unsheathed—not a good sign—and four other fierce looking fellows having stern words. She hung back to try to get some context before barging in, half-cocked, with skin so white and eyes so round, she would stick out like a sore thumb.

While Mina focused on listening, she couldn't help but notice the older one had long gray hair and a mustache, as well as an eye patch over his right eye with scars running underneath it. Her blood began to boil because she instantly knew who he was.

"The audacity of your presence in my garden calls me to violence, Kogen. What in the seven Hells brought you here?" Geezer was wound so tight, Mina thought he would snap at any moment.

Smugly, Kogen replied, "I hear you have an adopted daughter; foreign, but fiercely beautiful. Surely by now you know there is nothing you possess that I cannot take from you. I may no longer be head general of the shogunate, but I still possess great influence in these lands and my eyes are legion. So, let us have a look at her. Let us see if she is worthy to lay beneath me."

Mina had to trust in Geezer and reign in her explosive anger. Who the fuck was this guy thinking he could just waltz in here, boss Geezer around in his own home and force her into sexual submission? This motherfucker.

Kogen pompously motioned with his right hand for Geezer to bring her forward; however, before he could withdraw said hand, Geezer chopped it off cleanly at the wrist with his sword. The action was so swift, no one even knew it had happened until the pound of flesh hit the snow. The other three samurai for hire gawked in disbelief as their heads were suddenly and savagely separated from their shoulders. The trio fell to the ground simultaneously in a heap, their blood turning the snow and winter lilies from white to red. Kogen slowly, incredulously, looked at the stump of his wrist, which sprayed body wine across Geezer's best dark wafuku robes. Before Kogen could speak, Geezer sliced through the top of his head, right between his arrogant lips. Only after he crumpled to the ground on top of his lackeys, did it slide off, revealing the crimson meat of his tongue and the white molars of his lower jaw.

Mina, stunned, ran to Geezer's side. "Holy shit. Did you just do that?"

Geezer sheathed his samurai sword and looked up to her with his sweet old smile. "Breakfast?"

Mina was too shocked to respond, so Geezer took her hand and led her back into the house.

"The Gods have smiled upon me this day," Geezer said through a mouthful of rice and radish. "Most likely because I've been helping you with your vendetta. Good karma."

Mina was still slack-jawed in front of her breakfast, but managed to croak out a response, "That was amazing. Simply amazing."

"Getting your enemy dialoguing is an even better distraction than showing them your balls—or tits in your case. Once you get them going, easy peasy Japanesey." Geezer laughed at his own joke. "I have to say. This is the brightest day I've had since before my sweet Ichika was murdered. I owe it all to you. Your spirit brought them here for me and placed them under my sword; that's what is truly amazing here. Thank you, Mina. You have honored me with your presence."

"I am the one who is honored," Mina said softly. "I have learned so much from you, and I am forever in your debt. You're like the grandfather I never had. You are family to me, and I love you."

Geezer bowed his head, hiding his tears. "You're the granddaughter I was cheated out of, and you are indeed family. My only remaining family, and I love you as well." They shared a deep and emotional embrace for a very long moment. Geezer went on to say, "I feel lighter than a cherry blossom on the winds of spring. You have set me free."

Mina wiped a tear of her own away now. "Satisfaction second to none."

"You have been listening to all my wise, old ramblings." Geezer beamed.

"Of course I have you miserable old goat." Mina smiled broadly as Geezer laughed heartily.

"Baaaaa, baaaaa," he hollered. "Now let's go bury those fools."

"Indeed."

The next morning, Mina woke to thunder, sleet and rain; while foggy and gloomy, the melancholy was somehow beautiful. She stretched and arched her back like a kitten in a ray of sunshine, then built a fire. She was thrilled Geezer had been able to exact his revenge on Kogen, but worried his people would soon come looking for him—for them.

Mina thought long and hard about it as she prepared breakfast for the two of them as she had for so many months. She would try to urge him to leave with her, to strike out on the open road in search of a new home and adventure; one far away from these lands and Kogen's reach. The West perhaps. While the thought of her and Geezer venturing out together warmed her heart, she knew deep down he would never leave Ichika. Not to mention, he was as stubborn as he was kind, but maybe—just maybe—she could talk him into it.

When finished preparing the last two eggs they owned, along with some brown rice, Mina mentally began planning her day. She would have to venture into the village one final time for more supplies, pack her sparse belongings, convince Geezer to leave, train if there was time, and get things ready for them to depart that night. She suddenly realized Geezer hadn't yet come down to help her with breakfast.

Curious, but she figured he was sleeping the sleep of the satisfied. She couldn't let him become too complacent; they had maybe two days before Kogen's men would be there looking for them—if that.

The table was set and the food ready to eat, but still no Geezer. Mina suddenly felt a knot tighten and squirm in her gut. She broke into a run up to the loft and almost crashed through the rice paper door. She saw Geezer laying there on his mat, turned away from her on his side. She took a deep breath and slowly approached him, tears welling up in her eyes.

"Geezer? You awake?" She asked almost in a whisper, knowing the answer, but refusing to believe it. "Hey, old man, it's time for breakfast—no sleeping in." Still no response. Mina dragged herself over to him and plopped herself down, his back still to her. She put a loving hand on his shoulder and nodded, "You old goat, we could have been outlaws on the road, getting into mischief and adventures, but you had to go and die on me." Softly crying now, "Who will I misbehave with now? Who will train me? Who will clip the Bonsai trees with me? Once again, I am all alone." She sobbed now in unison with the falling sleet and rain outside. She cried for Geezer and she cried for herself. She cried for her parents and for her loneliness.

Six hours passed with Mina sitting there like a statue, her hand on Geezer's still shoulder, loving him and not wanting to let go. Losing her parents was one thing, but this...this was heart-rending. She had spent over a hundred years with her parents, and they weren't dead, they were just imprisoned. Geezer, on the other hand, was dead and gone. There would be no more breakfasts or training. There would be no more wisdom or jokes; she felt absolutely devastated. She had never forever lost someone so profoundly dear to her heart. In just under two years, they had formed an ironclad bond—a family bond. It seemed somehow more severe, losing someone so close that you only knew for such a short time. Mina felt lost.

The temperature had plunged throughout the day and the ground had become hard and unforgiving. Nevertheless, Mina transformed into her yaggowar form and tore up the uncompromising earth next to Geezer's daughter's grave with ease. When she had a suitable resting spot for him, she returned to her female form and laid him delicately within the cold earth. She unfurled his favorite blanket over him as a death shroud, and placed the blood-covered winter lilies, along with the brush drawing Geezer had done of his daughter, on top. As she stood over the open grave, she spoke her heart, "I sure am going to miss you, Geezer. You opened your home to me—an alien stranger—and let me into your life...your heart. You were so kind and wise, and hopefully your wisdom will live on in me. I will feel your loss for as long as I live, but I am eternally grateful to have met you; to have seen you find closure and peace through bloody revenge. You give me hope that one day I will find it as well. Until then, I hope you and your family will watch over me and help guide me to my destiny. I love you. Goodbye to you, my friend...my family."

There was a grumble of far off thunder as the storm geared up to be a lot more than just sleet and snow. Mina filled in the grave by hand and stabbed the earth with the samurai sword she had broken when they first met. Its simple but elegant hilt served as the perfect memorial for a warrior who was strong, noble, honorable and kind, with a vulnerable soul that was scarred but not broken. Finally, she pierced the frozen earth next to the broken sword with his precious samurai sword. The two swords stood together side-by-side as they had and would stay that way for eternity.

Mina let the cold sleet, rain and snow wash the freezing mud from her body and awaken her mind as well as her flesh. She was ready. She cast a clever portal cloaking spell over the garden, graves and house, so it would forever remain as it was without ever having to worry about it being disturbed by anyone or anything. It now existed between realms, a quiet tomb locked in winter, fit for a master, his loving daughter, and the souls of their slain enemies. Only Mina could ever find it, and she planned to visit it regularly to pay her respects.

The snow was really beginning to come down now, so Mina folded up the brush drawing Geezer had painted for her of her parents, and placed it within her jet-black kimono, directly over her heart. Roughly three inches of snow accumulated on her head and shoulders as she lingered over the graves, not wanting to say goodbye.

Eventually, she moved inside and suited up in black bear and wolf furs by the fire. Pulling on the sleek seal-skin boots lined with sheep fur Geezer had helped her make, she couldn't help but feel rejuvenated and inspired. In due time, she would have her bloody satisfaction, but not yet. Not yet. Mina crowned herself with Geezers pointed straw amaboshi hat; the slice of her pale face surrounding those fiercely green eyes resembled a ghostly mystery of white and shadow. The furs piled around her body, neck and mouth were more to camouflage and hide her than it was to keep her warm against the unrelenting arctic wind. Mina didn't get cold. Feeling ready to depart, she slung her pack of belongings and supplies over her capable shoulders and prepared to take the first steps of her long and uncertain journey. A large pole and lantern hung over her shoulder from the pack to light her way through the bitter, black cold.

Mina took one last, long look at the house, the garden, and the graves before stepping off the porch and into the blinding cold. When she got her bearings, she looked once more over her shoulder to make sure the house and garden were forever obfuscated from view. There was nothing but barren cherry trees, bamboo and dark; all bending from the cruel wind. She turned into that wind and demanded it let her pass, and it did.

CHAPTER 2
A THOUSAND SCARS FOR YOU

Three days later, the morning sun reflected brilliantly off the deep virgin snow like cascading diamonds. "I am certain this is where Geezer's house was and where he lived for decades. I can't explain it, Daisuke." Fumihiro clenched his teeth in disbelief. "I've put eyes on the house and its garden a hundred times. I..."

Daisuke, a former samurai turned local magistrate, stood up tall in his smart uniform resembling their French and Prussian influencers. Gold buttons and frills from the shoulders would have a long journey to fashionable. The thick, gray wool coats offered a defense against the cold, but were cumbersome and heavy. "Are you also *certain* Kogen and his men were headed here? Why, for what business? Keep in mind, I am familiar with their history."

"I am told it had something to do with Geezer's adopted daughter. Apparently Kogen was...interested." Fumihiro blanched, acknowledging the irony of the two enemies' history repeating itself.

"I have also laid eyes on Geezer's house plenty of times, and this is exactly where it was. Look here," Daisuke pointed to the north side of a hibernating cherry tree, and outlined where he had carved a rabbit into the smooth bark long ago. "I used to fish these waters frequently. I remember when Geezer built his house. We frequently crossed paths on our way to the watering hole. His house *WAS* here. This is some kind of black magic. I want every magistrate from the village to coordinate with the government liaisons and..."

Fumihiro waited anxiously for his commanders' continuing orders, but they never came. Instead, the commander peeled apart from the centerline, spilling his steaming inner contents into the deep snow. Fumihiro gawked and croaked as the nine-foot tall Mayax rose in all his thorny glory behind the remains of Daisuki. The other-realm barbarian rose out of a portal beneath the snow like rapture. Naturally, he was followed by the other six Nevuscar who emerged from behind the barbarian, out of a black hole that eclipsed the morning sun. They were all equally terrifying to someone like Fumihiro, who failed to make sense of it all. Mayax's second and third in command directed what Fumihiro could only describe as four giant cats on sparking lightning leashes. The albino giants held the leashes in each hand as the ferocious felines writhed in front of them like Hell's hunting hounds. Mayax leaned down nose-to-nose with Fumihiro, the four monstrous jaguars sniffing the air eagerly from behind. Speaking Japanese, he addressed the captain by his proper rank, "Captain. I don't suppose you've seen a snow-colored woman, eyes of emerald, taller than you by two, and breathtakingly beautiful, have you?"

Fumihiro slowly nodded his head up and down. "Yes."

"Excellent. Where?"

Fumihiro brought the first finger of his right hand up and pointed directly down to the snow covered ground they were currently having a conversation on.

"Interesting." Mayax slowly looked around through the sunlight dancing off the snowy scenery. He then closed his eyes and breathed in the magnificent fragrance of the forest in winter. "Rake, what do the girls say?"

Rake, Mayax's second, was very tall—taller than Mayax—and very slender with huge, imposing hands. He was so white his skin was almost invisible against the snow. The maroon armor complemented his blood-red hair and albino eyes, which searched the minds of his yaggowar captives for answers. "It would seem this man is telling the truth. She was here. Her scent has dissipated by roughly three days, but it's here."

Speaking deeply and confidently, Mayax ordered the other Nevuscar to fan out and look for her. He then turned back nose-to-nose with Fumihiro and spoke again in Japanese, "Thank you for your help. I return you to the earth." Suddenly, Fumihiro turned to salt and blew away like ashes in the wind. Mayax stood tall, his black beard blowing in the bluster. Mayax spoke to himself, almost in a daydream, "Perhaps when my steel meets her stone, she will grant me the Right of Copunocture, and we may lie together before battle. I am eager to fuck some respect into her."

"Well, that's the problem with men like you, Mayax: always trying to earn respect with your dick." Mina was suddenly there behind Mayax like a daytime wraith. She was truly a specter to behold, wrapped in black furs and shrouded beneath Geezer's amiboshi hat.

"Well, you have me alone and at a disadvantage; maybe you want to fuck some respect into me?" Mayax was calm as a cobra, but ready for anything.

"You wish. You want to tell me how the hell you have Pentavi yaggowars leashed and at your command?" Mina pressed Beauty against the back of Mayax's neck. "Talk, warlock."

"Gladly. You took off so quickly last time, I wasn't able to educate you on how things are now."

"Educate me." Mina drilled holes through Mayax from behind with her eyes, enough that he could feel it.

"Once I joined the war in Reclon with my second in command, it wasn't long before the Pentavi surrendered. We crushed them relentlessly under our heel, which was the turning point in the whole war. Currently, there are only a little over a thousand of your sisters left. But, don't feel bad, there is only a couple thousand Sinteverete left as well. Certainly enough to keep the leash on you females, though."

"Oh, you unbelievable bastard. I will put you under the knife." Mina gritted her teeth roughly as emphasis.

"It will do you no good; besides, that's pretty far from unity talk. I thought you and your parents wanted to end the wars, *unite the clans*, and execute the Elders," Mayax said sarcastically, waving his hands around in a mockery of her.

Mina interrupted Mayax rudely, "The Elders. The fucking Elders. They are the cause of all our loss and sorrow. Both of our Elders have been conspiring against the Pentavi *AND* Sinteverete for a very, very long time now. You fools are just too obtuse to see it. Once the thrill of wagering on the outcomes of our spilled blood ceased to entertain them, they decided to replace us all with a more tractable breed that they can control and use to march across all the realms in conquest. My mother heard it from their own lips, dammit." Mina was exhausted trying to pound logic into this big oaf's head. "I'm guessing once they have total dominion over the Earth realm and all the others, they'll be done with you and your *Nevuscar* warriors. You, a freak of dark magic conjured without a womb, might want to start thinking about their plans for you and your pals once they have everything they want. Pretty sure they don't have any intentions of actually sharing anything with lowly soldiers like yourselves; most likely you'll have some horrible eternal imprisonment of some kind waiting for you at the end. A fitting reward. All because of greed. Unbelievable."

"The idea that our Elders are conspiring with yours is absolutely ludicrous and laughable," Mayax proclaimed. "It's true, they created my second in command and me with dark magic and no womb, but we were the first, critical step in the evolutionary process necessary in making our Elders truly immortal—instead of merely ageless. They are so close now. Very soon the Sinteverete Elders will achieve their immortality and the final piece will be in play for total domination over all the realms. Me and my second were the breakthrough they needed to figure it all out. At one time, immortality could only be bred, but no longer."

Mina ventured a question, "Then the Elders are not yet immortal, and I may still collect their heads. I appreciate the good news."

"This is not good news for you," Mayax assured her. "I promise they are very close now, with only one element left to obtain. Then it will be all out war on this realm, and all the others. There will be nowhere for you to hide then."

"I'll hide as long as I need to. One element you say?" Mina looked intrigued.

Mayax inadvertently divulged a look of concern that he had said too much.

"Is all that womb-less, dark magic the secret behind your immortal army, too?" Mina pushed.

Mayax snickered, "It is. They are obedient brutes who serve as a blunt, but necessary and effective instrument in achieving our goals.

The Nevuscar, on the other hand, are surgical precision tools that do not require equality, only purpose."

"A Steplescar army of mindless immortals, all of whom will run willingly into the meat grinder over and over again? I'll put it to you a second time; you really think they'll *need* you and the Nevuscar after they've massed their armies?" Mina laughed in Mayax's ear. "You poor dope. Think about it; the one downside to the Nevuscar is they have no kill-switch, and I'd be willing to bet blood to bone the Elders have perfected that oversight with their new breed of soldiers. You know, in case they somehow get unruly like the Pentavi did. Tell me I'm wrong."

Mayax was like a statue on the outside, revealing nothing; but on the inside, a slight change in his heart rate, detectable only to Mina and her acute feline senses, told her everything. "You may appear to be carved out of stone, Mayax, but your fast beating heart has betrayed you. Go on, tell me I'm wrong."

"Apparently you know everything, so I'll save my breath. However, I will say this: our Elders are indeed spoiled and weak, and far from battle ready. Not only will they need us to protect them until they become immortal, but we Nevuscar have been solemnly sworn command over their armies. It has been carved into our history and is law." Though his tone was confident, hearing himself out loud, Mayax suddenly wasn't so sure.

"Right, I'm sure the elite ruling class of Elders will do everything in their power to make good their promise to you. And what about someone like Bael? Wake up Mayax, you're crafting your own doom," Mina said, using Geezer's words. She was precariously close to feeling sorry for him, but quickly worked past the fleeting emotion.

"The Pentavi are our slaves now—bound by magic—and their Elders are our prisoners. We are building our armies of immortal soldiers, and the Sinteverete Elders will soon be truly immortal as well. You've lost the war, my beauty. You may as well acquiesce to reality."

"Beauty is a blade, mage," Mina said in a whisper that was a scream.

"So I keep hearing, woman. You'll see; in the end you will lay next to me as one of my many concubines, and you will beg *ME* for privilege. I might even free your parents to work in the granite mines of Val Tebrae. Do you really think one renegade Yasmani Ro will put to sleep millions of years of hard-fought war and victory? Your naivety is precious. What's your plan here? You can't kill me, and only by my grace have you not been cast into a pillar of salt and laid next to your traitor parents."

"I want to give you a little something small before you never see me again," Mina chided, with just the right amount of sass.

"I'm intrigued..." Mayax confessed as Mina reached from behind him, her eyes emerald slits beneath the amiboshi hat, and brought Beauty up to his chin. Mayax smirked. "This is theater, my beauty. You know you can't kill me."

Mina sliced Mayax from the right corner of his mouth to the crux of his eye, mirroring Vasser's single scar. "That's for my mother and father, you black-hearted bastard. It's not every day a Pentavi woman, a renegade Yasmani Ro no less, gets to demote the lead Nevuscar with a scar of warning."

"And the warning?" Mayax queried, genuinely wanting to know.

"If you keep looking for me, one day you will find me ready," Mina hissed.

"Are you not ready now, my beauty?"

"I'm not your beauty; besides, I don't want to be interrupted. I want to take my time with you, Mayax, formerly the Malevolent. And you'd do well to remember that." Mina licked the blood from the side of Mayax's face, relishing the taste of his body wine. "You taste like...a lamb. I hope you don't begrudge me the scar."

"A thousand scars for you, my beauty," Mayax promised breathlessly.

"You talk sweet, lamb," Mina whispered while kissing Mayax's cheek. "The name is Mina."

He spun around in a microsecond, pulling Velocet, his Cursed Cleaver of Black, from an armory portal conjured out of thin air. The mile of meat splitting steel boasted a vast, wide guillotine blade of black that screamed with the captured souls of his fallen foes. Mayax knew she was gone. "Damn, that's twice she's out-foxed me. Respect."

Rake came over the hill with his two Pentavi yaggowar's snarling and fighting against the lightning leashes like desperate, caged animals. "Behave," he ordered thunderously, sending a massive shock through the leashes, gentling their disposition drastically. Reluctantly, the two beasts obliged, but watched him with hungry eyes. Rake moved to the right side of Mayax, and without even looking at him spoke his new leadership name, "I am Rake the Rancor," and without hesitation he began ordering Mayax around, "Collect the other's and summon what's left of the Roses with Thorns. I want those bitches on the hunt for that fucking Yasmani Ro cunt right away." Rake bowed his head, and after a moment his armor became black, and Mayax's became maroon.

Mayax continued, looking stoically forward, "Understood."

CHAPTER 3
IT'S THE BITCHES THAT'LL GITCHAS

Present Day...

"It's you." A young man about the age of 17 said in front of Mina.

Mina was sitting at an outside cafe teaming with people in Cedar Knolls, NJ. The patrons hustled around purposefully, strangely unconcerned with the fact that part of neighboring Morristown had been burned to the ground not 32 hours before. The news was speculating it was a gas leak and assured everyone the police, FBI, Department of Homeland Security, and military were getting to the bottom of things right away. That was all these salty New Jersians needed to hear; nothing was going to stop their enjoyment of the late spring weather, after four months of freezing cold. Mina wore a snazzy, high-fitting black skirt, matching black stiletto heels and a tight, white midriff shirt with the words: "It's the Bitches That'll Gitches" emblazoned in red across the front. The heels added eight inches to her already unusually tall 78 inches. She sipped a latte, puffed a massive cigar and pulled her sunglasses down to have a look at the young man. "I'm sorry?"

"It's you, the lady who blew up Morristown. Damn, you're a tall drink of water. You a superhero or something?" The kid asked sincerely.

Mina masked her concern masterfully while making sure no one nearby was tuning into the conversation. "Maybe a supervillain," she offered nonchalantly. Figuring she should assess this development further, she encouraged him, "You want a soda?"

"I'd like beer better," he said testing the waters.

"Soda it is," Mina proclaimed; instantly liking the kid.

"Alright...and a meatball sub?" He was pushing it now.

Mina smiled, "Sure, kid. Have a seat." She pushed the empty chair in front of her out with her foot and gestured for the teenager to have a seat.

"Those things'll kill you," he said, motioning to her thick cigar.

"Not likely," Mina said confidently.

"My name's Avery; what's yours?" He was a handsome, brave, and somewhat foolhardy young spitfire, but he had nerve, and Mina respected that. He was well dressed, wearing a Hawaiian shirt with cargo shorts, and nice kicks.

"Mina. Nice to meet you."

"Nice to meet you. Great shirt, by the way."

Mina chuckled, "Thanks, I just got it."

"So, you gonna kill me or something?" Avery asked, less than fearfully.

"No, no, I am not going to kill you or something." Mina blew on the end of her cigar to get it cherry again and inhaled a big draw.

"So why did you torch Morristown?" He asked honestly, sitting down casually in the chair opposite of her.

"I, uh...lost my temper." Mina admitted while exhaling. "Maybe not my proudest moment, but a warrior's heart is hard to cage."

"I heard that." Avery picked up the menu and started perusing. "I feel like I have a warrior's heart, too. Hmmmmm, actually, I think I'll have the prime rib. My mom always told me not to eat anything messy on a date."

"Smart lady. So this is a date, huh?" Mina couldn't hide her smile. "And you're making me pay? Typical man." She took a huge pull off her Cuban and blew the smoke through her nostrils like a sexy dragon.

"Well, I was gonna offer, but seeing as though I got the goods on ya, I figure we'll call it even." Now it was Avery's turn to smile.

"Uh huh," Mina huffed, less than worried." You think anyone is going to believe a kid telling them a woman blew up Morristown with her superpowers?"

"Fair point. I wouldn't, anyway; you seem pretty cool." Avery peeked over the top of the menu to gauge her reaction.

"Yeah, well, I am pretty cool," Mina offered. "You're pretty cool too, kid; I guess we can be pals. Wanna tell me how the hell you recognized me?"

"I'm a drone pilot; well not professionally yet—but I'm gonna be. I live here in Cedar Knolls, and I saw the fireworks, so I immediately put my drone in the air to see what was up. By the way, you owe me a drone; it melted when I got too close."

"That sounds like a you problem," she said laughing. "I guess you got some pretty *dope* footage, too?"

"Dope? No one says that anymore," he said in a snarky tone. "Yeah, I got some *dope* footage. I got some nice shots of you naked too—that's for sure." Mina flashed her emerald eyes, and it was enough. "Don't worry, I'll delete everything," Avery quickly promised. "You're lucky I met you before I posted the footage and screen shots, which I was going to do tonight after I edited it all."

"Well, I guess we can add luck to my roster of attributes," Mina said coyly. "I don't suppose you saw any other drones flying around and filming, did you?"

"Yeah, but they were way too far away to get anything good. Too afraid you'd melt their drones. Amateurs, you know?" Avery widened his confident smile. "All the footage I've seen on social media so far has been shit, so..."

"I didn't see anything on YouTube that got me too worried," Mina said. "Kind of like all those ghost videos with barely recognizable human figures. I appreciate the info and the fact that you didn't publicly freak out on me and cause a scene. I'd say that's prime rib worthy." Mina flagged down the waitress and ordered the kid a soda and prime rib special, then a triple bacon cheeseburger for herself. As the waitress walked away, Avery suddenly looked disappointed at his order. "Let me guess, you want the triple bacon cheeseburger?"

Avery tried to be polite. "No, no, you're good. I definitely wanted the prime rib."

"Um hm," Mina knew better. She puffed her stogie, and the drifting smoke added an irresistible air of mystery to her. "So what's your story, kid?"

"Ummmmm, not much to tell really. As I said, I intend to be a drone pilot. I'm a junior in high school, I love horror movies, drawing, I suck at math, and I'm...recently single," the last part he emphasized with a wink of his eye.

"Yeah, me too," Mina confessed with a pained sigh and a sip of her latte.

"Is that why you...lost your temper?" Avery was kindly being diplomatic and treading lightly.

"I lost my temper because my ex fiance was a lying, cheating douche canoe who managed to be the only person in a VERY long time to make a fool out of me." She shook her head vulnerably. "All my training, all my education, and all my experience over the years and it only took one pretty boy with a talent for orgasms to turn me into a gushing, gooey bimbo who was ready to believe anything he told me. Ugh, no amount of showers can wash that shame off."

Avery was surprisingly well put together for a teenager, and didn't even blush at the word 'orgasm.' "Don't beat yourself up; a lot of the guys I know will lie, cheat and say anything just to see a pair of tits. It's not your fault for trusting him," he said confidently.

"Thank you, Avery; I appreciate that," Mina admitted.

"My girlfriend cheated on me too, with this real asshole at school named Allan. Right before I was supposed to take her to prom, no less. He's a senior—of course—and it had been going on for a while." Avery bowed his head sorrowfully for a moment, but was out of it in a flash. "Anyway, fate is a funny thing because here I am now having lunch with a gorgeous super...*something*, and I can feel the chemistry between us BIG TIME," he said with a hopeful, probing chuckle.

"While the chemistry is truly evident between us, it's still way too soon for us to be messing around looking for rebounds. I will say this though, your ex is a damn fool. You are a very handsome young man with a great head on his shoulders and any young lady would be wise to treat you as a prize."

"You really think so?" Avery asked sheepishly.

"Damn right. If I wasn't *much* older than you, I'd totally ask you out," Mina truthfully said.

"What, are you like 25 or whatever? Pffffffft, that's not so bad. I'm 17 and will be 18 in four months. My dad is 20 years older than my mother. Anyway, your ex is a fool, too. I mean, anyone I know—including myself—would be all tangled up trying to catch your eye."

"The ladies are going to be lining up for you, my friend. Also...Thanks. You make an old gal feel good." This kid was smooth and didn't even know it. Hell, he was more charming and intelligent than most adult men she'd met in the Earth realm. She found herself thinking she might look him up in 20 years and instantly thought better of it. Mina scoffed at herself; 80 years since World War II and her last fulfilling long-term relationship, and she was already chicken hawking teenagers with potential. Fuck sake.

After a bit more polite conversation, the waitress arrived with their food. She placed the monstrous burger in front of Mina and the prime rib in front of Avery, but after the waitress departed, Mina swapped the plates. Avery looked at her while blushing. "You sure?"

"Yeah, it's fine. I was thinking about getting the prime rib, anyway. Knock yourself out, kid." Mina wasn't lying; besides, everything happens for a reason.

Avery took a huge bite and promptly dropped catsup, mustard and some kind of sauce all over his Hawaiian shirt. He looked down, pissed, but not shocked, and then looked back up at her with embarrassed eyes.

"Mama knows best," Mina said, chuckling as she put her cigar down, then grabbed a knife and fork. She cut herself a modest piece of rare prime rib and politely placed it inside her mouth. She savored the flavor briefly, but wasn't able to enjoy it for long. Suddenly, there was a deafening chorus of trumpets sounding off behind her, loud enough to shatter several storefront windows along the road. "What the fu—" Then it hit her, it was the Roses with Thorns reveille. "Oh, fuck."

"What in the Hell is that?" Avery hollered in between thunderous trumpet blasts.

"That, my friend, is the real reason I'm still here in New Jersey. Run." Mina was up in a flash and pointed for Avery to run the way he had come. "Go now. GO!"

Avery took another big bite of his burger and ran like his ass depended on it, because it did. A few other patrons followed suit, but most people just sat or stood where they were, dumbfounded and clueless. When Mina was sure Avery made good his escape, she turned to face a significantly depleted regiment of only 15 Roses with Thorns warriors—all dressed in their respective Ceridome wraps and light battle gear. The lead General, dressed in nothing but her Ceridome wraps, had a myriad of steel and stone knives woven into her thick, long dreadlocks, giving her a strangely beautiful but nightmarish appearance. She also boasted a menagerie of scars on her face and body, telling a brutal story of life on the battlefield. She stepped forward with her long, serrated sword and addressed Mina curtly, "I am Lindria, General of the Roses with Thorns. And you must be *Mina*—Yasmani Ro, yes?"

Mina grabbed her smoldering cigar and strolled right up to within an inch of Lindria's face. "You got that right."

"While I'm far from sympathetic to a mutt pussycat like you, it would be in your best interest to come quietly with us now." Clearly, Lindria was overflowing with vitriol. "I knew your mother very well, and the idea that she betrayed the Pentavi in order to bed Sinteverete scum like Vasser, so she could later push you out of her like so much shit is—"

"Shuddup you spineless Bimbo." Mina pulled on her stogie as though she were Fidel Castro and blew a thick cloud of cigar smoke directly into her face. "We should be sisters, fighting for a unified clan, but until that fairy tale comes to fruition, why don't you just shut the fuck up."

Lindria smirked, "I figured you'd say something like that."

"You figured right, dude." Mina was out with Beauty now and was ready to rumble.

Mayax, in full armor, placed his hand gently on Mina's shoulder from behind. "Easy now, my beauty."

Mina didn't even turn around, "Well, I was beginning to think you were too good to come out here and get me yourself."

The bustling street of shops and cafes with their myriad of patrons was now as silent as a graveyard while everyone pulled out their cell phones and began filming in complete disbelief at the medieval drama unfolding in the middle of the street. Mayax forcefully turned Mina around. "So you burned part of this shit hole down because you were jilted by a lover? That's more pedestrian than I thought you were capable of."

"Well, that was only part of the reason…" Mina smirked.

"Pray tell the other?" Mayax was inquisitive, if nothing else.

"I wanted you to find me." Mina started heating up.

"Feeling strong, I see—" Mayax began, but was abruptly interrupted by Rake. Mayax betrayed a glimmer of irritation.

"Silence," Rake bellowed while stomping forward. "The two of you banter like old lovers; it's nauseating. Step aside, Mayax."

Mayax graciously stepped aside and Mina used the distraction to hit Rake full-on in the face with fire from her eyes. The blast knocked Rake's helmet off and forced him back several yards, his feet digging deep, bilateral trenches into the smoking asphalt. Mina's protective light sphere, very similar to her father's, enveloped her in brilliant bright translucent luminescence as she sashayed past Mayax, who let her walk by with a little smile. "Nice hat," she wise-cracked, while tapping his horny helmet.

Rake quickly stood fast, wiped a trickle of blood from the corner of his lips before suddenly realizing his helmet was off. Mina, seizing yet another opportunity, whisper chanted and turned Rake's eyes to stone. The ghostly, slender wraith, once so confident and composed, suddenly started frantically clawing at his eyes to release the hex.

"Don't think I didn't notice how you lot were incanting the last time I encountered y'all in the Mandala realm."

"Y'all?" Everyone asked in unison.

Mina rolled her eyes as she moved in close to Rake. Lindria and nine of the other Roses with Thorns warriors moved quickly to intercept her. Without even looking, Mina pulsed her light sphere and sent them flying back and crashing through buildings and windows. This spurred most of the gawking onlookers into screaming and fleeing the scene post haste. "I'm impressed you've moved past whisper chanting to thought incantation. You guys are full of surprises. Still, you need your eyes for that, sorcerer." Rake tried to go old school and whisper chant a reversal of the hex, but Mina was ready for him, "Nu uh uh-hhhhhhh..." She snapped her fingers, vanishing his mouth and nose. "And just for good measure..." she whisper chanted again and turned his right, spell casting arm to stone. "Why, you're just as gentle as a lamb now, aren't you?"

Mayax continued to hold back and fight a larger smile. The remaining Roses with Thorns and its ladies of war looked anxiously at him as Rake continued to flounder. The other five Nevuscar came forward and casually twiddled their thumbs while waiting for Mayax to give the order to move. Mayax, sensing their expectation, held up the palm of his hand, instructing everyone to wait. Bael snickered, "Looking to be promoted back to king shit of fuck mountain, huh? I can respect that."

Mayax cut him a pointed sideways glance. "Might mean a promotion for you too, but I doubt it."

"No worries, I enjoy being the ugliest," Bael offered truthfully.

"Well then, you better hope I never have to release your old friend, The Wrecking Ball," Mayax noted.

"Now that is one beautifully ugly motherfucker," Bael reminisced. "I miss that dickless scab. You leave this bitch over here unchecked long enough though, and you may just have to release him."

"Rake can handle himself," Mayax promised in a suspiciously sarcastic tone.

"She's got some salt to her, that's for sure. Just like her fucking mother. I mean, she managed to scar all your beauty a hundred years ago." It was Bael's turn to cut Mayax a pointed glance.

"Indeed. Keep talking like that, though, and I'll have to release Vasser instead." Mayax threatened light-heartedly while watching on with interest as the skirmish unfolded. Bael shut up.

Mina levitated up to be breath-to-breath with Rake, who sensed her presence and gave up his struggle. He straightened rigidly, knowing any further fighting was futile. All he could do now was stand there and wait for Mayax to give the order to save him.

"You Sinteverete swinging dicks are all the same, I swear." Mina looked over her shoulder at Mayax to gauge his response, only to see him smile politely at her and show no signs of retaliation. "Well, maybe not all the same," she admitted, while placing her right, white-hot hand over the left eye of Rake's face. For a warlock with no mouth, he managed to scream admirably from the inside as Mina melted the left side of his face off. "Hard to scream without your cry hole, huh, Undying one?"

Rake retaliated by using his right hand as a stone club, and shattered it over Mina's head, but she barely noticed; her sphere of light protecting her. She pressed her molten hand deeper into Rake's face and closed her hand around his stony left eye, reduced it to dripping, liquified magma, "Like a scorpion with four stingers, I pluck at thee," she said laughing loudly while withdrawing her right hand and heating up her left. She positioned herself to burn Rake's right eye out when Mayax finally gave everyone the nod. The five remaining ladies of The Roses with Thorns, along with the other five Nevuscar, sprang into action and dog-piled onto Mina, imploding her light sphere, and forcing her to the ground.

Mayax blinked his eyes and returned Rake's mouth, nose and right eye. "You can scream now," Mayax assured Rake, who glowered at him with his one remaining eye that promised comeuppance. "It's the bitches that'll gitches," Mayax added with an acidic snicker. Mayax then turned his armor back to black and Rakes to maroon. "Now move over there out of the way," Mayax ordered. Rake obliged with a lowered eye, picked up his helmet with his remaining left hand and put it roughly back over his head.

Mayax moved over to where Mina was being held down and looked at her for what seemed like forever. "I guess folks only underestimate you once."

"Sometimes more than that," she teased. Suddenly, the hands holding her down began to smoke and smolder until they all released her simultaneously with a shriek. Even the Nevuscar turned her loose and stepped away, not wanting to add any scars to their skin stories that day. Mina stood elegantly and brushed off her shoulders. "I'm about to demote all you rotten Nevuscar motherfuckers; and then the bitches of the RWT and I will have a little chat about what it means to be sisters of the Pentavi." The five Nevuscar knew exactly what was up, and didn't want to risk any demotions, so they instantly dropped through portals they conjured beneath their feet. "Fucking pussies," Mina chided. Mayax, on the other hand, held his position firmly, but the other five Pentavi warriors decided to follow the Nevuscar and got the fuck out of there. The ladies of the Roses with Thorns regrouped with the nine others who continued to pull themselves crestfallen from the rubble. The other five Nevuscar joined them and they all hung back from a safe distance while Mayax sized Mina up.

"Alone at last," Mayax coaxed. "I don't suppose you'd like to revisit my proposal of Copunocture."

"You're so old-fashioned; but no, I'll pass. I only fuck for love and pleasure. But I'm happy to burn your eyes out." Mina found her stogie on the ground, blew it off, and placed it back between her clenched teeth. Then she grabbed up Beauty, laying a few feet to the right.

"Perhaps another time—for Copunocture, not the burning my eyes out." Mayax said seriously.

"Fair 'nuff,'" Mina offered with another wink.

Lindria pulled herself roughly from the rubble within the building Mina had propelled her through and realized she was smack dab in the middle of a gun store. "Well now; let's see if human weapons measure up, shall we?" She held both of her first two fingers from each hand to either side of her head and began incanting. After a moment, she picked up an AR15 semi-auto and disassembled it like a 30 year Marine veteran. She used her fingers to snap off the contact patch between the hammer and sear and expertly reassembled the rifle with some yummy extras. "There, that should make you a fully automatic force of retribution." She loaded several magazines, strapped a couple into her Ceridome wraps, and slapped one into the housing like a boss. She pulled the charging handle back and released it, loading a round into the chamber. Locked and loaded, she conjured fire from her left hand and lit her thick dreadlocks ablaze. Her hair was now an inferno, with all manner of edged weapons clanging and banging from within. Fierce as fuck, she climbed out of the destroyed storefront and let her eyes find Mina. "Let me show you how bad girls do…" She drew down on Mina and let the AR rip.

Without warning, the rifle began to crack like thunder as Lindria unloaded straight at Mina. The familiar sound of gunfire sent the few remaining pedestrians frantically running for shelter. Unfortunately, Mina caught a bullet in the upper center of her left arm, excruciatingly shattering the humerus within. She cried out and clapped a hand over the wound as two more grazed her shoulder and neck. She launched herself over a parked minivan that Lindria promptly peppered with rounds.

Mayax was caught off guard as well and dove out of the way as Lindria, now bullet drunk, screamed and fired with careless abandon. Mina slammed her back against the far side of the van and regrouped. "Well, that was unexpected," she managed, before healing and sealing her wounds with a whisper chant. "Dammit, that's gonna scar. Ugh, Christ, that was almost fucking game over." She closed her eyes and encased herself within her protective sphere of light. "Alright you fucking twat, let's see what ya got." Mina flung the van out of her way like it was a Tonka toy and called Lindria out. "Bang, bang, kiss, kiss bitch." Mina blew Lindria a kiss that promptly extinguished her halo of fire and opened a portal directly behind her. Lindria, her head smoking and her thunder stolen, scowled at Mina as a thousand tentacles suddenly wrapped around her and dragged her kicking and screaming into the portal to God knows where. Several other giant tentacles forced the portal open even wider and started grabbing at the other Nevuscar and RWT as though they were candy for the beast.

Most of the remaining Roses with Thorns took a page from Lindria's battle book and made a B-line straight for the gun store. "I don't think so." Mina flung a flaming power sphere straight at the armory, with every intent of blowing it straight to Hell, but Mayax was able to blink it out like blowing on a match.

Mina caught Mayax's eye. "Naughty, naughty; mama spank." She brought a fountain of magma straight up out of the ground underneath him like a volcano and engulfed him in a column of liquid lava. Unfortunately, this gave the other Roses with Thorns their opening to get inside the gun store and begin arming up.

Mina was more focused on Mayax now that she had her protective shield to keep the inevitable bullet symphony at bay. The magma pillar stretched up hundreds of feet into the air, before cooling to hard rock, trapping the lead Nevuscar within—for the moment. "Okay, Mayax the Malevolent; now for your buddies."

Rake answered her from behind by reaching inside her protection sphere and clapping his one massive mitt around her face and head. "You miserable, mouthy stray. Let's fit you for a leash, shall we." Rake pulled his hand back, revealing a lightning leash tethered to Mina's neck.

"You really think..." was all Mina could muster before Rake delivered a million crackling currents directly into Mina's throat, forcing her to scream out and fall to her knees.

"Yes, I really think." Rake said poisonously. "I cannot heal what is gone, but I will take your eye and your hand as my own. Then, I will endeavor to heap as much pain and humiliation upon your disfigured shoulders as I can creatively come up with. You will always know that you are mine."

Mina began to unbelievably grin up to Rake through sparking teeth and forced herself back to her feet as he futilely turned up the electricity to unimaginable levels. She grabbed hold of her leash and tore it from her neck as though it were made of tissue. "Hey nubby, if you were me, and I was you, I'd get the fuck out of my way. "

"Tough talk," Rake grumbled.

"Who's tougher than this bitch?" Mina said confidently, hitting her chest with Beauty, clasped firmly in her right fist.

Rake looked to the other five Nevuscar and the few remaining ladies of war, who continued to wrestle violently with the tentacles from another realm; Bael, in total Bael fashion, rode a tentacle like he was a rider in the Kentucky Derby; all the while laughing and whooping it up. Rake then looked back to the gun store where a majority of the Roses with Thorns were still getting their shit together.

"It's just you and me again, mage," Mina said, chomping on her stogie. "Beauty is thirsty for your body wine. Surely you can see that with your one big, beautiful red eye." Mina sensed she had the upper hand and was smearing it right in Rake's face.

"I grow weary of these shenanigans." Rake blinked that one beautiful red eye and the mechanical innards of a nearby car blew out the side of the left front quarter panel and snaked like animated intestines across the road towards him. They coalesced into a heavy metal make-shift, metallic gauntlet for his right hand, which he clenched in a show of force. He blinked again and the portal to the tentacle world drew closed and wetly clipped off the squirming appendages, leaving them to writhe in the street like giant beached eels. Rake blinked a third time and Lindria came crashing down out of thin air, all the fight in her extinguished like her smoky dreadlocks.

"Well, you're no fun," Mina said, catching sight of the RWT ladies of war emerging from the gun shop, armed to the teeth and biting at the bit. "I don't like these odds…" Mina whispered to herself, as she began plotting her exit strategy.

Suddenly, as if by providence, the police, a helicopter, and swat arrived in force, pulling all focus away from her. The cops began getting into position when Mayax exploded dramatically out of the high reaching stone column. The rocky shrapnel perforated the helicopter and sent it spiraling out of control into a nearby two story commercial building where it crashed apart and burst into flame.

The police instantly opened fire on Mayax as he stepped forward, the upper rock pillar crashing down behind him like an avalanche.

The bullets pinged ineffectually off of his thorny armor as he drank in the situation. His gaze settled upon Mina, who was standing approximately 20 yards away and looking ready to leave. "Not so fast, my beauty." He blinked and her protective sphere turned into a wrought iron cage around her.

"I told you, the name's Mina, fuck face," she shouted before trying to whisper chant her ass out of there.

"It's no use trying your magic, Mina. Just sit tight for now; and, if you will excuse me for a moment…" Mayax turned his attention back to the Roses with Thorns, who were eagerly awaiting his go ahead to open fire—but he had other plans. He blinked his eyes at the cops who were still shooting at him wildly, and without warning, every one of their guns turned to salt and disintegrated out of their hands like sand in an hourglass. The police gawked, amazed at him for a moment, before turning to flee. Mayax waved his right hand and a wall of hot sulfur engulfed them. Rake, along with the other Nevuscar, joined Mayax at his rear.

"Go watch Mina," Mayax ordered Rake, who reluctantly stomped over to where she was and pouted. "All this fighting is invigorating to be certain, but it's missing something," he turned his gaze to Mina, "...Ah yes, Copunocture."

Mina rolled her eyes and sheathed Beauty within her Ceridome wraps. "Well, don't look at me; I told you I'm not into fight-fucking. I'm down for a lot of shit, but that ain't it."

"You don't know what you're missing. In any case, have it your way." Mayax conjured a nice, big, juicy cigar between his lips, and snapped his fingers like striking a flint. The action created an impressive little flame on his right pointer finger, which he promptly used to fire up the Havana.

Mina, still clenching the long cold stub of her expired stogie between her teeth, frowned pitifully, "Now that's just wrong."

Mayax drew deep with a wide, ostentatious smile. "Damn, that's even better than smoking a wrap of Deadman. I can see why you love it." He puffed on it for a moment to really rub it in, and when Mina looked ready to cry, Mayax tossed the cherry cigar to her. "Since you can't conjure in there..."

She caught it like a ninja catches stars and spit the old one at Rake. "You can keep that nub, nubby." Planting the fresh stogie between her luscious red lips, "I hope you don't think this means I'm going to take windy walks with you down the shore."

"I respect your feistiness; it really gets my blood going, and puts your scent in the air..." Mayax raised his nose to the wind, sampling it.

Mina blew a big huge cloud of cigar smoke in his general direction.

"Hmmmmmm," Mayax playfully hummed. He looked over to the Roses with Thorns and summoned all fifteen over. As they strode suggestively his way, they slung their guns and sheathed their swords. Mayax began pulling his armor off, including the helmet—knowing Mina couldn't whisper chant in his mage cage. When he was down to a leather loincloth, he turned back to Mina. "Last chance..."

Mina smiles, "I don't suppose you could conjure me a bottle of wine too?"

"You're fucking spunky for a little thing." Mayax obliged, "Enjoy the show."

Mina picked up the bottle before it even had a chance to fully materialize. "Ugh, a chardonnay? Whatever, whatever, it's fine." She plucked up the cougar-sized wine glass Mayax provided and emptied the full bottle into it. "I know, I know, but I don't drink from the bottle."

The Roses with Thorns began draping themselves around Mayax eagerly as their Ceridome wraps fell to the ground. The only thing that remained were their guns and swords. Mina rolled her eyes and hollered from her cage, "It's okay, don't mind me. I'll just be over here judging your entire performance. No pressure. You're gonna do just fine, champ."

Rake began to disrobe, but Mayax stopped him. "Rake, you keep an eye on her—no pun intended." Rake angrily pulled his armor back on in a huff. "There's a good lad."

Mina couldn't help but snicker at Rake from her cage. "How is it that you're up there and I'm down here, but I feel less like a piece of shit?" She sipped her massive wine glass and winked.

"Keep joking cun..." Rake began but Mina let out a huge, impressively long and loud burp.

"BUUUUUUURRRRRRRRRPPPPPPPPPP, oh man, sorry about that. I used to drink sake with an old Samurai; you know how it is? Yeah, you know how it is."

Rake turned away with daggers in his eyes. "It's going to be you and me again real soon."

"Yeah, yeah, do you mind stepping to the right a little so I can," much louder now, "get a good look at how bad a lover Mayax is?" Rake gave her no response. "Meh."

The Roses with Thorns were well-versed concubines of Copunocture and enjoyed taking their hatred of the Sinteverete out on them during the angry sex act. Copunocture was always a consensual, but violent, battlefield orgy that blurred the lines between pleasure and pain, as well as subjugation and release. The ladies of war began stroking, kissing, and petting Mayax before getting rougher and rougher. It wasn't long before some of the ladies began partially letting out their Alma, or soul smoke, so they could use their sharp claws and teeth. Two of the RWT exhaled their Alma entirely and transformed into their huge, sleek yaggowar forms. Roaring, then purring, the two apex predators curled up together like a couple of twelve ton house cats. They provided a fur covered foundation for the unrestrained bacchanal about to take place on the main-street intersection in broad-daylight, inside war-torn suburban Cedar Knolls, New Jersey.

The other five Nevuscar rose out of portals beneath their feet to join in the debauchery and began stripping off their armor in anticipation. Bael, already naked and too ugly to fuck, liked to hang around the periphery and stroke his ruined cock while watching everyone with lurking eyes. The four higher-ranking Nevuscar paired up with several Pentavi seductresses a piece and led them behind the two yaggowars, knowing Mayax was the main event. Mayax and the remaining six Roses with Thorns began to tangle up in one another indecently. He greedily reeled in a different woman in each hand every two minutes and licked them from head to toe. He let slip sweet words, "to be inside you, either with my steel or my flesh, is the home of the warrior's heart."

There were teeth upon him, just to the point of drawing a small taste of blood, and claws, harsh but meticulously careful not to scar. There were lips and labia, sweet with battle sweat, for Mayax to taste and enjoy, after the ladies lewdly pleasured themselves with his serpent tongue.

Suddenly, there was a battle cry from above that tore through the area like a shockwave and froze everyone in their tracks. Lindria, her hair a fiery halo of Hell once again, shrieked from the destroyed roof of a looming building overhead and leapt down five stories with her sword pointed straight at Mayax's heart. "This Heaven will feel like Hell when I'm done with you," she screamed with every intention of stabbing him straight through the heart. Mayax knew it too, making him all the more hot to have her. With a microsecond to spare, he conjured a portal over his heart, and her sword sank harmlessly into another realm. He closed off the portal, snapping the blade into oblivion at the hilt and disarming her completely. With a monstrous, firm hand, he grabbed her left foot and dragged her on her stomach across the backs of her Pentavi yaggowar sisters. Mayax, three times her size, hoisted her—flaming hair and all—upside down, high into the air by her left leg in order to separate it from her right leg. In an instant, he sank his serpent tongue deep inside her sweet mound and gave her no mercy. "This fire will burn us both," he promised as her flames engulfed them. Mayax, levitating them into the air, knew better of it and already had a protection spell cast in order to shield himself from the passionate fire. Lindria was a hard-bitten Pentavi priestess of peril, nourished on millions of years of conflict, and the two intertwined like twin comets hurtling through the galaxy looking for a planet to crash into and obliterate.

The other Pentavi ladies of war were not about to go unsatisfied and unceremoniously yanked the two fucking fighters back down to the living bed of fur and muscle to rejoin the melee. One wardress of the Roses with Thorns savagely smothered Lindria with her clit, while the other ripped Mayax's leather loincloth from his hips and brazenly forced herself onto his enormous cock. She sank to the base and let out a cry that could easily have been pleasure or pain—most likely both. Lindria ferociously devoured the Pentavi warrior's pussy that was drenched in perspiration thanks to the contradictory sensations of fight sex. Mayax turned his attention from Lindria's fuck flower to find the mouth of her sexual wardress. He slowly slid his snake tongue down her throat, all the way down to her pleasure center below—from the inside. His tongue found Lindria's, and they wrestled over the warrior's clit from both ends. She exploded with multiple orgasms, giving them both a taste of her squirting nectar.

Mayax, still invasively tongue kissing the wardress and Lindria simultaneously, pulled his impressive length of manhood out of the weak and withered woman of former wrath who dared to climb atop him. She crumpled at his feet, reeling from her instantaneous and explosive climax. He conjured with both hands, and his one massive cock suddenly became five. As if lambs to the teat, five of the fiercest Roses with Thorns warriors eagerly stepped up and penetrated themselves through various orifices, forming a heaving meat sextuple. Lindria climbed down and kicked one of her lower ranking Roses with Thorns soldiers off of Mayax's main cock and took it for herself. She was the only warrior in the whole regiment who could truly handle it. The Sinteverete Nevuscar sorcerer proceeded to ass-fuck, pussy-fuck, and face-fuck all five warrior women at the same time to the rhythm of approaching military Black Hawk helicopters.

The three choppers arrived and began swiftly unloading their arsenal of rockets and chain guns directly at Mayax and the main event. Thunderous explosions erupted along the perimeter of the impromptu orgy, as thousands of bullets ripped through the asphalt and devastated the surrounding buildings. Mayax, having cast a protection spell over the area as well, was less than concerned about the intruders, and more focused on completing his sinful and salacious sex act right there in the middle of Main Street. The explosions and violence in the background only served to further excite the ladies of war being pleasurably punished by the Undying One. The four Roses with Thorns warrior women were all on their hands and knees now, taking it from behind and about to come in unison, as Lindria rode their backs on her back and received the best of Mayax's pounding. Lindria straddled the barbarian's hips with her thighs and pulled him deeper inside her as a catastrophic crescendo built within her. Without warning, they all reached an apocalyptic level climax at the same time and Mayax bathed them in thick long ropes of alabaster colored cum from each of his rigid members. Lindria lapped at it as a kitten laps milk, hissing and clawing at the others to selfishly get her fill first. Mayax unabashedly swung his five monstrous phalluses in Mina's general direction and let her have a good, long look.

She sat there in the cage, gobsmacked, wide-eyed and scarred for life; the impossibly full glass of wine clutched firmly and untouched in her right hand, while her cigar sat forgotten between her pursed lips. Mayax grinned, loving the look on her face, and incanted himself back to one impressive singular penis. Giving Mina one last look, he conjured his thorny black armor back around his body and stepped off the backs of the two yaggowars.

Mina starred at Mayax and downed the entire glass of wine in one impressive gulp. She dropped the glass, which shattered on the street beneath the cage, and pulled her cigar from between her teeth. "That wasn't awkward for me at all."

"Well, now I know what it takes to impress you," Mayax quipped, as another huge explosion erupted beside them. He nonchalantly turned his head back to the Black Hawks circling above. "Oh yes, I forgot about them. A moment please..." Mayax turned and levitated up into the air to face the three helicopters on their home turf. The other Roses with Thorns and Nevuscar suited back up and stood by awaiting orders for reinforcement.

Rake continued to stand close by but was eager and preoccupied with joining the fight. Mina used the distraction to look for any way out of the cage, but there didn't seem to be one. Suddenly, she heard a familiar voice whispering to her from behind a nearby pile of rubble, "Mina, hey." It was Avery. Oh God, it was Avery.

"What the hell are you still doing here?" Mina mouthed more than screamed.

Avery just shrugged his shoulders as if to say, "I dunno, but you're welcome." She frantically waved him away, but he bravely, and foolishly, snuck up right to the edge of the cage. "Can't you explode your way outta this or something?"

"If I could, don't you think I would have by now?" Mina asked with angry emerald eyes.

"I guess so. What can I do; how do I get you outta there?" Avery diligently looked for a lock, release or any kind of access, but there was none.

Without warning, Rake suddenly appeared behind Avery, towering over the teenager like a monolith. "What have we here? A little...*boy*?"

"I'm all man, pal." Avery spoke defiantly.

"I'll just bet." Rake smiled, revealing his shark-toothed grin and raised his new metal gauntlet high in the air for a death blow.

Mina shuddered, "No, wait."

Just then, a blast from above hit Rake hard in the chest and sent him ass-over-elbow into a wall of fire. Mina, shocked, looked up into the air and saw Mayax levitating there, his hand still smoking. He looked annoyed, but quickly turned back around and began powering up big time to scorch the earth. Only Bael of the Nevuscar and a few Roses with Thorns had seen his uncharacteristic act of charity, but you could tell they were perplexed and didn't like it much. Mina had only seconds to get out of there and save Avery before Rake crashed the party again. She thought at the speed of a supercomputer and an idea suddenly came to her. The cage may be able to block her magic, but not her Alma. She quickly exhaled her soul smoke in one great gasp and transformed into the second largest yaggowar ever, next to her mother. The sheer size of her feline form expanded and shattered the iron cage like tinfoil and set her free. Avery gawked at her, frozen and amazed as she seized him in her massive maw and took off with him like a lioness with her cub.

Mayax saw Mina abscond with the young man, but worried not. "Run rabbit, I'll catch up to you later." More military Humvees and vehicles of war arrived, and the soldiers ran around the area like ants with a purpose. Additionally, several fighter jets streaked by overhead with deadly intent, and began circling back around to attack. Mayax huffed in aggravation, and rather than turn everything to ashes, he motioned for the other Nevuscar and Roses with Thorns warriors to join him in taking leave. They all took a look around and reluctantly agreed that this was not the time to declare war on the Earth realm, so they conjured portals beneath their feet and dropped out of sight—everyone except Rake. He pulled himself from the rubble and glared at Mayax before blinking out. Mayax sighed deeply. "That woman will be the ruin of me." Right as the military got into position and prepared to launch a massive offensive, Mayax blinked out of midair, leaving them all wondering what the hell had happened.

Chapter 4
Fresh Outta Fucks

Mina made sure she and Avery were deep inside the Frelinghuysen Arboretum before gently placing him down and shifting back to her female form. She only had the Ceridome wraps to cover her now that previous transformation had shredded her clothes. "Damn, I loved that shirt." Avery was clearly trying to wrap his head around everything, so Mina attempted to calm him. "I guess an explanation is in order here?" she managed in a clumsy tone.

"That was the coolest fucking thing I have ever seen." Avery blurted out loudly.

"Shhhhhh," Mina put her finger to her lips and quickly silenced him.

"Oh my God," he desperately tried to whisper. "You really are a fucking superhero."

"No I am not, but we need to get our shit together in a hurry and get the fuck out of here." Mina looked around to make sure she hadn't been followed. "Be quiet and do exactly as I say."

"Totally." He was smiling ear to ear.

"This is not something you should be enjoying," Mina scolded. "Now, where do you live? I'll drop you at home and you must never—EVER—speak of this again, to anyone."

"What, are you kidding me? Oh man, don't sideline me now. We're a team, like Batman and Robin, or some damn thing. I can help."

Mina grabbed Avery by his stained and scorched Hawaiian shirt and reeled him in to within inches of her burning, green eyes, "We are not a team. Understand? You are in incredible danger here. If they find us...It would not be pretty. I need to get you home as soon as possible."

"Will they be able to find me there?" Avery asked frantically. "I mean, can that tall fucker track me to try to get to you?"

Mina thought for a long moment and bowed her head. "Fuuuu-uuuuuuuck."

"See, so you have to take me now. Ha ha. You can't let me go home and risk them finding me." Avery knew he had a point and drove it home. "Looks like we're a team after all." Avery couldn't hide his excitement. "Look, I can help. I'm not sure how yet, but I promise I won't slow you down."

Mina shook her head and rubbed her eyes with her hands. "Fuuuu-uuuuuck."

"Is that superhero talk for we're a team?"

"Absolutely not. I'm guessing you have a mother, father, sister, and or brother..."

"Um, all the above," Avery admitted, shrugging his shoulders.

"Fuuuuuuuuuuuuuck," Mina gasped again and rubbed her head some more, "Okay, okay, how long can you reasonably stay away without raising suspicion?"

"I dunno; I have another week of school left before summer break. After that, I can say I'm at Todd's house for...maybe a few days. I don't know though, my mom will be all over the place looking for me, especially after you nuked Morristown, and your pals fucked up Cedar Knolls."

Mina thought long and hard. Any options seemed elusive or preposterous. Finally, she spoke, "Ugh, I think I might have something..."

Avery perked up, "Oh yeah. Sweet, what?"

"So, I'll, uh...have to enchant them and wipe you from their memory—but just until we get things sorted out. When the coast is clear, it will be easy enough to undo. Christ, I need a cigar."

Avery thought about it for a quick second. "Okay, I'm strangely comfortable with that."

"We can stay at my friend Auri's house while we figure out our next moves. She's a very nice, super cool, sweet Irish rose, and well, kind of...how do I put this..." Mina scratched her head, "a demigod—of sorts—but completely safe. And rich, with a lot of resources."

"Wow. A demigod. This day did not go the way I thought it would this morning when I was eating my Captain Crunch," Avery said, torn between excitement and crippling fear.

"Not a demigod *exactly*, more of a...seriously high-ranking demon I guess you could say—never call her that by the way."

"Holy shit, a DEMON? No fucking way." Avery was swimming inside his head now.

"Don't call her that. Besides, she is known as a..." Mina cleared her throat, "a...Well, her official title is..."

"Ohmigawd, spit it out," Avery demanded

"She's an Executioner, okay. On occasion an interrogator, a torturer, and a punisher," Mina blurted out, "but usually an executioner—but super nice." "Jesus. And who does she execute, interrogate, torture, and or punish?" Avery asked, his voice cracking.

"Criminal demons mostly, but the occasional rogue God; you know. Fortunately, there aren't many of either, so she has a lot of time on her hands. You'll love her, trust me."

"Is SHE single...and age appropriate?" Avery asked, changing lanes quickly.

"Uh, no. She is definitely not single," Mina said, scoffing. "She is married."

"Crap, is her husband going to come home and freak out that we're there?" Avery asked fearfully. "Is he an asshole or something?"

"You've heard of Satan, right?" Mina raised her eyebrows. "Well, that's her spouse."

"Dude. This is me with my mind blown."

"Yeah, yeah, just try to act normal when you meet her," Mina pleaded. "She's shy about it all."

"Shy? Fuckin A. Will I get to meet him—Satan, I mean?" Avery asked, changing lanes yet again.

"You mean, her?" Mina corrected.

"Get the fuck outta here. I always knew being a drone pilot would change my life, but this. This is just fucking bananas."

Mayax, along with the other six Nevuscar and the Roses with Thorns, stood before the newly completed, sinister Sinteverete Temple within the Val Tebrae realm. The freshly constructed temple sat atop the ruins of the old one, and boasted new, elaborate corkscrewed architecture that spiraled up toward the heavens for miles in looming, infinite blackness. Hundreds and hundreds of miles of salt flats surrounded it, and thorny black and red Deadman trees that bore fleshy flowers and jagged branches. Mayax conjured an entrance, and they all stepped in.

Once inside, the Roses with Thorns broke off to the left and down a dark, foreboding passageway. When they were out of sight, a massive iron gate crashed down behind them, sealing them within. The Nevuscar continued forward into the stony, shifting, MC Escher-esque labyrinth that morphed and spun around them precariously at impossible angles. Anyone who didn't know how to navigate the complex, enigmatic maze would surely be crushed, impaled, or pushed into a yawning abyss by the morphing structure, but Mayax and the other Nevuscar strolled through it like they were window shopping.

Upon entering the Elder's vast, stone chambers, Mayax was always impressed by the outrageously high, domed ceilings that were held up by tall, stout columns displaying ornate, intricate carvings of their sacred runes depicting the same blue dwarf star of the Mandala realm. Further into the chamber there stood seven ostentatiously decorated thrones with precious metals and jewels covering every inch. The Master Elder's throne sat in the middle of the other six smaller thrones, all with their backs towards the entrance. The Master Sinteverete Elder spoke out in a creepy, childish voice that echoed ominously throughout the vacuous chamber, "You still do not possess the Yasmani Ro?"

"No, Master Elder," Mayax answered unabashedly. "However, she is no longer trying to hide, so it will be easy for us to locate her again. I warn you though: she has become very powerful and formidable. She represents the best training of both clans, and we're no longer hunting her; she's picking a fight."

"You suggest I should fear this mongrel minx, Mayax?" The Master Elder needled in that ghastly, youthful voice. "All we ask is that you bring her to us—ALIVE."

"I am aware you require her Alma for the dark Ritual of Estuche." Mayax reminded him. "Only the soul smoke of a Yasmani Ro born of fire and ice during the blue dwarf star eclipse can make you pristine, unmarked and immortal; all your beauty and wisdom forever preserved," he continued, suspiciously sarcastic. "You will be immortal like us Nevuscar—but not like us. You will be so much more." He bellowed too enthusiastically. "Untouched by hurt or blemished by scars. You will never have known suffering or strife, and you never will." Mayax proclaimed overdramatically. "You will be the supreme beings and bring all the realms together under your gorgeous rule."

The Master Elder giggled impishly and maniacally clap his hands together in quick succession from behind his throne. "Magnificently said, Mayax. You sing the words like swallows from your lips. Truly a poet and rabble rouser of inspiration."

"You flatter me, Master Elder." Mayax said in a practiced and well rehearsed tone. "It means a great deal to me, knowing I inspire loyalty and unity amidst you all. Always a place at the table for us, yes, Master?"

"At the head of it, Undying one," the Master Elder smirked. "Now bring me the mongrel, Mayax. Earn your place at the table."

"Master."

Rake could barely hide his contempt.

Auri opened the front door to her lavish mansion in the hills wearing a brightly colored exercise outfit, and saw Mina there in nothing but her Ceridome wraps, with a teenager that couldn't take his unblinking eyes off her.

"Well, I've been expecting *you*." Auri declared. She was a stunningly beautiful woman, with blood red hair, green Irish eyes and rosy cheeks. She was tall at five eleven, but nowhere near as tall as Mina. "You know you're all over the Internet and television fighting with Nevuscar and

the Roses with Thorns, right? Good Lord, look at the state of you."
She bellowed in a thick Irish accent. "And what's with the kid?"

Avery stood there slack jawed and stared at her wide eyed. "Nice
place."

"You told him everything about me, didn't you?" Auri scolded.

"Yeaaaaaah, well, sort of. Lighten up though, I can always wipe his
memory," she assured Auri as she shoved her and the kid inside, but
quietly shook her head "no" to Avery.

Once inside the sprawling, ostentatious home, Auri lambasted
Mina. "Jesus Christ, Mina. You destroyed a major township in New
Jersey after I explicitly told you not to overreact. That's the last time I
mix in with your relationships. Then you come here after giving Cedar
Knolls the same treatment and becoming Internet famous, looking
like a wartime refugee—Fuck sake."

"I know, I know, I'm sorry. Can I please borrow some clothes?"
Mina begged.

"Ugh," Auri rolled her Irish eyes and stomped up the elaborate
staircase towards her bedroom. "C'mon bitch." She hollered down to
her, waving her up the stairs.

"You sure she's not going to execute us?" Avery asked in a genuinely
concerned tone.

"If she executes anyone, it'll be me, so you're good. Just don't...say
anything or touch anything and stay here. I'll be right back."

"Can do," Avery promised, saluting Mina.

Mina chuckled, "Don't...don't salute me," then rushed up the
stairs after Auri. She crept into her bedroom and called out, "Auri?"

She responded from her gargantuan walk-in closet, "You got some
'splainin' to do, Mina." When Mina joined her in the ridiculously
huge walk-in closet, Auri pulled a tight T-shirt off a random hanger
and tossed it to Mina, "I believe this is one of yours."

Mina held it up to read the print on the front, "Fresh Outta Fucks." She smiled, "Yep, that's mine. Thanks girl." Mina pulled it on over her wraps and selected a nice pair of tight black pants from a shelf. "These okay to borrow?"

"Yes, yes," Auri said curtly, exiting the closet and crossing the room to sit on the lush bed that was the size of a football field. "Now, you wanna explain to me what the actual fuck is going on?" Auri plopped down on the bed and crossed her legs in an expectant, parental manner. "Yes..."

"So, um, yeah, I made a rash decision in the heat of the moment, and now I'm just dealing with it," Mina explained nonchalantly.

"Well, that's pretty fucking reductive," Auri huffed. "And what about the kid out there? How the Hell does he figure into things?"

"He...uh...saw me blow up Morristown with his drone." Mina expressed sheepishly.

"Wow. So you kidnapped him? Unbelievable. Not that it matters now anyway. The media is connecting what happened in Morristown to what happened in Cedar Knolls. You can't believe the unbridled speculation going around. And they have your mug, along with the others, plastered everywhere."

"No, no, I didn't kidnap him. I'm protecting him," Mina said reassuringly. "And yeah, I guess it's not a stretch to connect those two things. I may have to adjust my age to stay undetected. It's...frowned upon to go younger, but I sure as hell ain't going older."

"I wish I could adjust my age. At least I age very slowly—and gracefully. Anyway, more on that in a minute," Auri digressed. "And what did I tell you on the phone? What did I specifically say? I said, 'DON'T DO ANYTHING RASH', didn't I?"

"Yes, you certainly did," Mina said, bowing her head like a chastised child. "What can I say? I'm prone to whimsy."

"Whimsy? Dude, you incinerated half of Morristown and a church, not to mention about a thousand people, and then fought a battalion of barbarians from another realm in front of a few hundred people with cell phones. Somehow 'whimsy' just doesn't quite say it."

"I mean, yeah, what the fuck do you want me to say? Don't piss off a Yasmani Ro. My bad."

"Damn girl, you stink of the drink too," Auri observed, waving her hand in front of her face. "REALLY?"

"It's a very long story—there was wine and Copunocture involved; we can get into all that a little later." After a moment's consideration, "And, I'm sorry, but am I really being lectured by Satan's executioner—slash—wife? Give me a break. Shit, what about that time you called me from Vegas, high on Deadman and covered in the blood of a hundred mercenaries because you, and I quote: 'were given bad intel.'"

"Yeah, well, toh-ma-to, to-mah-to," Auri said. "You didn't see that shit on the prime-time news, though, did you?"

"Well, you have me there," Mina relented.

"Shuddup and get your ass over here, girl," Auri said, patting the bed next to her and holding open her arms. "I'm sorry Roland turned out to be a lying, cheating shithead. I'd offer to execute him, but—you know—you already did."

Mina's shoulders slouched as she walked over, sat down on the bed next to Auri, and gave her a big hug. "Thanks, honey. He must have been a total sociopath, anyway; I never once detected any change in his heart rate or blood pressure when he was lying his balls off straight to my face."

"This is why I'm married to a woman, and the men we bed are always lawless demons and slaves," Auri noted, stroking Mina's hair gingerly.

"Don't let the Christians hear you say that," Mina joked, and instantly regretted it.

"You know, religion here in the Earth realm has given the Hell realm such a bad name, and we just take it on the chin." Auri began to launch into another one of her myriad tirades surrounding religion. "It's so unfair. Hell serves a very important function. We operate a prison for all the rotten souls and evil entities, so they don't keep breeding and spreading. You know, without us keeping them in check, all the realms would be lousy with wicked, awful shit. Furthermore, our support is the only reason the Earth realm is as powerful as it is to begin with. We've invested in this shit hole and the souls on it, so whether we like it or not, we have to protect our investment—even if no one fucking appreciates it. I mean, HELLO. Our protection and services are the only reason the Sinteverete haven't tried to take over yet, and is the main reason this cluster fuck of a realm isn't overrun."

"I can tell you right now that demons and demigods are the least of your worries; you're going to have big problems with the Sinteverete Elders now that they have subjugated the Pentavi, built an immortal army, and are dangerously close to perfecting immortality for themselves. I promise you they are gearing up for an invasion." Mina was solemn and serious now.

Auri tried to lighten the mood, "Yeah, yeah, yeah, they've been singing that song for many hundreds of thousands of years now. Even with their dark magic on the rise, that's not a fight they want to pick—at least not right now. I don't see them getting a lot of traction trying to take on the Earth realm military alongside our legions of enforcers, anyway. Smug pricks."

"Shit, you don't know the half of it, sister," Mina snorted. "You and Bee better watch those fuckers real close, though," she added sincerely, while tenderly rubbing Auri's shoulder.

"I'll put it on the list. Work has been an administrative nightmare these days." Auri shook her head in anger. "So much fucking paperwork and red tape now you wouldn't believe it. You know I haven't executed or interrogated anyone in so long; it's just been all BS work. Bee has tried to keep things flowing smoothly, but there's this demigod, Bob, who's the director of the board, trying to push her out and replace her with one of his guys. It's a whole thing."

"Bob? Really?" Mina had a hard time swallowing that name for a demigod.

"Yeah, I know, right? And he chose that. Anyway, he's such a typical dangling dick. Makes me fucking sick." Auri feigned gagging. "He wants to scrap the current model completely and give up the prison business altogether. He actually said the realms should be handling their own garbage for themselves. He wants to get in bed with the politicians here on Earth, the Elders in your realm, and the overseers in all the other realms so he can muddy the waters with bureaucracy and rise to the top," she proclaimed in mock grandiosity. "The most frightening thing is, he has a lot of support down there."

"I'd watch that brazen Bob," Mina warned, wagging her finger. "He offers exactly the kind of dirty dealings the Sinteverete will be looking to exploit. Fuck, this thing keeps getting bigger and bigger."

"You ain't lyin.' Good advice though, I'll pass it along to Bee. Now, about your fugitive status, do you guys need to hide down below for a minute, or what?"

"I really appreciate that," Mina proclaimed sincerely. "Avery might need to hang with you guys for a bit until I sort this shit storm out. The Nevuscar and Roses with Thorns would be fucking insane to try to start trouble here. Shouldn't take too long to mind-erase his family, kick the Nevuscars' asses, collect the heads of all the Elders, and bring our clans back together; you know, another Tuesday night."

"That's quite a to-do list. Yeah, I don't see the Sinteverete knocking on this door looking for trouble anytime soon, so we would be happy to host the young man. Keep in mind, he may see some shit around here that you'll have to mind-erase as well," Auria said, winking.

"I figured; fuck, I better mind-erase his family soon," Mina groaned and rolled her eyes. "When is Bee getting home?" Mina asked.

"She's caught up at work but should be home in the morning. She's going to love seeing you again. It's been a long while since we all hung out."

"Indeed. She'll be okay with Avery here, right?" Mina inquired, concerned about putting them out.

"Oh yeah, it's all good," Auri assured her. "Teenage boys are her bread and butter, so I'm sure she'll love him." To this, they both laughed loudly. "Wanna...fool around until she gets home? She would absolutely love to come home to that."

There was a gasp from around the corner of the bedroom door as Avery struggled to contain his hormones.

"Ugh, no, let's deal with the horny teenager's family first. Besides, I have to get my head straight; I'm pretty sure the lead Nevuscar, Mayax, is crushing on me," Mina speculated.

"Oh. My. God. Do tell." Auri's focus totally shifted to girl talk as she slapped Mina's knee. "Holy fuck—you're into him."

"No, I'm not. I assure you, I am not," Mina said, trying to convince them both. "I mean, he's got five dicks, but...No, no, no. This is me changing the subject."

"Five dicks, you say? Jesus Christ, if you don't wanna crack at that, Bee and I certainly do. I saw him on the Internet, all hot as fuck in that Reclon armor. Damn, I could hit that."

Mina slowly turned her head to look deep into Auri's eyes, "Please shut up."

Avery suddenly peeked his head from around the door frame. "Who's got five dicks?"

They both devolved into laughter once again.

It was night now, and the air was cooling. While it was a clear night, there were no stars visible due to the excessive light from the neighboring cities. "Alright, kid, what's your home address?" Mina asked Avery outside on Auri's bricked private road.

"It's 384 Marne Road, Cedar Knolls, New Jersey," the youth rattled off effortlessly.

"Okay..." Mina punched the address into her phone and got the location. "I think you'll enjoy this next part," Mina teased.

"Cool. All I ask though, is that you don't blow up my family," Avery said sincerely.

"Fair 'nuff,'" Mina said, concentrating on the GPS coordinates on her phone. She began to whisper chant, and a portal opened up right next to them; on the other side of it, Avery could see his house.

"No way. That is so fucking epic. You have to show me how to do that." Avery was like a kid in a candy shop.

"Maybe sometime. C'mon, let's go." She pushed him roughly through the portal and followed him in. Instantaneously, they were on the other side and she pulled him behind a tree, casting a long shadow. From there she transformed herself into an 18-year-old girl, conjuring her clothes to fit, and could immediately read Avery's interest.

Avery, "I didn't know you could do *that*."

"I'm going to need you to put that thought right out of your head, youngster." Mina was stern to drive her point home.

"What? Oh, yeah…totally, no, no. You are hot, though." He looked longingly at her. "Jeez. Will you go to prom with me?" Avery blushed.

"Dude, we have such bigger fish to fry right now," Mina said, getting frustrated. "I'll tell you what, if we survive all this, I'll think about it."

"I'll take it. Man, that would burn Kendra's ass so bad." Avery became lost in the what ifs.

"Focus kid," Mina shook him. "I need to be in close proximity to everyone in your family for this to work. Got anything in mind?"

"Uh, yeah," looking at his watch, "We usually eat dinner pretty soon, but I have to warn you, my family is tragically embarrassing. Like on a different level, embarrassing."

"What family isn't? This should be pretty interesting." Mina rubbed her head as though a migraine were coming on.

"Good point. Oh, my mom will most likely be totally insane since I haven't answered her 99 million calls all day and you guys recently blew up downtown Cedar Knolls. I'm starting to see a pattern here, by the way. I'll tell her we were out and my phone broke. Still, though, brace yourself."

"Jesus, kid, wasn't it you who promised me you wouldn't be a burden?" The headache was finally upon her. "Okay, whatever, let's just get this over with. I assume they wouldn't be thrilled with me smoking a cigar in their house?"

"Haha nooooo." Now it was Avery's turn to push Mina ahead. "C'mon, this'll be weird."

"Yeah, I know," Mina said, huffing like an angsty teenage girl. "Ugh, hormones. I forgot how much I hate being this age."

The moment Mina and Avery stepped through the back door, there was an onslaught of heated, concerned questions hurled at them. His mother was at the forefront of the cacophony. "Oh, dear Lord in Heaven, where the hell have you been?"

"I'm really sorry mom, my phone broke and I got stranded—," he began to explain before his dad cut him off.

"Listen up, Avery. It is completely unacceptable to stay gone all day and not answer your phone when there are literal riots and explosions happening in the streets. Jesus Christ, you had us worried to death."

"And who is this?" Avery's mom demanded, pointing sternly at Mina. "Are you the one who had him out gallivanting around all day during a damn national crisis?"

Mina, who was over two hundred years old and trained in more than four hundred and sixty styles of fighting, looked like a helpless deer caught in the headlights of a truck. "Uhh, no. No, I had to go get him. He—uh—his friends had to leave because of everything that's happening...you know, with the riots and all...and he got stuck on the other side of town, where I live. So, I went and picked him up and brought him home as quickly as I could." She kicked herself for not having a better story prepared. Next time, she promised herself.

Avery's parents snapped their heads around for verification, so he quickly spoke up. "Yeah. Yeah, Todd's truck broke down and I had to call Mina. This is Mina by the way. We're going to prom together."

Mina quickly gave Avery 'the look,' but didn't have time to truly drill it home before Avery's mom was all over her again. "I see. Nice shirt, Mina," Avery's mom said in a pointed tone.

Mina looked down at her shirt, kicking herself again for not thinking of changing it sooner, "Oh, this, haha, well, you know—my uh, yeah."

Mina just bowed her head as Avery tried to smooth everything over. Mina wanted desperately to just start handing out mind-erasing spells, but she had to wait until his brother and sister were present. As if on cue, Avery's little sister rounded the corner to the kitchen giggling as 4-year-olds do. "Affrey in trouuuuuuble," she managed, while shaking her plump little finger at him.

"Shut up—I mean, no Lilly, it's just a misunderstanding is all..." Avery started but was cut off yet again by his mother.

"You are in big trouble, mister, so we'll just have to have a little talk about prom later. Thanks for bringing our irresponsible, inconsiderate son back to us, Mina. Take care."

"Oh, actually mom, I was hoping Mina could stay for dinner," Avery ventured with an awkward smile. "And where's Jefferson at? Is he here?"

"Wow. Just wow. And since when do you care if Jefferson is here? You know, things are going to change after school ends and you start getting ready for college, mister. Mina, you're welcome to stay for dinner," she acquiesced reluctantly.

Mina snapped back into the conversation impressively, "Thanks. That's really very nice of you."

Avery's mom cut him a disappointed gaze, huffed and said, "Well, I'm Mrs. Burlington, and this is Lilly," she said in a calmer tone, pointing to his little sister. "And JEFFERSOOOON DINNER," she shouted, "is upstairs."

Mina smiled a broken smile, "Can't wait to meet everyone." Then spoke inaudibly from under her breath, "and fucking mind-erase this whole encounter for us all."

"I like her, Avery," Mrs. Burlington offered. "Much nicer than that Kendra girl. Oh, she was awful. Mina, are your parents going to be worried about you with everything that's going on?"

Mina stuttered, "Oh, uh, no, no; I called them already. They're uh, in—Morocco anyway." Morocco, she thought. Ugh, immediately after saying that, she wrinkled her eyes and wished she hadn't.

"Ohhh, how exotic. Well, I'm glad you're responsible enough to keep your parents in the know, and I hope you'll tell us all about it over dinner."

"Yeah, totally," Mina lied again.

In an instant, Avery's older brother, Jefferson, came barreling around the corner to the kitchen and froze in his tracks when laying eyes on Mina. "Ma what's for dinner? Oh, hello there." Mina raised her eyebrows in a silent greeting. "I'm Jefferson; what's your name?"

"Hello, I'm Mina. Nice to...meet you."

"The pleasure is all mine," Jefferson said, trying to be smooth. "Mina, love that name. So, what are you doing hanging around with this clown?" Jefferson asked, hooking his thumb at Avery.

Mina leaned in close to Jefferson's ear and whispered, "We're lovers."

Jefferson smiled wide and shook his head in big-brotherly approval. "Niiiiiiice." He then slapped Avery roughly on the back and plopped down into a chair at the table.

Avery spoke up, "Well, now that we're all together..." He looked pensively over at Mina.

"Oh, yeah, yeah, right—the thing..." Mina placed both hands on either side of her head and began to whisper chant quietly. For a moment, Avery's mother and father looked at her like she had two heads, but quickly glazed over and began drooling. "Alright kid, we have five minutes for you to grab your shit and us to get the fuck outta Dodge before they wake up and wonder why two strangers are standing in their kitchen."

"No pressure." Avery stepped around his dumbfounded family and bounded up the stairs. Jefferson stared slack-jawed up at Mina with a thread of drool trailing from the corner of his mouth to his shirt.

"That's a good look on you," Mina joked, looking at her watch. After a few minutes, Avery came running down the stairs in essentially the same outfit he had on earlier, only clean. He had his backpack full of stuff slung over his shoulder.

"Alright, let's save the world, or whatever." He was clearly over-joyed to be embroiled in this otherworldly adventure, and Mina couldn't deny him that. It was her fault he was in peril in the first place.

Mina sighed, "Okay, okay, let's get the hell outta here."

"Copy that." Avery confirmed. Mina opened the back door, and they stepped out onto the rear deck. She conjured a portal back to Auri's private road, and they quickly moved through it.

Meanwhile, back inside the house, the Burlington family was sit-ting down to dinner, oblivious that they were short one family mem-ber.

CHAPTER 5
THE BLOOD RED ROSES

M ayax sat solemnly upon a large, cold stone seat, detailed with elaborately carved etchings, in front of a massive, organic edge, black granite slab that served as his work surface. It was piled high with books, scrolls, papers, candles, potions, iron mixing pots, sacrificial tools, a huge cauldron in the center that bubbled with some sinister concoction, and amazingly, a very impressive computer setup with five screens. The sparse items were set within the dark, stony, shadowy confines of his vast, lonely living quarters. There was a fire pit in the middle of the barren floor with a circular iron cage around it and a roaring bonfire inside. There were also rows upon rows of ornate bookcases with shelves that stretched up into the void of darkness above, but no bed or comforts of any kind. The Nevuscar never slept, and they never relaxed because they were forever in pursuit of something.

Currently, Mayax was in pursuit of a reprieve from his troubled thoughts. He smoked a tight roll of Deadman and toiled over his dark imaginings. Mayax thought for a moment, shrugged his shoulders and conjured his roll of Deadman into a Cuban Cigar. "Damn, that really is good," Mayax murmured to himself as he pulled from the stogie and inhaled deeply. Thinking now of Mina, her words wormed their way through his mind like maggots in marbled meat. The Elders had gravely sworn their allegiance to the Nevuscar and carved the decree into their Historical Tablets, but what did it all really mean? It could just as easily have been theatre designed to maintain the Nevuscar's loyalty. There was no real binding consequence, should they decide not to honor their word. The Elders smacked of aristocracy and elitism as well, with their precious jewels, pretentious ornaments, and their flamboyantly gaudy robes and thrones—forever with their backs to us all. Would it be so far outside the realm of possibility to consider they were all being used? And then there was the audacity of the Master Elder choosing such a small child's age. No one had ever actually seen the Master Elder in the form of a child because their backs were always to them, but you could always hear it in his voice. Mocking, daring a challenge—or picking a fight. Whatever it was, it did not sit well with Mayax. Furthermore, were the Pentavi Elders truly imprisoned within their temple? He had never actually seen them in chains. There were four Pentavi Elders left after the revolt, but maybe they had negotiated some kind of beyond-the-curtain arrangement and had a hand in subjugating the rest of their Pentavi Clan in exchange. It would explain Layluna's massacring three of her own Elders, Vasser's insurrection, and their subsequent relationship. And Mina, right there at the center of it all; the personification of the entire story. Mina...

He couldn't for an instant imagine his Elders in cahoots with the Pentavi Elders, but he couldn't avoid thinking long and hard about everything. If there was some way he could see the Pentavi Elders imprisoned with his own eyes, without illusion interfering, or tipping off his Elders, that would serve as confirmation. Any allegiance the

Sinteverete Elders had with the Pentavi Elders would cement their deceit.

Mayax was over a hundred years old, and unique because of his origins. By all accounts, he was a very young Sinteverete, if he could even be considered one at all. He was the result of black magic, not conception; created with a dark heart for dark deeds by dark masters. Even the other Nevuscar treated him differently; trepidatious and weary. Rake, on the other hand, was a competitive sibling. He may have been created by the same dark magic, but he was vastly different. More angry, impetuous, and hateful. Mayax was a brutal enforcer to be certain, but not one without a moral compass or honor. He searched for meaning and reason in his deeds, and the more he searched these days, the more he didn't like what his black heart was telling him. Betrayal was in the air.

Dark magic was his creator, but he had a soul; whether it was black as pitch or not, it was there. For instance, he never once thought for even a moment that he would consider saving the life of a human insect in order to spare the feelings of a Pentavi *woman*. Is that why he had saved the child? He wasn't sure; the feelings he was having recently, more specifically surrounding Mina, were completely alien to him. At the time, it had just struck him as the right thing to do. Picking on fragile, defenseless animals was beneath him. Being a bully was a hollow bastion used to shelter weak and fragile spines and elevate delicate egos. Mayax considered an analogy: there is a big difference between killing a rabbit to eat and killing a rabbit out of cruelty.

Mayax had always felt different from the Sinteverete, even when compared to his five Nevuscar comrades. All the other Sinteverete had a very long history of hating the Pentavi, whereas he was only trained to hate them. He actually admired them as strong, honorable warriors who possessed strength and heart. Lindria and the Roses with Thorns had been his greatest resistance during the ending of the war in Reclon, and now they fought fiercely by his side with every fiber of their being. They had guts, and guts were enough.

When it came to Rake, he shared a connection and brotherhood with him, but it was complicated and combative; they were yin and yang. Even the other Nevuscar didn't care for Rake much at all. They clearly preferred things when Mayax was in charge; Rake was cruel, emotional and unpredictable.

Contrarily, the similarities he shared with Mina, like her age and unique conception, suddenly struck him. What's more, he felt indescribably drawn to her in an irresistible way. She possessed an unbreakable spirit and legendary skill. Her warrior heart was immeasurable and her Alma was stronger than a thousand jaguars. Mayax knew she would never be captured alive, much less allow herself to be delivered a prisoner to the Elders. He was beginning to think there might be too many immortals in the kitchen if they were successful in capturing Mina's Alma and performing the Ritual of Estuche. As it stood, they still had a kill-switch and could be liquidated in battle; however, after the ritual, there would be no stopping them. It began to sink in, just how much faith the Sinteverete Elders required when it came to their oath and loyalty. His confidence was shaken.

Mayax thought it best to have a conversation with someone who had extensive experience with the Elders and the situation at large. Someone who had concerns and questions so compelling it drove them to action. Someone who risked everything to rage against the machine. He decided to discuss things with Vasser and see if he could gain a little perspective.

As Mayax strolled through the whirling death machine that was the interior of their toxic temple, he thought about the questions he would ask Vasser. He wondered if Vasser would even help him, considering Mayax was the one who had imprisoned them and was currently hunting their daughter.

Mayax took a casual walk past The Paradox Stronghold where all the Steplescar were bred, raised and aged by accelerant magic; then trained to destroy. The Steplescar were a truly nightmarish breed; bald, with coarse, textured skin that resembled scar tissue, and faces void of mouths, noses and ears—all the elements that aid revolt—their only features were two red eyes set deeply within their gaunt, sandpaper faces. Eyes that sought only one thing—death. Their uniform was an imposing mixture of taunt black leather flaps and straps; worn underneath hard, heavy black armor that was dressed with spikes, chain, iron scales, and studs. They were just over half the size of Mayax, but their numbers and mindless obedience made him leery. Mayax pondered another thing Mina had intuited about the Steplescar having a kill-switch. The Elders had studied him and Rake intimately in order to figure it out, so he was aware of the detail. Damn, that girl was razor sharp; beauty was indeed a blade, and it ran in their family.

Mayax arrived and entered the trophy chamber, which doubled as a prison for many souls, including Vasser and Layluna. This vast, sterile room of rock, stone and shadow was as silent as a crypt, when in fact it was one. Every trophy either contained the screaming souls of the imprisoned, or some remnant of a fallen foe, be it ash, tooth, bone, or blood-covered steel and stone. Mayax always felt the power of this room when he walked in; it was simultaneously astonishing and humbling at the same time. It meant something to be in here.

The Malevolent one continued his walk past rows and rows of incalculable trophies, until he arrived at his most precious: the towering, exquisite obelisk of white Pentavi granite with the rune of two embracing lovers etched into its surface. He hesitated there for a moment, invigorated with the prospect of talking with the Sinteverete's most deadly warrior.

Mayax ran the palm of his hand over the smooth surface of the tomb and remembered the first day he met Mina there in the Mandala realm, so innocent and beautiful.

Young like Spring, but with a certain understanding of the universe. While she had only been warned about the savages of war during talks over a roaring fire with mommy and daddy just before bedtime, she had never had to actually endure the nightmare herself. She had trained relentlessly her entire life—for hundreds of years, in fact—but had never really needed to apply it until now. She was an apex predator, denied prey for so long that she was now spoiling for a fight. That's how villains are made, Mayax thought. It's true she had morality, heart and soul, but would scorch the earth if provoked. She had a little bit of darkness within her, just as Mayax had a little bit of light. She was impulsive, but lucky; far from battle hardened, but absolutely deadly. She was like an untested weapon of mass destruction, and Mayax found her to be an alluring enigma. When she was kicking Rake's ass and holding her own fighting the Roses with Thorns, he could sense she was only using a small fraction of her power—whether she knew it or not. Once she realized her full potential, he felt it would far surpass simply being the best trained warrior of both clans. She was destined to bring forth a reckoning; the Yasmani Ro, born of fire and ice.

Mayax withdrew his hand from the pale granite slab and blinked his eyes; instantly, a seam appeared within the monolith and withdrew like liquid to reveal Vasser's head. The warrior in stasis awoke instantly, his red eyes glowing, and snapped his pale face around to see Mayax standing there. "Mayax..." Vasser spit more than spoke his name.

"It is I. How goes your torment?" Mayax asked, not meaning the question as an insult; rather, he was genuinely curious.

"Every second you keep me away from my family is one you will later have to serve tenfold in punishment under my Blade of Black." Vasser promised vehemently, through the sweaty tangle of his white hair. "But, you know this already; why have you opened the door to my cell?"

"Explain to me how a warrior of your magnitude, the former dreaded head of the Nevuscar for millions of years, would trade everything for a fucking pussy cat?"

"You dare call my wife a 'pussy cat?' That woman is the fire in which I burn, and you will know those flames too one day—I promise."

"Maybe in Copunocture," Mayax goaded, then regretted defaulting to trivial jabs below the belt. "Listen, I did not open the cell to your cage to trade petty quibbles. I respect you and your wife for the warriors that you both are. I respect Mina for the warrior she has become—"

Vasser scoffed. "What do you know of Mina?"

"I know she is born of fire and ice, which makes her special." This elicited a probing look from Vasser. "I know her power and wrath are in their infancy. I know she is beautiful…" Mayax caressed the matching scar Mina had given him. "…And that Beauty is a blade."

Vasser narrowed his eyes. "And that blade will cut you, but apparently I don't have to tell you that. So the two of you have crossed stone and steel?" Vasser probed further.

"No. She gave me this as a warning, and no one has EVER given me a warning I considered legitimate. Mina is fierce and I've learned not to underestimate her."

"You keep her name off your tongue, wretch, or I will cut it off and wag it in front of your serpent eyes."

Mayax ignored the threat and breathed the air. "I know you would try. You know, I can still smell the honey and lavender on you, old man."

"YOU FUCKING—" Vasser screamed, but Mayax cut him off with a finger to his own lips.

"Shhhh," Mayax quieted him. "I ask you again; why sacrifice everything for a woman? Why become a traitor to your clan and its Elders after so long serving as their loyal right hand? All to become a fugitive family, only one member away from being together again in a prison of Pentavi granite?" Mayax almost whispered the last couple of words before suddenly raising his voice and fist in demand, "Why, dammit?"

Vasser began to try to whisper chant, but it had no effect and he sighed in resignation. "I'm sorry, but your magic is ineffective here," Mayax told him solemnly. "Please understand, I ask you these questions because..." Mayax trailed off.

"Because *why*?" Vasser hissed miserably.

"Because I wish to make sense of your revolt and subsequent love of our sworn enemy. It's very compelling. What did you discover that caused such a divergence in your path? What did you learn of our Elders?"

"Ahhhhh, the Elders," Vasser reminisced. "Do you really want to know? I wonder. I do nothing for your pleasure, pig."

"Might be in your best interest, old man. I am...conducting an investigation and require this information. In exchange, I could offer you something..." Mayax teased.

"What could you possibly offer me, mage? You've taken everything from me." Vasser bellowed from the pit in his stomach.

Mayax blinked his eyes and the Pentavi granite became like liquid again, and receded to reveal Layluna's bowed and unconscious head. Vasser studied Mayax very carefully. "Dammit, I want her with me."

Vasser demanded. Mayax sighed and dissolved the granite around them, allowing Vasser to catch Layluna in his arms before she crumpled to the ground. Vasser looked up to Mayax with a mixture of unending rage and immeasurable gratitude. "You wish to know? I'll tell you. They lied, asshole." Vasser screamed at Mayax. "They have lied about *EVER-Y-THING*. The purpose of the Great Divide was engineered by BOTH the Sinteverete AND the Pentavi Elders; all so they could gamble on the outcomes of our spilled blood. And when that didn't proffer one clan reign over the other, the Elders from both clans decided to unify and get rid of us all. Then, they were going to build some army of mindless Nevuscar, and become truly immortal themselves. The Sinteverete and Pentavi Elders have been united for a very long time; unified in our subjugation, unified in our extermination, and unified in domination over the realms. Wake up, you poor fool. Wake up before it's too late. If the Elders have not discovered true immortality yet, they soon will. And when they do, you will be right next to us in a slab of Pentavi granite. You and all the other Nevuscar. Then your Sinteverete brothers and the Pentavi slaves will all be executed."

"An interesting theory, Vasser." Mayax concluded, rubbing his bearded chin.

"It's no theory, Mayax. I heard it from their own lips. I saw it with my own eyes." Vasser screamed but was careful not to disturb Layluna in his arms.

"That sinister little imp, the Master Elder, took great pleasure in telling me this. So tell *me*, how far along are they in their wicked designs? Do they have their army? Are they immortal? And who authorized this investigation?"

"This investigation is mine, and mine alone," Mayax said in a thunderous tone. "I don't need authorization. However, it appears you and I share a suspicious nature."

"Is that right?" Vasser examined Mayax with his pointed eyes for any sign of comradery, but it just wasn't there yet. "When you finally open your eyes to the world around you, Mayax, we will be here. Your brainwashing at the hands of our Elders is criminal, but the real crime is not learning the lesson." This seemed to hit Mayax in the gut like a fist.

Layluna suddenly stirred in Vasser's arms. She blinked and cleared her magnificent green eyes and saw Vasser there, amazingly smiling down at her. She immediately broke into tears and hugged him desperately in her arms. She kissed him passionately and whispered a promise of her undying love into his ear. They held each other for a long moment, feeling the electrical connection for as long as they could, all while Mayax watched on with incredible interest. This was what love looked like. It was so foreign and incomprehensible to him, yet he was no stranger to it. Seeing them this way, feeling their heat, pulled his thoughts back to Mina. Mina... "Enough," Mayax suddenly shouted.

The two soul mates maintained their embrace but focused determined eyes on the sorcerer barbarian standing tall before them. Layluna scowled with poisonous eyes. "*You.*"

"Yes, me," Mayax confirmed.

Layluna studied his scar. "I see Mina gave you something to consider."

"Agreed. It would seem the three of you have," Mayax confessed. "Now, charming as this conversation is, I've woken you with purpose. Tell me, if I were to see the Pentavi Elders in chains, how could I be so certain it was them?"

Layluna looked bewildered and confused now. "What the Hell are you talking about?"

Mayax sighed deeply. "I want to know that your Elders are indeed prisoners of the Sinteverete instead of conspirators—as you suggest."

Layluna squinted her eyes, trying to catch up on events surrounding her clan, and see through to Mayax's soul. "Tell me, mage, have you seen the Pentavi Elders dressed in chains? I'll bet not. But I wager even if you were to see them imprisoned, it would be a ruse. I saw their conspiracy with my own eyes, but you don't have to take my word for it—go see for yourself."

"How," Mayax demanded.

"Every Pentavi woman since Zol has secretly been given a mark at birth by their mothers. This rather unassuming mark, about the size of a blueberry, was branded on the soft flesh under the right shoulder, above the axillary."

"Go on..." Mayax encouraged her in a more forthcoming tone.

"The mark illustrates the Alma, or soul smoke, inherent in every Pentavi woman." Layluna weakly raised her right arm and showed Mayax the mark above her armpit. "The mark was a hard kept secret among the Pentavi women; none of the Sinteverete men, or any of the Elders, were aware of the ritual. It was done in secret to honor the fourteen Elders—the firstborn—who were considered perfect, unmarked and unblemished."

Mayax was intrigued. "I see. Did you brand Mina with this mark?"

"No," Layluna said, more to Vasser than Mayax. "I broke with tradition because our Mina is the truly perfect one—not them. Seek out our Pentavi Elder captives, and seek the mark. If it is absent, you have the real Elders, but if it is there...you've been had. Now, let us out. We will help you find this truth and retribution. We are not your enemies, dammit."

"We are not allies either," Mayax pointed out.

"Why not?" Layluna demanded through her tears of mixed emotion.

"I'm not sure yet," Mayax admitted.

He blinked his eyes and the white Pentavi granite became liquid again, only this time, instead of sealing them inside separately, it sealed them together within a lightless, stasis bubble of prison rock. Inside, Vasser and Layluna kissed and held each other tightly, promising one another they would soon get out.

Vasser and Layluna sightlessly clutched one another in the inky blackness of their prison. It was as if they were floating through space, just the two of them, together. Suddenly, the prison felt less like Hell and more like Heaven. Here, they didn't have to worry about war, fighting, death, or vengeance; here, they could be together forever, locked in a loving embrace. They no longer required food, or water, or air; they had each other in stasis, their love preserved forever—but forever caged. Did it really matter, Layluna wondered? Love is love, when experienced together, and here they had that. But then Layluna's thoughts found Mina.

"Mina will need our help," Layluna spoke aloud to Vasser. "We need to get out of here."

"I know, my love. We will." Vasser promised, kissing Layluna softly on the lips and exploring her wild hair with his wanton hands. "For now, I'm just so grateful to have you in my arms once more. Your absence was a hell I cannot ever again endure."

"It seems like a dream, but here we are. I won't waste a second wondering why." Layluna feverishly kissed Vasser again, her hands now finding his leather fastenings. "I want you now. I need you inside me to know you are truly flesh and not fantasy." Layluna's hands toiled fervently to get Vasser's leather garments off, while he slowly dragged her long, black robe down to her feet. In an instant, Layluna had Vasser's strapped leather uniform on the bottom of their cage, and his Absence of Light cloak off and around them like a blanket. He felt her face with rough hands and projected her beautiful visage inside his head, but it was not enough; his eyes were greedy for her. He knew he could not conjure any significant magic in here, but he could manage a very small, weak, light sphere the size of a firefly, so they could lay eyes on one another. Under the faint light, they wept in each other's presence. It was the first time one had seen the other since they were captured in the Mandala realm, over a hundred years ago. With his hungry hands, Vasser explored every inch of her body, still dirty from the garden on Mandala so many years ago. Each second locked in the granite had been torture; they could only think, but were unable to move, hear, or see anything—complete sensory deprivation—but they found a way.

Layluna looked deeply into Vasser's eyes, fraught with shadow from the dim, flickering light. "I could feel you in there, my love. Your heartbeat, a rhythm, a vibration through the rock no prison could contain. I retreated inside myself, but your heartbeat was always there to remind me of you."

Vasser caressed her face with his hand. "No prison can ever keep us apart. I could always feel your heat there burning behind the cold stone, assuring me you were close and alive."

"That heat is about to burn you, dear husband," Layluna moaned, breathing in his honey and lavender fragrance to the point of intoxication. "I missed your scent more than anything else in the world."

"For me, it was the taste of you," Vasser said breathlessly as he ran his forked tongue over the dewy landscape of her neck. "Tasting you was always one of the greatest pleasures of my long life."

"Taste me now," Layluna begged through bated breath. Vasser didn't waste a microsecond and dove deep inside her starving clit with his ravenous tongue. Layluna's spine cracked with electricity and arched as Vasser savagely lapped her into a frothy frenzy. She exhaled some of her Alma and tangled her claws deep inside his long, white hair, pulling him deeper inside her. After only a brief moment, Layluna bathed her lost lover's serpent tongue in sweet orgasmic body nectar that was sweet and tangy, which he licked up like a thirsty hummingbird. Wanting her kiss, Vasser ascended the length of her body and shared the nectar with her in a crazed kiss. He knew she loved her own taste almost as much as he did.

Layluna couldn't stand the anticipation any longer; the many years spent separated now behind them, "Vasser, my light, my love, you are the marrow in my bone. I have never wanted you more than I do right at this moment."

Vasser caught her words with his lips, replying in a ragged breath, "We are forever bound together by devotion, purpose and vengeance. There is no love that burns as bright as ours."

In a desperate, fleeting moment, Layluna wrapped her legs around Vasser's waist and brought him deeper inside her, sending her over the precipice and plunging them both into a heated rhythm. They ebbed and flowed with one another in perfect harmony; like undulating ocean waves, they crashed into one another with increasing tempo. Vasser gripped his wife's hips firmly, remembering all too well the pain of her absence, while Layluna refused to let him withdraw, fearing he might vanish from her sight like before.

Neither could stand to close their eyes or blink for even a second, afraid the reunion may be some trick of the mind, or cruel hallucination brought on by extreme solitude. Layluna rode Vasser tenaciously until she could sense he was about to climax. The anticipation drove her over the edge and she drenched Vasser's throbbing cock before going down on him to taste herself once again. She cupped his balls in one hand and pistoned him in and out of her mouth with the other. Vasser gasped for air in the airless chamber until he found the edge of his climax, then propelled himself over it. After projectile ejaculating down Layluna's throat, she siphoned as much of his sweet, honey-flavored cum into her mouth as she could and drank deep, relishing his flavor.

Vasser collapsed next to Layluna and spooned her underneath his Absence of Light cloak. "I would rather snuff out my immortal flame than ever go that long without you again. I swear this to you now, death before disunion."

"Death before disunion," Layluna repeated intently. "Now, before we fuck a hundred more times, how are we getting out of here? We have to find Mina and help protect her."

"This prison extinguishes magic, and without it, there is no way to break free. However, I believe we may have made an ally in Mayax."

"You really think so?" Layluna asked rhetorically. "That miserable, black-hearted mage—no offense—is miles away from helping us. I could smell Mina on him, Vasser. She clearly gave him that scar as a comeuppance for our imprisonment. There is no way he would join with us—or her—unless he had some twisted ulterior motive. It's irrelevant anyway; I will tear this fucking cage apart with my bare hands to find her if I have to," Layluna screamed so loud within the tiny cell it momentarily deafened them both.

Vasser quickly rolled over and softly kissed her trembling lips. "Be calm, my love. Mayax would never have come down here to investigate had he not made a significant journey towards suspicion already."

"Well, he better hurry the fuck up and screw his head on. I can't stand being sidelined like this for so long," Layluna cried, fraught and anxious.

"Mina can handle herself; trust me. Not to mention, if he had captured or killed her, he would have rubbed it in our faces. She is still out there, and most likely the one putting them on the defensive. Don't forget, the barbarian actually imprisoned us together this time, so he's coming around. Let him go investigate your supposedly imprisoned Elders; I'll bet he'll be begging us to help him soon. Just try to be patient." Vasser went to kiss her lips again, but she turned her head.

"You remember how I feel about you telling me to be patient and relax, right?" Layluna emphasized this statement with a biting, sideways glare of her eyes.

"Of course, my love," Vasser relented.

"Alright then, I guess there's nothing left to do but wait. And what better way to pass the time in a cage together..." Layluna's sharp eyes became sexy eyes, and she grabbed hold of his cock underneath the cloak. "Ready for another round, warrior?"

"It would be my pleasure..." Vasser whispered in her ear.

Mayax was lost in angry thought as he made his way briskly to the Sinteverete stockade, where the Pentavi Elders were supposedly being held captive. The Sinteverete temple swirled around him like a medieval torture device, while his thoughts swirled dangerously in his head. Everything Vasser and Layluna said was starting to add up. He already knew the Elders were selfish, pretentious, pious beings who sought to control and own everything throughout the realms, but he always thought they would reward the Nevuscar with authority over their armies. He also thought the Sinteverete clan would no longer have to fight when they invaded the realms thanks to the Steplescar army, rather they could focus on furthering their intellect and honing their sorcery. Now he wasn't so certain. The tapestry of his world seemed to be unraveling and revealing a very ugly stain behind it. The Sinteverete was a brilliant, proud clan with men who fought and died for a cause they unwaveringly believed in. He had fought next to them, believing the same impossible lie, and felt their loss when they died in battle next to him. Was he really a fool to have trusted his Elders? He would soon know the answer.

When he arrived at the Sinteverete stockade, he marveled at how ominous it appeared from the outside. There were two massive doors, shiny and black like spilt tar, with intricate, ornate, colossal, metal locks in place that promised no soul inside would ever escape. They stretched high to the stone ceiling, with black chrome hinges. Thorny spikes protruded through the surface as though it were a live insect.

Two heavily muscled Sinteverete guards in silver and black leathers looked shocked to see him. Mayax cleared his throat and looked impatient as the two massive guards quickly dropped to their knees in penance. "Lord Mayax." They both proclaimed in unison.

"Rise," Mayax ordered.

The larger guard to Mayax's right spoke up, "To what do we owe the pleasure?"

"I wish to see the Pentavi Elders—*now*," Mayax instructed.

"Of course, commander. This way..." The guard instructed the other to remain while he whisper chanted open the huge prison gates to certain Hell. The guard led Mayax to the Pentavi Elder's prison cell, side-by-side without a word for what seemed like forever. Upon arrival at the cell door, Mayax conjured a view portal to within and took a look. There, wrapped in thick chains, were the last remaining four Elders of the Pentavi—or at least what he presumed were the last four Elders, considering he had never laid eyes on them before.

"Let me inside," Mayax ordered.

The guard seemed flustered and uncomfortable. "I beg forgiveness, Undying One, but we have been instructed by the Master Elder never to allow ANYONE inside."

Mayax considered this, "And at this very moment, are you more afraid of the Master Elder—or *me*?"

The guard pondered this quickly and withdrew his skeleton key to let Mayax inside. Mayax snorted at the guard and strolled confidently past him.

Upon entering, the four presumed Pentavi Elders all quickly looked up in unison. They were all rail thin, mistreated, malnourished, dirty and beaten. Two of them wore long, gray dreadlocks woven into their hair, and looked to be an attractive 60ish years of age. The other two appeared much younger—twenties, maybe; one was frail with short, deep red, and savagely cropped hair, while the other had black, shoulder length hair and was missing her left arm. They were tall, pale white and barely clinging to life, but defiant with their eyes.

One of the two older women spoke softly like a sledgehammer, "Mayax the Malevolent. Isn't this a treat? What brings you to our lavish accommodations?" Mayax took note of a long ragged scar across her neck, forcing her to whisper when she spoke.

"Silence," Mayax barked, then pointed to the seasoned upstart. "You, on your feet."

She glared at him with a snarky smile, "I haven't the strength, Undying One."

Mayax stomped over to her, frustrated, and grabbed her right arm by the chained wrist. "Then allow me to give you some assistance," he hissed before roughly raising her high into the air and eye-to-eye with him. He stared through her with his burning black eyes until she faltered and looked away. At that moment Mayax knew but looked under her dangling arm anyway; and there it was, right above her armpit, her Alma mark, small and unassuming like a mole, just as Layluna had said it would be. He nodded his head slowly up and down in grim disappointment. This Pentavi woman was no Elder. She continued to look away and whimper within his crushing grasp. Mayax shot a demanding look at the other three Pentavi women, who also looked away in shame. "So, now I have my answer." Mayax relaxed his grip on the woman and gently brought her down until her bare toes touched softly on the cold rock beneath them. She found her feet and managed to call upon the strength to stand on her own.

Mayax began to growl softly at first, but it didn't take long for the sound to rise exponentially in his throat and became a thunderous, guttural roar that echoed through every hall in the Sinteverete temple, cracking the wall of the cell from floor to ceiling. The guard came rushing past the Pentavi women to see what the disturbance was; only to find Mayax standing there like a God of war with gritted teeth, clenched fists, and angry eyes. "Commander Mayax, what is it?"

Mayax towered over the muscled guard like a monolith. with murder in his eyes. However, the look quickly faded and was replaced by a cold emotionlessness. "Forget your fear at this moment. You are...Bonefield of the Sinteverete guard, are you not?"

Bonefield froze, afraid to respond at first, but found his belly, "I am."

Mayax asked him flatly, "Do you swear allegiance to me or the Elders?"

Bonefield didn't know how to respond. "I...I'm sorry, I don't understand..."

"It's a simple, but gravely serious question. Do not respond out of fear for your life, just respond truthfully. Who are you with?"

Bonefield couldn't wrap his head around the gravity of the question, and tried desperately to weigh his answer keenly. After a very long time, he raised his head, looked Mayax straight in his eyes and replied, "The Elders."

"I understand, brother. I do." Mayax actually began to tear up, faced with the cruel realization of his new life from this point forward. He wavered under all the terrible decisions he would have to make from now on. "If you stand with them, you kneel for me."

Bonefield, knowing exactly what it meant, bowed his head and kneeled before Mayax. The Undying One conjured Velocet, his cursed Cleaver of Black, slowly out of the portal armory inch-by-terrifying-inch; until its full, imposing length was visible. Like an executioner, Mayax raised the behemoth beef splitter high above his head and prepared to drop it square on the nape of Bonefield's neck. "I grant you a warrior's death. Your soul will be free from my cursed Cleaver of Black, but your head will belong to me."

"Thank you. commander," Bonefield said without fear.

"I am no longer your commander," Mayax lamented as he dropped his cleaver like a guillotine, severing the sorcerer's head from his shoulders. Mayax looked up to see the other guard standing there at the door, wide-eyed and terrified.

"I...will stand with you, Mayax." The smaller guard managed through a trembling tongue.

"Coward," Mayax growled before disemboweling him, as though he were horizontally spatchcocking a chicken. Now covered in blood,

Mayax looked to the Pentavi women, who were utterly dumbstruck. He spoke directly to them, "Do you stand with me, or your Elders?"

All four of the Pentavi women stood now on quivering, but confident legs, and looked him dead in the eye. The older woman Mayax had interrogated previously finally introduced herself. "I am Viss Vascene, and I know you, mage. You cut my throat and killed my wife right in front of me; along with 12 of my sisters during the end battle of Reclon. Their souls are locked within your cursed Cleaver of Black, you miserable cocksucker. But I'll stand with you."

Mayax humbled, nodded his head graciously and unbelievably smashed Velocet explosively against the wall. The spectral black steel broke apart like shattered ice, freeing the countless screaming souls within. Mayax was left holding the black iron handle with a big, jagged, triangular shard protruding from it like a megalodon shark tooth. Mayax never wavered, but a single tear ran down his scarred cheek and into his beefy beard for the loss of his beloved Velocet.

Viss Vascene peered skeptically through her gray dreadlocks. "Quite a performance."

The other older Pentavi prisoner stepped forward, brought her hands and arms up over her face, then withdrew them to reveal she had transformed into a much younger, strikingly lovely woman. "I am Sistell. You murdered my best friend, then personally put me in chains...and I'll stand with you."

Mayax nodded approval.

The two younger Pentavi women rose together and stood weakly, then spoke in unison, "We are the twin sisters of Savvoy."

The red head spoke first, "I am Osha. You destroyed my home, executed seven Pentavi sisters from my battalion during the trials...and I'll stand with you."

Lastly, the brunette twin spoke, "I am Amira. You cut off my arm in battle and destroyed an entire battalion of Pentavi warriors right in front of my eyes. You presumed me dead, and piled them on top of me in a mass grave. I had to claw my way with one arm through their mangled corpses to see the light of day again...and I will stand with you."

Mayax nodded nobly, then unbelievably bowed his head to them. They all shared an electrified look of absolute shock with one another before snapping out of it and returning the gesture.

Mayax motioned towards the dead guards as he attached Velocet and Bonefield's head to his belt. "You need to get your strength up."

Without warning, all four Pentavi women screamed out their Alma, shifted into full yaggowar form, and wildly began devouring the fresh meat and viscera. They were so hungry they even ate the bones, which they crunched loudly between their massive molars. When finished, they transformed back into their female forms, but were naked and covered in blood. Mayax conjured sleek, black, stylish lightweight armor around them, and smiled. After a moment's consideration, he conjured an armory of wicked, serrated edged weapons out of thin air. "I hope you ladies of war will find this armament suitable."

"And then some," Viss Vascene acknowledged with a murderous grin.

Amira quickly chose a spiked mace gauntlet, which she strapped to her left arm stump eagerly.

Viss Vascene addressed the other ladies in her whispered tone, "We will wear the blood of these first fallen as war paint. Keep it replenished as it fades, for it represents our independence day. From this day forward, we are the Blood Red Roses."

They all suddenly bellowed a "HU-RAH" in unison.

"Alright then, Blood Red Roses, I propose we storm the Elder's throne chamber immediately and make war."

"Yessssssssssss," Viss Vascene hissed, claiming her leadership of the Blood Red Roses with the single word. "We can catch them off-guard and off-balance. They won't be anticipating shock and awe in a time of their spoiled complacency."

"It's agreed then." Mayax suddenly punched straight through the cracked wall of their cell, instantly reducing it to a pile of gravel. When the dust settled, he stepped through the gaping hole and onto the narrow stone path that stretched out in front of him, hugging the right side wall. The Blood Red Roses closely followed behind him, and emerged ready for anything. There were colossal spinning gears overhead that descended from above and threatened to mutilate the female intruders, but Mayax grabbed hold of a central cog and ripped it violently from the ceiling. There was a bone-chilling screech of metal on metal as the other gears stripped their teeth and shattered their axles. Mayax tossed the mega-machine part into the gnashing teeth of another deadly contraption of carnage, closing in on them from the front. The gruesome metal monstrosity chewed on the massive cog, only to choke, smoke and grind to a halt. Mayax grabbed hold of it and forced it off their slender path and into the yawning abyss to the left of them. Behind it stood about twenty Sinteverete soldiers, their General, and about a thousand Steplescar warriors.

CHAPTER 6
BORN OF BLOOD

M ayax addressed the Sinteverete General politely, "Do you stand with me, or the Elders?"

The General wrinkled his brow. "What's that? Are you joking? How can we stand with you when you stand with loathsome Pentavi spume? Have you somehow been bewitched or beguiled? Explain yourself."

"I explain myself to no one," Mayax snarled, "much less a lowly worm like you, *General*. Now, do you stand with me, or the Elders?"

"We stand with the Elders, of course. What in the realms has gotten into you, Mayax." The General queried, trying to put his head around the impossible situation.

Suddenly, a voice from behind the General parted the Steplescar army, "I know what's gotten into him," Rake called out mockingly. He was wearing a black, torn piece of leather across the eye Mina had taken. "One sniff of pussy, that's it."

"Crass, Rake," Mayax replied like a disappointed parent. "It has absolutely nothing to do with Mina, and everything to do with our treacherous Elders. I know trying to convince you of anything is a waste of time. Enough talk, action now." Mayax levitated up off the labyrinth passage and beckoned Rake with his hand to join him. Rake obliged and levitated up into the air to meet him.

With the two of them squaring off, the General and Viss Vascene locked eyes. She chuckled, her gray dreadlocks swaying through the tense air. "Say when..."

The General shouted out a command to attack, "Kill them all." The massive regiment of Sinteverete warriors surged forward with murderous intent.

Viss Vascene quickly cast a hex on her long, serrated sword and leapt boldly off the edge of the precipice into the abyss. She plunged the cursed blade into the descending side of the stone pathway all the way to the hilt and rode it down several hundred feet before stabbing her dagger into the stone to hit the brakes. Above her, the Sinteverete army continued rushing forward, their sights set on the three remaining Blood Red Roses, who were more than ready to rumble. Viss Vascene, using the dagger as an anchor, withdrew her sword from the wall, spun around gracefully and sliced horizontally across the rock face, splitting it like a loaf of bread. The weight of the thunderous army above met the weakened, narrow pathway, and it crumbled dramatically underneath their stomping feet. Suddenly, it began raining rubble, Sinteverete soldiers, and Steplescar warriors dangerously around her. The falling army took random, vicious swings at her, but could not connect. Laughing, she used her sword and blade to climb back up the wall to her sisters. The Steplescar army, void of any conjuring abilities, tumbled pitifully into the maw of the void down below, while the Sinteverete warlocks levitated and teleported themselves back to the safety of the path above. The Blood Red Roses were there waiting for them. Right off the cuff, Osha and Amira took out eight of the dark sorcerers with their sword and mace skills, evening the odds a bit between them. Sistell didn't want to chance fully shifting into a yaggowar on the slender walkway, so she let out just enough of her Alma to use her claws. She leaped onto the ascending wall to the right like a spider, ran along it sideways for several yards, and came crashing down on the heads of several other Sinteverete sorcerers. She kicked one right back off the edge with a chuckle, sunk her sword to the hilt into the scalp of another warlock's head, and brought the blade vertically out the front of his face, neck, and chest. His body wind sprayed rubies like a jeweled fountain down into the darkness. Sistell then pirouetted back around and viciously cut the top of another Sinteverete's head off, sending his long-haired scalp flying in front of his dying eyes. More and more Sinteverete soldiers massed around the Blood Red Roses and the fight heated up.

Meanwhile, Mayax and Rake circled one another, high in the air, each waiting for the other to make a move. "I know you and I have had our differences, Rake, but you would do well to hear me out right now," Mayax encouraged him.

"Honestly, there is nothing you could possibly say that would sway me from collecting your head." Rake was grim but calm. "I've tolerated your insufferable arrogance for far too long now, and even took it easy on you when I was in command, but those days are over, *dear brother*. You have finally met your fate as a traitor in the eyes of the Elders, and once I have your head, I will cast your body into the acid oceans of Reclon to be lost in the depths forever condemned to dissolve and reconstitute for eternity."

"Very creative. Look, I respect that you have made up your mind, brother. No matter what happens, you might soon stand tall against the Elders, and they will either be weak and vulnerable, or immortal and unstoppable. The choice is yours."

"You really do take me for a fool—like yourself—don't you?" Rake laughed. "You miserable, dopy simpleton; I have known about our Elders and their alliance with the Pentavi Elders for some time now." Rake revealed unbelievably.

Mayax darkened like a storm cloud. "Explain, brother."

Rake relished the opportunity to dialogue, "First of all, I am not your brother, fool, nor would I want to be." Mayax let slip a look of shock as Rake continued. "*I* was the first. *I* was the one created by dark magic. *I* was the one that cracked the immortality code for the Elders. And *I* am the one who will lead the Nevuscar, the Sinteverete, AND the Steplescar armies like a pestilent plague across the realms." All of Rake's emphasis landed on the letters 'I.'

"Talk about arrogance," Mayax pointed out.

Ignoring him, Rake went on, "*You*—and I'm really going to enjoy telling you this—are the forbidden and flawed product of the womb." Rake laughed maniacally. "That's right, *dear brother*; you are a one-of-a-kind, Yasmani Ro Nevuscar, and direct descendant of the Master Elder. HAHAHAHAHAHAHAHAHAHA." Rake cackled like a one-eyed joker. Continuing with pleasure, "You are the illicit byproduct of our Master Elder's weakness and a Pentavi Elder's shrewd pursuit of position." Rake savored the unavoidable shock etched into Mayax's eyes. "Lock me away, it's a crime to feel this good." He bellowed in jest. "Your mother, a conniving Pentavi Elder whore, seduced the Master Elder and convinced him to match her age at fifteen in order to bed him. She planned to use sex as a manipulation in order to solidify her station by his side, but inadvertently became pregnant. She knew the Master Elder would kill you both once he found out, so she blackmailed a Sinteverete conspirator to turn you into a Nevuscar while you were still in the womb. Unfortunately for her, the Master Elder did find out and executed her, while she was still pregnant, along with her conspirator. After the Master Elder pulled you—a tiny little babe—kicking and screaming from your mother's bloody corpse, you became the Yasmani Ro born of blood. He planned to imprison you...but he just couldn't do it. Another sign of his incalculable weakness. Apparently, you reminded him too much of...*him*. The Master Elder decided to try to pass you off as a brother to me; another child of dark magic like I was, in order to bond us together throughout our training. He managed to hide his bastard son from everyone in plain sight."

Mayax erased any further emotion from his face. "Go on..."

Gleefully, Rake replied, "Poor Mayax, not as in the know as you thought, huh? You see, after I was given life through the dark ritual of Matr Faltous Estuche, my creation unlocked the secret behind true immortality."

"Do tell," Mayax inquired.

"Happy to," Rake said, clapping his mismatched hands together with joy. "I was conjured by your elders and their sorcerers, then made to crawl here through a fetid portal from a malignant realm of pure evil known as Faltous Estuche, or the Dark Realm. I was a tiny, blind and determined little fetus made of true malevolence and dark magic, brought into the world by wicked warlocks. After I was studied relentlessly by the Sinteverete Elder's most esteemed sorcerers, it was determined that while I was truly immortal like the Nevuscar, I lacked the soul inherent in all Nevuscar born of the womb—like you. This taught them many things about crafting their Steplescar army using dark magic, but more importantly they learned that the only way to bind immortality to the Elder's souls using dark magic, outside of the womb, required a special Alma sacrifice of the Yasmani Ro born of fire and ice."

"Mina," Mayax said flatly.

"Indeed; all the Sinteverete need now is your current crush. After they sacrifice her and extract her Alma, they will offer it to the God of Faltous Estuche," louder now, "architect of the Steplescar army, Lord of the Dark Realm," melodramatically screaming now, "ATHAN ASIOS—MY CREATOR ," quiet again, "in exchange for immortality. And, in exchange for immortality, the Pentavi Elders sold out their females to us for slavery and experimentation. Additionally, they promised to help the Sinteverete track down the Yasmani Ro of fire and ice. So far, the ladies have held up their end of the bargain."

Mayax shook his swimming head, "And how did you come to know all this? Your origin—my origin, the Elders coupling, their conspiracy..."

Rake giggled and that shark-toothed grin appeared underneath his ruined eye. "I'll get to that later, but first the best part, *dear brother*. The Master Elder, knowing I never liked you, promised me your head when everything was over and done." Rake squealed like a banshee. "Yep, it's true. Calculating and treacherous, aren't they? They promised I would be the one to lead the Steplescar army across the realms. They promised I would be the one flush with purpose and prize." Rake raised his hands like a televangelist.

"You're the fool Rake if you think those selfish fucks will give you anything other than a prison cell for your prize," Mayax not feeling so stupid now.

"Of course they won't honor their promises." Rake proclaimed light-heartedly, crushing Mayax's brief reprieve. "I'm not as willfully blind as you are. No, no, I'm not putting any faith in those weak, self-serving clowns. First, I'll imprison you as described earlier; I'm certain the Master Elder will be howling for your face and pecker on a platter after this little escapade—bastard son or not. Then, when you're finally out of the way, I will kill all of the Sinteverete and Pentavi Elders, take control of the armies, crush all the realms, and make Mina my number one concubine. I'll be sure and fuck her in front of your weeping eyes every night until the end of time."

"That'll be the day," Mayax growled. "You're a deceitful dog, Rake; worthy of the Elder's disloyal nature."

"Stop, you're going to make me blush," Rake joked.

"Enough. How did you know? Tell me," Mayax demanded.

"A flea told me," Rake revealed, smiling.

"Be serious," Mayax scolded.

"I am being serious," Rake admitted. "There are some unexpected benefits to being a prince of the Dark Lord Athan Asios. For instance, when I was a small boy—before you were even born—I realized I could control the lower beings in all the realms; like rats, bats, and insects. Not to mention I'm discovering new talents all the time. I have eyes and ears everywhere, in all the realms, my friend. There is nothing you've done since being born that I haven't known about, and there is absolutely nothing that happens anywhere, anytime that I can't listen in on, or see."

"I should have known your superpower was crawling in the dirt with the rest of the bugs," Mayax barked.

"There are lots of things you should have known," Rake pointed out. "It's how I knew you were here, snooping around the Pentavi prisoners. It's how I know EVER-Y-THING that goes on around here, and in the realms."

"I always knew we were different, Rake, and I'm pleased now to know why. Thank you."

"My gift to you. Something to hold dear to your heart as it floats in an ocean of acid, or toils in the belly of some beast below the surface."

"And if I win, I'll be sure to give your head a good home," Mayax promised. "Right here, on my fucking belt." He pointed to a spot next to Bonefield's still dangling head.

"If you think you can take me, take me," Rake beckoned, before yawning ostentatiously.

Mayax needed no further invitation and brought the broken Velocet around in a deadly semi-circle, but Rake instantly teleported out of the way. He reappeared behind Mayax and clapped his metal mitt over the barbarian's head and helmet, snapping off one of the high reaching horns and crumpling the steel to his scalp. Mayax cried out in agony, but wrenched his head free and spun around to face Rake with a frustrated frown. Rake smiled, "Incidentally, I wasn't quite as weak as I've been letting on all this time."

"What other tricks do you have up your sleeve, Prince?" Mayax pulled off his ruined helmet and dropped it into the void, letting his coal colored hair flow around him like a storm.

"Allow me to demonstrate," Rake announced as he grinned ear to ear. The grin widened impossibly, revealing savage, and still growing, pearly fangs. His other teeth became jagged shards of white tooth, and the nails of his left hand grew to razor-sharp daggers. His voice was much deeper now—possessed—with a tone that shook bone, "I should like to taste your body wine now, mongrel."

"Not this day," Mayax said confidently. Rake gestured with his iron gauntlet for him to bring it. Mayax responded by blinking into fifty mirror versions of himself and attacking Rake simultaneously from all angles. Unfortunately, the soulless dark one slipped them by disappearing into shadow. Suddenly, every shadow within the great hall became a wraith and attacked the Mayax illusions, dispersing them into nothing. Then they turned on Mayax, coming together like smoke and coalescing to form Rake, his hands firmly holding the Yasmani Ro's wrists. Mayax broke the hold with his incredible strength, but took one on the chin from Rake's gauntlet. Mayax pulled away, blood trickling from his lips. "First blood; I'm impressed."

"I'm not interested in impressing you," Rake screeched.

Mayax flashed a look through his black eyes that froze Rake in midair. "You've been holding back all this time for sure, but I get the feeling Mina would still legitimately beat your ass."

"That mutt of a minx?" Rake chortled like a hundred demons laughing in unison. "I'm afraid not, old boy." That said, Rake was on him in a flash, doling out a barrage of devastating blows that rocked the barbarian's world. Dazed and dizzy, Mayax fought hard to tip the scales, but Rake was inches away from sinking those massive fangs into his neck. Mayax forced his hands inside the Rake's yawning jaws, shredding them, and jacked them open like a crocodile's. There was a loud, wet snap as the bones in his mandible crunched and splintered, and the wraith's mouth suddenly split apart at the corners, tearing towards the back of his head.

Rake brought his gauntlet around defiantly, but Mayax released his grip and caught it. Now it was his turn to offer a show of strength, and he began crushing the iron prosthetic in his unyielding grip. Rake's jaw snapped and crackled back into place, but his mouth came together at the corners with long, ragged scars; a joker's smile. Rake vanished and reappeared several yards away to regroup. "Looks like we both have a couple new skin stories."

Mayax examined his scarred hands and shook his head, "It would appear so, although it's nothing to smile about."

"I'm not smiling," Rake said, trying to frown.

"My mistake."

Rake rushed in again, hands outstretched and grabbing. Mayax met them with his own, and a fierce power struggle ensued. Each one forced the other back and forth until it was fairly obvious their strength was evenly matched. Mayax knew immediately if he hoped to beat Rake, he would have to outsmart him. Easier said than done, considering how sinister and underhanded the dark one was.

Mayax chanced a look down below and saw the Blood Red Roses, in female form, eating the heart out of the Sinteverete General. A moment after, they began figuring out their next move—which he hoped would be helping him gang up on Rake. Unfortunately, below the victorious and wrathful ladies of war, he could see the Steplescar army climbing back up to the top of the path like relentless robots. Their textured, featureless faces were trained unemotionally on the fighters above, with one singular motive: destroy. Below them, only the red eyes of a thousand more Steplescar soldiers could be seen emerging from below the dark depths. Mayax wagered they didn't have much time before the tables turned disastrously against them. In the fraction of a microsecond it took him to think all this, Viss Vascene caught his gaze from below, read it, and followed it over the edge of the stone pathway to the ascending Steplescar army. "Fuck's sake," she gasped, unable to yell. She loudly clanged her blade and sword together to get the other Blood Red Roses' attention, and they instantly knew what to do. Without their Ceridome wraps, they were at a disadvantage, but quickly compensated. Letting out a little of their Alma, they clawed their way up the rock face toward the main event between Mayax and Rake, and away from the emerging Steplescar soldiers.

Rake saw the Blood Red Roses on the rise and started rethinking his position. "Can't take me yourself, I see; you have to call in your killer kittens of war? Pathetic."

"It's a wise man who accepts assistance when he needs it." Mayax divluged while conjuring a solid, large circular platform of energy beneath his feet. The Blood Red Roses were quick to join him on the swirling disk in defiance of Rake. The five unlikely comrades stared Rake down, begging him to attack.

Rake pondered this a moment before addressing Mayax. "I presume you and your whores are on your way to the throne room—yes?"

Mayax, already knowing where this was headed, replied, "I and the Blood Red Roses are, yes."

"I see," Rake stalled, rubbing his chin thoughtfully. "I'll tell you what; I'm going to join you. The enemy of my enemy is my friend."

Mayax stiffened and drilled holes through Rake with his black eyes, looking for a setup. "I'm afraid we're not auditioning for talent just now."

"We both want the Elders dead, yes? Together we are stronger, and they certainly won't be expecting an attack from the two of us. Why not ally and eliminate them so we can have the battlefield all to ourselves? Just you and me at the end, the way it should be. What do you say?"

Mayax looked over his shoulder to Viss Vascene, who nodded her support of the idea. "They are a slippery sort, especially that little imp," Mayax conceded. "It is agreed then. Be warned though, Rake, I am fucking watching you."

"Awwwwwwww, don't be so serious?" Rake jested, tracing the scars of his new permanent smile.

"We'll follow you there," Mayax ordered, gesturing forward with his hand.

"You're not in command of me anymore, fuck face. You and the bitches can float right there alongside me."

Mayax snorted in reluctant agreement.

The implausible, motley crew of six patchwork warriors arrived at the gigantic, metallic, black and lavishly decorated doors to the Edler's throne room. After only a second, Mayax abruptly kicked it open with his big, black boot. As the massive twin doors parted and swung open, they were greeted by several thousand Steplescar soldiers standing between them and the back-facing thrones.

"I don't suppose you know where the kill switch is on these things, do you?" Mayax asked Rake genuinely. "Do any of your mosquitoes have intel on that?"

Rake gave him a tired look. "No talk that I've been privy to."

Mayax nodded, "It would appear our plan of attack should consist of dismemberment, incapacitation, banishment, and/or imprisonment. Be clever."

Sistell chimed in, "Can we eat these things?"

Mayax responded with a chuckle, "I wouldn't recommend it. They would most likely disagree with you."

Sistell, "Well, that's disappointing; I'm still starving. I knew I should have eaten that last Sinteverete soldier, but I wanted to stay light on my feet for the big fight. Now, here I am, without so much as a snack."

"Struggle through," Mayax encouraged her respectfully.

From over the heads of the many Steplescar, awaiting the order to attack, came the adolescent voice of the Master Elder, "What have we here? Another short-lived rebellion? I must say, this is not the collection of insurgents I would have expected to see. Rake, you and Mayax have betrayed us? After everything we've done for you? Ungrateful scamps."

"Perhaps it was our upbringing...father." Mayax hit a nerve with that one.

"Silence," The Master Elder suddenly roared in a deep and threatening voice. "Your insolence knows no boundaries."

"I find it interesting that *you*, a perverted, immature little whelp, would condescend to enlighten *me* about impudence," Mayax pondered. "You are a puny, selfish, treasonous tadpole, and I will have your head. Why not face us. You and your six soft-handed Elder simps. Put eyes on your destroyers."

The massive round stone that served as foundation to the seven thrones suddenly came to life and turned slowly to face them. The Steplescar army continued to obediently and patiently wait to be let off the leash, as the throne stone completed its one eighty turn. When they were all face-to-face, the five Nevuscar warriors levitated down from the ceiling, behind the Elders. They were ready to defend their masters, but careful not to set eyes on them.

"Brothers," Mayax called out to the Nevuscar. "Stand with us; stand with liberation. No longer serve these spoiled, self-righteous elitists."

Of course, it was Bael who responded first, "I never thought I'd see the day you and Rake would be working together; much less in sedition." He began to reminisce. "I was around long before you two, and I plan to be around long after both your heads are in a trophy case. I faced Vasser and his slut, and I'm still here. Not to mention, I had the honor of seeing our clan defeat the Pentavi, and rise to power. Here we are, on the precipice of seeing all our efforts come to fruition, and you want me to throw all that away on your *word*? You who have served and experienced so little? You have some fucking balls on you, youngster."

"At least I have balls, you disgusting, crusty eunuch," Mayax hollered, before turning his attention to the other four Nevuscar. "And you four, does this spineless reptile speak for you as well?" They turned and looked at one another to carry on a silent conversation with their eyes for an uncomfortable amount of time.

Eventually, they turned back to Mayax and Rake. Zone, the former third in command of the Nevuscar, now lead, addressed them, "I am Zone the Zealot, and for all his boorish bravado, Bael is right." Zone was a handsome man, with angular features, no facial hair, and a slim, muscular build. He had mid-length, dark rusty collared hair and elegant, black, segmented armor. "We have invested too much of ourselves in this clan, and I am afraid change at this point is impossible. Mayax, we still consider you a brother; one of legendary, fearsome and formidable skill, but we must despise you now. Rake, we have never felt a soulful connection to you. You are a deadly, bloodthirsty fighter, and we respect that, but you are far from honorable. We must despise you now as well."

Mayax bowed his head and nodded in understanding. "I understand, brothers. It will be my honor to cross steel with yours."

Zone also nodded. "It will be our honor as well. I must admit, I have always wanted to fight you."

Mayax looked Zone dead in the eye. "Sorry to say, I don't think it will end well for you."

"We shall see..." Zone promised stoically.

Rake chimed in, "I'm just happy to be here, see," he said, pointing to his unnatural smile.

The Master Elder finally rejoined the conversation, "Glad that's all figured out. Now, before I give the order to crush you two traitors, and these," laughing now, "four, frail and starving females, I'd like to address the elephant in the room—if I may, Mayax?" The Master Elder, looking directly at Mayax now, with the other six Elders following the conversation with interest.

"Please do, father," Mayax encouraged.

Rake turned to Mayax and whispered into his ear, "The little fella doesn't look anything like I pictured. The others sure, but him—he gives me the creeps."

"Be silent, Rake." The Master Elder called out in his typical juvenile voice.

Rake shrugged his shoulders, "What?"

The Master Elder ignored Rake and focused back on Mayax. "I am NOT your father; rather, I am the father of an experiment gone wrong. You were the control group; a means by which to compare our experiments on Rake and test the soul equation."

"Only after I was made a Nevuscar in the womb, why else kill my mother? You can't sell this to me as something you planned. You are a weak-willed pervert who got caught trysting with a young Pentavi Elder—in that tasteless, garish, adolescent form no less—and had to spin it all for everyone to make it work. You are pathetic." Mayax was truly flabbergasted.

"LIES! LIES! LIES!" The Master Elder screamed over and over again, while banging his hands in a tantrum.

"Shame on you," Mayax grumbled.

"How dare you judge me—I am ageless. I was alive at the dawn of time; you are the infant here. Not that I feel the need to explain myself to the likes of you, but I choose the form I please, just as you have chosen yours. And after all, I am the Master Elder," he screamed.

"This is truly a spectacle. I accept the fact that you contributed one half of my genetic material, but parading yourself around in that puckish goblin body will earn you no mercy from me; I will grind your bones to make my bread," Mayax proclaimed.

"You think your brute force coupled with this laughable sundry of mismatched has beens is enough to put to bed my millions of years of experience and survival? To say nothing of my army of obedient, deadly, immortal soldiers. You underestimate me, barbarian."

"Do I?" With that, Mayax began shoving and forcefully pushing his way through the Steplescar army, still awaiting command. Now he was out with Velocet and ready to start hacking away. The Blood Red Roses shrugged their shoulders and began following Mayax into the crowd.

"Still working on the team dynamics, I guess," Rake said, levitating up into the air above the poised legion of faceless, immortal fighters.

The Master Elder turned his head quickly left and right to address the other Elders, "Look at that. I've never before seen such boorishness. The audacity." The other Elders answered only with grimly concerned faces. The Master Elder shrugged them off and ordered the Steplescar army to "ATTAAAAAAAAAAAAACK."

As if a switch had been thrown, the entire Steplescar army suddenly jumped to action. In a flash, they were out with their steel; eager to find the tender bellies beneath the bloody, lovely ladies of the Rose. Others dog piled on Mayax, who was almost double their size. He barely acknowledged them, his eyes trained solely on the Master Elder. Dragging them roughly across the ground, the fighters struggled to hang on to his arms and legs. Several warriors clung to him with claws and blades plunged into his back in order to hang on, but it barely fazed him.

The Master Elder clapped his hands together in excitement and called out to Mayax, "You'll be as ugly as Bael trying to come at me head on."

"A thousand scars for you," Mayax screamed, his onyx eyes flashing directly at the Master Elder.

"Bring it, barbarian..." the imp whispered.

Bael, Zone, and the other three Nevuscar levitated up to meet Rake, high in the air. Zone called out to Rake, "This hardly seems a fair fight; and you should know, we will not be pulling any punches."

Rake, "I've seen all five of you fight your best fight, and it's nowhere near my level. Allow me to introduce you five to the *real* me." Rake suddenly began to hulk out freakishly; doubling, tripling, and quadrupling in size. His enchanted armor grew and expanded to accommodate his unearthly transformation, while his teeth and nails grew out like bone knives.

Zone faltered, looking at Rake transform. "Good Lord, what have you become?"

"It's what I've always been, Hahahahahaha," Rake's voice was thunderous and echoing now. "I have a special treat for you, Zone. One that will help you see things my way."

"Impossible—" Zone began, but it was already too late. Rake suddenly transported behind him, his mouth a yawning, cavernous hole, lined with shards of greedy teeth. He clamped his monstrous hands around the smaller Nevuscar's shoulders from behind, and without mercy, sank his fangs into the Undying one's neck, all the way to the gums. Bael and the other three Nevuscar gawked as the giant, parasitic leech sucked Zone into a withered husk.

"What kind of unholy abomination are you?" Bael bellowed hysterically.

Rake pulled his bloody, dripping fangs from Zone's desiccated neck and replied, "You have some nerve calling *me* an abomination. Have you looked in a mirror lately?" Rake held up Zone's leathery, pale, shrunken form by the scruff of his destroyed neck, "You look a little like THIS," he said, throwing Zone's floppy body at Bael.

The scar-riddled sorcerer caught it and stared into the sunken face of his former friend at arms. "I've never seen anything like this." In an instant, Zone's eyes suddenly shot open, along with his mouth, which now contained hundreds of long, pointed teeth. He hissed in Bael's frightened face before being thrown like a hot potato back towards Rake. Zone caught himself in mid-air at Rake's side and levitated back around to grin demonically at Bael with his anorexic, angular features.

Zone gasped in unnaturally, zeroed in on Bael, and launched himself, fang-first at him. Beal instantly shrieked like a coyote and floundered backwards. "Whatthefuck..." Bael barely managed to catch the ravenous wraith before its teeth found his flesh. He flashed a desperate look to the other three Nevuscar. "Well, don't just fucking stand there."

Coming out of their shock, two of the Nevuscar rushed in to aid Bael, while the third, Ashen, announced himself as the new leader of the Nevuscar. "I am Ashen the Abhorrent," he proclaimed as the sleek, maroon form fitting armor that clung to his athletic, slender frame in flexible segments suddenly changed to black. His short, choppy, blonde hair danced in the wind as he rushed Rake head on.

Cackling, the hideous vampiric behemoth unsheathed Somhaine—his Cursed Blade of Black—for the first time in a long time and met Ashen blade to blade in a shower of sparks.

Down below, Mayax stomped, smashed and carved his way through the swarming Steplescar army like a bulldozer, but was getting little traction. There were several soldiers still trying to hang on to his thrashing back like cowboys at a rodeo. The Blood Red Roses did their best to clear the way and stay alive, but fighting this army as opposed to the Sinteverete army was vastly different. These grotesqueries didn't care about catching a sword to the face, because they were essentially walking scar tissue as it was.

They just kept coming and coming; relentless and robotically driven by their masters. "They just walk like zombies face first into your steel," Sistell cried out to her sisters of war. "How do you defend against that?"

The twins answered in unison from their precarious position, "We'll let you know when we figure it out." The girls were desperately pulling out all the stops, with only three arms and a mace between them, just to keep from being overwhelmed by the sheer numbers of Steplescar soldiers. "We'll never make it like this," Amira pointed out.

Viss Vascene, encircled by a coalescing mob of Steplescar, was inclined to agree. She banged her sword and blade together to call the Roses back in preparation for a retreat. They rejoined her side with grim prospects for making a safe exit. They all turned to see Mayax still wading through the sea of Steplescar soldiers without a hint of wavering. Sistell called out to him, "Mayax, we are leaving." He ignored her and continued his lumbering rampage of useless destruction. Viss Vascene, not known for her patience with people, threw her blade end over end, hitting him in the back of the head with the handle. The hard 'thunk' managed finally to get his attention. He swung his head around to see the Blood Red Roses all frantically waving him back.

Gritting his teeth in angry frustration, Mayax bellowed loudly and brought his furious fists down like twin asteroids colliding with the earth. The impact sent the Steplescar soldiers in his general vicinity flying away like paper dolls; while the shockwave blast rippled outward and forced many of the other soldiers to their knees.

The Blood Red Roses quickly joined hands in the middle of the mosh pit and began spinning with their swords held out like a carousel of carnage. They shredded the Steplescar soldiers into quivering, pulsing piles of body parts and meat, but it wouldn't stop them for long. Bathed in their blood, the ladies fought their way over to Mayax, who was trying to make sense of the skirmish Rake was having overhead. "RAKE," Mayax called out loudly, "Let's go."

Rake was hammering Ashen with Somhaine and had him on the ropes, so he was reluctant to retreat. Zone was inches from Bale's throat, with the other two Nevuscar urgently trying to hold him back. Rake finally responded, "What? We're crushing these guys." Mayax raised both his hands palm up and thrust them at the heaving crowd of Steplescar closing in around them. "Okay, okay," Rake relented. He and Zone instantly transported down to where the others were. "Where to now?" Rake asked justifiably, while shrinking back to his normal size.

"Mina," Mayax said, then looked strangely at Zone. "What's this?"

Rake looked at Mayax, then at Zone, then back at Mayax again, "Him? Oh, this is Zone the Zombie, and he's my eternal slave now."

"Great. Him I liked." Mayax huffed. "Okay, let's get the fuck out of here..." Mayax conjured a portal to Earth underneath their position and everyone weightlessly fell through it into Central Park, Whippany New Jersey. On their way out, Rake grabbed a Steplescar soldier by the ankle and dragged it through the portal with them.

They all landed roughly in an open field north of the park's center. There was no one around, but the military still had a presence close by. They squatted down and looked around, as Mayax lambasted Rake, "Why in the Hell would you bring that thing here?"

Rake rolled his eyes. "I want to see something..."

"What could you possibly want to see with that?" Viss Vascene whispered.

Without another word, Rake fiercely bit the faceless freak on its neck and hunkered over it while slurping loudly. Everyone turned away in disgust as he drank the blood of the single Steplescar soldier. However, after a moment, Rake gagged and tossed the mindless pugilist away. "Ugh, poisonous dog." He spit and wiped his gory mouth. "That thing has no soul—like me. There's no enslaving these things."

"Great, so now what the fuck do we do with it?" Sistell asked briskly, as the Steplescar soldier found its feet and began looking wildly around.

Rake grabbed it back up by the scruff of its neck, hoisted it up and examined its eyes for a minute. "Fuck. I was really hoping I could control them. That's disappointing." Shrugging his shoulders, he conjured a portal to Reclon and dropped the squirming soldier through it as though he were discarding an apple core in the trash. The portal closed and Rake looked back up to everyone. "I'm sure he'll make lots of friends there." Meanwhile, Zone stood behind them, hunched over, breathing heavy and fast, with foam and drool flowing out of his toothy trap like a hyena. He had eyes as big as dinner plates now that were piss yellow and pupil-less; with bony hands that were drawn up, crooked, and clawed like hooks. Rake patted him on the back, "He's fine."

"Just keep him the fuck away from me," Mayax grumbled.

"Fucking A," Viss Vascene agreed.

"How are we going to track down your girlfriend?" Rake asked Mayax.

Mayax sighed and glared at him. "First thing first," Mayax conjured the arsenal portal, reached inside, and withdrew the Ceridome wraps belonging to the Blood Red Roses. "I believe these are yours."

The ladies eagerly grabbed the wraps out of Mayax's huge hand and sorted through them to find theirs. Viss Vascene croaked out a back-handed thank you. "Thanks. Could have used these earlier."

"You're welcome." Mayax offered, ignoring her curtness. "It's lucky I found them at all."

The Blood Red Roses let the enchanted wraps slither inside their armor and wrap around their naked bodies underneath like old lovers. Osha hugged herself. "It's been so long since I've worn these. I felt so lost without them…"

Viss Vascene's wraps snaked inside her armor, but a strap wrapped itself around the gruesome scar across her throat that Mayax had given her not so long ago. She spoke with a strangely modified voice now, "Thank you, Mayax," she said reluctantly. "While I can never call you friend, I can appreciate you throwing away everything you've ever known in order to do the right thing."

Mayax bowed his head. "And I can appreciate how hard that must have been for you to say. Maybe one day, we'll find our way to friendship."

The twins, Osha and Amira, spoke in unison with sultry tones, "Perhaps a little Copunocture is in order to get to know one another better."

Amira added, "It's been a very long time."

Rake instantly began pulling off his armor, "I thought you'd never ask. I got left out last time," he added, shooting Mayax a pointed look.

"We don't have time for this," Mayax barked. Looking at the twins, "Unfortunately, the clock is working against us." Now looking to Viss Vascene and Sistell, "With Rake and I on the outs, the Master Elder will be looking to obtain Mina before we can get to her. It's a race now."

Rake began disappointingly putting his armor back on, "Unbelievable."

"Hold on Rake, we have to do something about our look if we are to blend in," Mayax pointed out. He blinked his eyes, and they were all suddenly wearing black swat gear with bulletproof padding, glossy black boots, and a large DHS insignia stenciled across the chests.

Sistell looked at Mayax, scar-faced, bearded and burly; then to Rake, vampiric with long red hair, pale skin, and a leather strap over his destroyed eye. They both resembled humongous, 10-foot-tall barbarians, who oddly enough were crammed into military flack suits. Then she looked at Zone, who just looked—wrong. "Yeah, we're going to blend right in."

Mayax looked at Rake and hooked his thumb back at Zone. "Is there anything you can do about that?"

Rake raised his eyebrows and exhaled sharply, "Sure." He snapped his fingers and Zone straightened up, closed his frothy mouth, and hovered there in mid-air like a pale ghost. "Better?"

Mayax sighed and stood up. "Not by much." Everyone stood up with Mayax and looked to him for instruction. After a few beats, he slipped back into his role of leadership, like putting on an old pair of pants. He looked around at the motley crew. "Mina will be thrilled to see all of us on her doorstep."

CHAPTER 7
KILL SWITCH

M ina was exhausted from all their escapades the previous day, and slept in. Needless to say, when Auri came rushing into the guest room where she was pleasantly dozing like a wild Irish rose, she was less than excited. "Um, honey, you're going to want to come downstairs—RIGHT. NOW."

"Yeah, yeah, whatsup," Mina managed while wiping her mascara smeared eyes.

"Let me put it to you this way, don't do anything rash," Auri said in her Celtic lilt, before putting on a big, false, sunny smile.

Mina shot straight up in bed and hastily began pulling on her clothes from the night before. "Please tell me there's not a fight waiting for me down there."

"No, no, I think you're good. Just, uh, keep an open mind," she strongly suggested while shrugging her shoulders.

Mina scampered past her and bolted down the spiral staircase, ready for anything. She stopped cold when she hit the tenth step and saw Mayax, still in the DHS flack suit size 64, towering inside the grand room. "What the actual fuck." Her eyes turned to fire in a hurry. "Well hello, lamb."

He quickly turned to face her. "Mina, WAIT." He held up his enormous hands in front of himself disarmingly, trying to defuse the situation. "I can explain."

She hung on the banister for a long moment, drinking him in, and poised to throw down, "Mother fucker, I can't wait to hear this." Behind Mayax, Mina saw Avery playing the VR headset, completely oblivious to everything going on around him, and threw up her hands, "Really?"

Unexpectedly, Rake rounded the corner into the grand room and followed Mayax's gaze up the stairs, "Oh, hey Mina." He waved non-chalantly while using an entire coffee carafe as a mug. "You...want some coffee?" He asked, raising the pot after taking a drink. "Your gal pal knows her grounds. Fucking delicious."

Mina was gobsmacked, but felt Auri put her hand on her shoulder to calm her down. She looked to Auri, then to Mayax, then to Rake. "What the fuck, y'all?"

Just then, Bee, aka CEO of Hell, aka Queen of the Damned, aka Satan, aka Auri's wife, came walking smartly into the room with eight-inch stiletto heels clacking loudly on the Calacatta marble floor. She was wearing a gorgeous black and red skirt suit, as well as a frilly pink and white apron, and carrying a tray full of scones. "Mina," she tittered. "I'm so glad you're up. Come on down here and have some scones and coffee." Bee looked to Mayax, then to Bonefield's severed head still dangling from his belt. "Yeah, let's go ahead and do something about that right now, huh?"

It took a second to hit him, but Mayax quickly scrambled, un-hooked the head from his belt and stuffed it into a portal to some-where. "Sorry," he offered sheepishly. Bee smiled thankfully in return.

"Ahhhh, I get it," Mina said. "I'm still asleep and this is a crazy fever dream fueled by watching too many TikTok videos before bed last night. Am I right?" Mina speculated half-smiling with her makeup smeared across her face from sleeping on it.

"No such luck, I'm afraid," Bee said, making an exaggerated sad face. "But it appears things are heating up for an all out realm war. Yay," she added, strangely giddy and excited.

Mina came lumbering down the stairs in yesterday's clothes, her makeup a mess, and her hair wild. Bee met her at the bottom with the tray. "After you get some breakfast in you, we can see about getting you cleaned up," she said, smiling as politely as possible.

Mina cut Bee a sideways glance with half-shut eyes and nipped her hospitality in the bud. After a seconds long stare, she snatched a scone off the tray and began munching it. "Thank you, Bee. I love you, and I appreciate your playing host to me, the kid, and the fucking Apple Dumpling Gang here. I promise I'll have everything sorted by tonight, and get these clowns out of here."

"No worries," Bee proclaimed with over-the-top sweetness. "It's been so long since I've seen you, and meeting all these new friends of yours has been such a wonderful surprise."

"I saw you three weeks ago, Bee, and stop being so damned polite; I know this is a terrible imposition." Mina slapped her head and shook it in disbelief. "I was told there is coffee...?"

Out of nowhere, Zone, still looking like a floating fresh corpse, handed her a coffee mug. Rake poured her a cup from the carafe he was drinking from with a fake smile. After an epic eye roll and shoulder shrug, Mina began sipping the coffee. She sat on one of the high stools at the wet bar, adjacent to the playroom. "Sooooooooo, anyone want to tell me what in the name of Captain Kangaroo's red suit is going on around here?"

"Who's Captain Kangaroo?" Amira asked as she and Osha entered the room from the hall bathroom.

Mina gawked, "Who's Captain Kangaroo? Who the fuck are you?"

"Oh, I'm Amira, and this is my twin sister Osha," she said sweetly before pointing with her left arm mace. "That salty, sexy, silver-haired lady over there sitting stoically by herself in the corner is Viss Vascene, and that's Sistell, a few seats down. We are the Blood Red Roses."

Viss Vascene waved, and Sistell scoffed, "What, no miles long title of embellishment before my introduction? I thought we were friends."

Mina shook her head up and down rapidly, "Okay, okay, this just keeps getting better and better. Anyone else?"

Auri came up to Mina and spoke softly in her ear, "I think that's everyone. They just uh...showed up here this morning; the big bearded one, Mayax, said it was imperative that he speak with you right away. They were all very polite and promised they weren't here for trouble, so Bee let them in and started making breakfast; you know how she is."

Mina gulped down her coffee and marched over to Mayax. "Okay big boy, start talking and make it good. First off, how the hell did you find me?"

After a deep breath and a sigh, Mayax began his multi-faceted explanation. "It was Rake who found you, using a murder of ravens who have been watching your comings and goings around here with much interest." Rake saluted Mina, who scrunched her mouth in aggravation. Mayax continued, "What can I say? Your parents were right, and I was a fool."

"I love a man who can admit when he's wrong. Points to you. Go on..." Mina thrust her empty cup at Rake, who filled it again with that same sarcastic smile. Mina fished a cigar out of her purse, sitting on a couch-side table, and chomped it between her teeth. She began eagerly patting her pants pockets, looking for a lighter, but Bee cleared her throat and shook her head. With a sigh, Mina put the cigar back into her purse and let Mayax continue.

"I had to see it with my own eyes. I spoke to your parents—" Mayax began.

"You spoke with my parents? Where are they? I want to see them right now." Mina slammed her fist on the small table for emphasis.

"I have not been able to set them free yet, but I will, I promise you," Mayax assured her.

"You're fuckin' A right you will."

"In order to do that, collect the Elders' heads, and unite the clans, we have to be smart about this. I've already tried the direct approach in collecting my Elders' heads, but that didn't go over so well."

"Haha, no shit," Rake added smugly.

"Their army of Steplescar warriors is far too vast and formidable to take head on," Mayax continued, "so we'll have to find a better way."

"Tell me everything I don't know," Mina demanded.

"This will be a long story..." Mayax moaned as he began to launch into everything, but Rake butted in.

"Oh, for fuck's sake. Your newfound diplomacy is exhausting," Rake said, throwing up his arms impatiently. "You are Yasmani Ro, born of fire and ice, and it is your Alma the Master Elder seeks in order to make himself truly immortal. Mayax found out he is also a Yasmani Ro—born of blood—from the Master Elder, and some bitch Elder from your clan who has since been executed. He and I were experimented on throughout our lives so the Master Elder could create his Steplescar army of immortals. I was the only one created through black magic. I don't have a soul, and we are only allied to eliminate the Elders. The Blood Red bitches over there were prisoner patsies, used to hide the Sinteverete Elder's alliance with the Pentavi Elders, but they have joined with Mayax and myself, for now, in order to strengthen our numbers. Once the Elders are dead, I plan to take control of the Steplescar army, kill all you motherfuckers and claim the throne for myself. After which, I'm coming for *this* realm, your realm," pointing to Bee, "and all the other realms. Oh, and Mayax thinks you're cute. There, you're all caught up." Rake drained the rest of the coffee. "I'm going to brew another pot." He got up and went into the kitchen, leaving everyone there awkward and quiet in the sprawling mansion's sitting room.

The air was thick with uncomfortable silence for only a second until Avery pulled off his VR headset and turned to Mayax. "Hands off Mina, pal, she's taking me to prom."

Mina laughed nervously, "I told you we would see about that. Now, let me try to unpack all this…"

Before things could get anymore uncomfortable, Bee quickly saved the day, "Well, that was informative. And very concise too. Everyone, if you haven't grabbed a scone, please do and join me in the kitchen for some scrambled eggs and bacon. Ladies," Bee extended her hand, inviting them to follow her. "You too, Avery." Avery started to protest, but read Bee's eyes and shut up. Everyone left Mayax and Mina alone to hash out the alliance and figure out their cluster fuck of an arrangement.

Mina and Mayax sat silently on opposite ends of the long couch in the sitting room. On one side, Mina looked like a tiny porcelain doll when compared to Mayax, who looked like an oversized grizzly bear. Mina finally broke the silence, "So, you think I'm cute, huh?" she prodded Mayax, who promptly began blushing hard.

"Rake was paraphrasing..." Mayax assured her.

"So, then, you don't think I'm cute?" Mina countered. She was far more skilled at the art of flirting than Mayax was; however, it was all lost on him and he scuttled her ship by being honest and direct.

"I don't think you are cute; I think you are beautiful."

"Oh, well..." Mina said, flummoxed.

"Aren't you going to tell me how beauty is a blade?" Mayax joked.

"No. Gosh...But it is..." Mina crossed her arms across her chest and started pouting. "Ugh, I need a smoke." She reached into her purse and pulled out the cigar from before, finally found a lighter, and fired it up. "'Tis better to ask for forgiveness than beg for permission..." Mina fired up the stogie and inhaled deeply. "Ohhhhhhh, that's the stuff."

Mayax conjured himself one and lit it with his finger, trying to look cool. "You've got me hooked on these things now. Just have to be right about everything, huh?"

"Yep," she said quickly. "Being right is kind of my thing. Now, let's talk about how we're going to make all this right."

After a draw on his stogie and a bit of contemplation, Mayax kicked things off. "The first priority is to keep you safe and away from the Elders. I want you alive and I want them vulnerable."

"Already, there is a problem with your plan." Mina pointed out with a gesture of her Havana.

"What's that?" Mayax asked, perplexed.

"First of all, I'm not some delicate dove who needs protection, certainly not from the likes of *you*; and I'd expect you to know that by now. Second, I intend to collect those heads with or without you and your pals, so you better start learning how to accept that. I will have bloody revenge for myself and my parents; we deserve it. I mean, you've already cheated me out of part of that equation by being so damn rational now that you're in the know. I think I liked you better when I hated you."

Shaking his head in reluctant agreement, Mayax ventured some common ground. "I understand, and thank you for appreciating that I'm trying to change my engineered mindset. I was a soldier, doing my job."

"You know that's what the Nazis always used to say—I should know. Anyway, my father required that same consideration from my mother, so you're welcome. People deserve a chance; except Rake; that fucker is on my shit list."

"Mine too," Mayax chuckled. "I know him pretty well, considering, and I think he will be an asset as long as we keep our eyes on him."

"If you say so," Mina acquiesced. Changing the subject she continued, "What can you tell me about the Steplescar army? What are their strengths, and weaknesses—if any?"

Mayax thought on this for a moment, "Unfortunately, they have many attributes, and few weaknesses. Their primary strength lay in the fact that we cannot kill them in battle, or at all, as far as I can tell. Our only hope is to fight them as if we were fighting Nevuscar, but comparing the two is a stretch; they are a completely different breed. Additionally, they number in the hundreds of thousands and are growing exponentially every day. Once the Elders figured out how to create them without a womb, soullessly through dark magic, they have been busy breeding them like roaches. You were right about them having a kill switch though, unfortunately I do not know what that is. I suspect Rake does, but he will never divulge that to us. I gather he aims to find a way to control them, and use them against us."

"Alright, until we figure out their kill switch, we'll have to improvise and be creative. Have you tried burning these things? Like incinerating them, completely reducing them to ash," Mina wondered.

"It's worth a try, but we don't even know if it'll be effective. All fire ever did to the Nevuscar was make us uglier. I suppose if it was hot enough, maybe, but again, it's hard to draw comparisons."

"Let's put that in the maybe category, then. What else? They aren't capable of conjuring; can't we just transport them to the Reclon realm or some equally hostile and horrible place?"

"It's a possibility, but until we eliminate the Elders and the other Nevuscar, they can just keep bringing them back. Imprisonment has always worked best on the Nevuscar, but there's just so many of the Steplescar; I don't know how we would pull it off."

"Ok, maybe we can enchant them? Turn them against the Elders?" Mina asked hopefully.

"They have no souls; enchantment won't work on them." Mayax pointed out.

"Fuck." Mina drew anxiously on her cigar, hoping the answer would come to her in a puff of smoke. It did not. "If only we had one, you know? One we could study, experiment on, see what makes 'em tick. Is there any way to get our hands on one?"

Mayax stroked his beard in thought and puffed his Havana. "Rake brought one through with us when we arrived, but transported it to the Reclon realm when he realized he couldn't control it, like he could Zone. There is no telling where that thing is in Reclon by now. Probably in the bowels of a titan. I suppose we could track it and trap it."

"Oh, well, since we have all this fucking time on our hands. I mean, what the Hell, Mayax? You had one of those freaks and it didn't occur to you to try and contain it so we could gather intel? Fucking amateur hour." Mina threw up her hands in disbelief. "Christ, this is hopeless."

This drew a deep inhale and exhale from Mayax, who had clearly reached his limit. He stood up, and let her have it. "I have been nothing but patient and respectful to you since the day we met, even when we were on opposite sides of the fight. I found your reckless, brash, petulant personality invigorating and strangely charming at first, but it is starting to wear thin. I don't care how powerful and skilled you are as a warrior, you are of no use to me—or your cause—if you can't learn to work with others. Even without a soul, Rake knew the value of working together. We have a great deal of preparation needed in order to complete all of our objectives." Mayax's words were coming hard and loud now. "I don't give a shit about our past, only what's going to happen in our future, if we'll even have one. It's time you start learning how to function as a *we* instead of a *me*."

Mina's eyes began to smolder like green embers, "I find it interesting that you would insinuate that you were patient and respectful to me since the first day we met, considering the first day we met you imprisoned my parents and forced me to run and hide for a hundred years. Not to mention, Mr. Johnny-came-late-to-the-fucking-show, you're a Nevuscar barbarian with much blood on his hands. The audacity of you lecturing me about ANYTHING is staggering."

Every atom in the air seemed to vibrate with tension now. "Wasn't it you that incinerated five square blocks of this human zoo because of your wimp boyfriend's infidelity? Spare me the hypocrisy. And to be clear, I'm not *lecturing* you, I'm encouraging you to be a part of a team, something I have a lot of experience in, and you do not. Maybe if you can keep your temper in check, we might be able to accomplish something."

"Motherfucker," Mina whispered acidicly through clenched teeth, having reached her limit as well. She stood up now, all six feet six inches of her, and levitated into the air so she was face-to-face with Mayax. "You think I have a temper? You ain't seen nuthin' yet…"

"Oh please. Am *I* supposed to be afraid of *you*?" Mayax taunted.

"You're fuckin' A right you are." Mina wasn't joking.

"I'm sorry to disappoint you, but—" That was all Mayax was able to get out before Mina conjured a portal to Reclon behind him, and kung-fu'd his ass straight through it. He tumbled backwards into the brutal battle realm, with her close behind. His cigar left his lips and spiraled end over end behind Mina, who still had hers clamped securely in her lipstick smeared mouth.

Moments later, Bee walked into the room with two fresh cups of coffee. "Hey you two, thought you might be in need of a warm up—. Mina? Mayax? Well, how do you like that? Is that fucking cigar smoke I smell."

The portal to Reclon opened up and spit Mayax out onto the edge of a huge glacier in Reclon's arctic. He landed explosively on his back, breaking through fifteen feet of permafrost, and almost went over the edge. Mina suddenly landed on top of him with her legs on either side, her midnight hair blowing fiercely in the arctic wind, and her white skin disappearing in the blowing snow. She grabbed the front of his bullet-proof vest to sit him up before knocking him down. Mayax caught her next punch in his coarse hand and painfully crushed it like wringing out a wet washcloth. "Well, if you must have it, have it then." He rose up out of the crater and hoisted her high into the air by her crumpled fingers. Mina cried out as he tightened his grip, then propelled her cruelly down through the petrified ice. She exploded out the plummeting side of the glacier's slope, ten thousand feet above the rocky ground, and fell stunned towards the jagged stones below. Naturally, she still managed to keep the cigar clenched between her beautiful teeth. She came to within fifteen feet of colliding with the deadly landscape, but Mayax snatched her up by the collar of her shirt before she touched down disastrously. She raised her head and looked him in the eyes with her own that burned brighter than a million suns. Mayax yelled in agony as she burned his retinas out and had to release her quickly. She kicked him in the balls, doubling him over, and unleashed a flurry of punches, jabs and chops to his head, neck and torso, putting him on the defensive. Bellowing, Mayax let loose his battle cry and decked her right across the chin, finally knocking her cigar out. He then dragged her like a ragdoll, dazed and confused, through the air at a hundred miles an hour. Once he was above the glacier again, he shook her violently. She responded by placing her white-hot, right hand over his heart, and melting straight through his uniform to the pale flesh beneath, where she left her brand. Mayax quickly grabbed her arm and ripped that fire from himself. He crumpled her hand into a fist and held it within his own, keeping the majority of the heat inside her palm. Unable to free herself, she became enraged and powered up big time. Mayax clapped his other hand around their joined hands and struggled to contain the fire inside. He began to yell loudly through his beard as the heat threatened to melt his face off. Mayax put every ounce of strength into trying to contain the liquid lava that was brewing in her right hand, when she suddenly let go of the air in her lungs and screamed out like a banshee.

Mina's left hand suddenly began to smolder and smoke with fire, but the fire this time was blue and the smoke was the kind of vapor you see coming from dry ice. Mayax could already feel the fierce cold radiating from it, a hundred times colder than the surrounding blizzard. Frost began forming on his nose and lips before his beard became thick with it. Seconds later, he could barely breathe the frigid air that threatened to freeze his lungs solid, and he had to let her go. Mina broke free triumphantly with one hand dripping burning hot magma, and the other hand blowing like the eye of a blizzard hurricane. She seemed shocked by this and marveled at the duality of power she never knew she had. Then she turned her gaze back to Mayax and smiled devilishly. Clapping her hands together, she created a shock wave of fire and ice so powerful it knocked Mayax out of the air like a bird hit with a stone. He plummeted unconsciously towards the same rocks below as Mina howled victoriously, not at all herself. Quickly, she came around and noticed Mayax about to plow face-first into the rugged terrain of Reclon's worst arctic shelf. She instantly transported down to him and grabbed hold of the back side of his flak vest, and halted his descent abruptly. He came to, held like a babe in arms by her single right hand, and he smacked it away. Levitating in the air on his own now, he studied her carefully. "What the fuck was that?" Mayax demanded.

"I...I don't really know," Mina confessed truthfully while looking bewildered at her hands. "I have no idea. Holy shit, though, I feel like I just doubled my power, and that's saying a lot. Even before that, I felt like I was strong enough to take the whole fucking Steplescar army on by myself, but now...now, I feel like I could crack this whole fucking realm in half."

"Born of fire and ice," Mayax said as though he were in a daydream.

"Yes. It would seem so. You...you helped me unlock my full power..." Mina said softly to Mayax. "Unbelievable. I feel absolutely invincible."

"Great, and I thought you were an arrogant female before," Mayax chided.

"What the fuck did you just say to me?" Mina growled, one eye fire, the other ice.

"Nothing." He replied instantly, shaking both his hands and chuckling now. "For fuck's sake, I didn't say anything."

The fire and ice left her eyes, and she was calming again. After a moment, she started to giggle and couldn't contain it. Mayax rolled his eyes melodramatically and started chuckling along with her, "Got to watch that temper, my beauty."

"Good advice," Mina said, winking at him with her special brand of wink.

They hovered there in mid-air amidst the unforgiving winds of a Reclon blizzard and tried to enjoy the brief moment of levity; brief being the key word here. Without warning, a swarm of savage, white, long-haired yetis, about the size of a large silverback gorilla, emerged from the snow and ice beneath them. They grabbed and snatched them out of mid-air and forced them roughly to the ground. Instantly, they were caught up in a flurry of gnashing teeth and grabbing claws. Mayax was quickly out with Velocet and started turning the snow red with a frenzied flurry of ax wielding. Mina had Beauty out immediately and began to hack and slash alongside him.

After only a minute, the two warriors began to appreciate the gravity of their situation as hundreds of thousands of the hairy beasts began converging on them from beneath the snow. Mayax was suddenly being dragged down into the sublevel ice caverns below by the hundreds of clawed hands around him. Mina knew if they got him down there, it would be game over. She heated up her aura, incinerating many of the feral creatures in her wake, then clapped her hand around Mayax's and raised him high into the air. Unbelievably, the multitude of voracious snow creatures began piling on one another and climbing themselves in a fraught competition to be the first one to get to their meal.

"Fuck all this shit," Mina screamed, and used her hand of ice to bring the entire glacier down on the writhing mass of blood thirsty abominable snow beasts. They wailed unnaturally as the mountain of ice came crashing down on their heads, burying them beneath like a thousand-foot-tall avalanche. Mina and Mayax collapsed on the frozen tomb, weary and drained. They tried to catch their breath when they suddenly heard snarling and clawing from underneath, "Christ, enough already." Mina and Mayax levitated high into the air, where she began to power up like a nuclear reactor.

Mayax raised his eyebrows in astonishment as her levels kept climbing. "Keep it going, girl; let's see what you got."

Mina continued to suck energy until she was bright as a supernova star about to explode. Her hair suddenly began to glow white, with a blue halo, and her eyes burned pupilless as though they were twin suns. After a few more seconds, she unleashed a blast of power that detonated on the surface like a comet smashing into a planet. The impact disintegrated hundreds of miles of the frozen tundra below, then sent a massive pyroclastic cloud of steam and vapor barreling up towards them at a thousand miles an hour. Mayax couldn't believe his eyes. "Uh, we may want to get out of here."

Mina agreed and grabbed hold of Mayax's war-torn flak suit, yanking him forcefully through another portal before the blast hit them head on. Instantaneously, they found themselves floating in outer space, surrounded by brilliant stars and beautifully colored, swirling nebulas; all spinning around them as though they were in a planetarium. "How is this even possible?" Mayax wondered out loud.

"It's okay, I have a protection sphere around us," Mina assured him.

"No, I mean, this...this place. It exists in a dimension somewhere between realms. This is like nothing I've ever seen before." Mayax tried to look at everything all at once, but still couldn't get his head around it.

"What, you can't transport to the in between?" Mina asked, surprised.

"No, I can't. And as far as I know, no one else can either." Mayax was truly stunned.

"Oh, I thought anyone who could conjure portals could transport here. I like to come here every now and then when I need some peace and quiet." She shrugged her shoulders as though it were no big whoop.

"You are truly special and unique." Mayax shook his head in disbelief. "I've never seen anyone do the things you do. You are a force of nature, Mina." Mayax suddenly turned to look deeply into her eyes. "I find myself...caught up in you..."

Without warning, Mina suddenly kissed Mayax deeply and forcefully on the lips, unleashing all the pent up sexual tension that had been building exponentially between them since the beginning. The flood gates finally swung wide, and threatened to drown them both, but they hung on to each other for dear life. Mayax wrapped his massive, muscular arms around her, but was careful to be tender. Mina, put both hands behind his head and threaded them into his long, flowing hair, reeling him in closer to make love with their lips.

They breathlessly danced their tongues over one another while Mina tore off Mayax's vest and shirt in frenzied anticipation. Upon shredding his clothes, she saw the branding of her hand over his heart and looked remorsefully into his eyes, "I'm...so sorry, I didn't realize—"

Mayax shushed her with a kiss, "I told you, I would gladly take on a thousand scars for you." He held up her right hand and placed it like a puzzle piece on top of the scar over his heart, "You will always have my heart in your hand."

"This...is all moving so fast for me," Mina said, her head swimming.

Mayax loosened his hold on her, "It is for me too. Perhaps we need to slow down and take stock of everything. We're getting swept up in some intense emotions and we don't want to complicate things. There is something special and important happening between us, and I would hate to—"

Mina cut him off, "Fuck it." She kissed him again, her lips like twin embers in a roaring fire. Mayax needed no further coaxing, but slowed the tempo down in order to savor every moment. He delicately began easing off her T-shirt and tossed it into the void. He cupped her breasts in his hands, that had never known such supple softness throughout his entire life. Over a hundred years of only training and fighting had deprived him of such a simple, compelling pleasure that he could scarcely comprehend it.

Mina matched his pace and began undoing his belt buckle slowly, deliberately. She felt his excitement like a gift and pressed herself against it in sultry expectation. She rhythmically rode his rising erection through her pants until she was soaked. The galaxy spun magnificently around them, but was somehow less impressive than the beauty of these two finding themselves. A comet streaked by, illuminating Mina's green eyes, and Mayax threatened to fall in love with her right then and there.

Mayax couldn't take it any longer and slowly edged her pants, along with her panties, down past her ankles and off her feet. Mina brought Mayax's pants down and he quickly kicked them away. They stared into each other's eyes forever, their bodies pressed flesh to flesh. Mayax stole another kiss before gently laying her back, gravity all nonsense now, and making his way down her quivering belly. He lingered there, savoring the taste of her salty perspiration, before finally helping himself to the sweet honey of her juices. "I've fantasized many times about this, but never dreamed you would taste so good." Mina cried out as he brought his hands underneath her ass, then raised and tipped her like a cup running over, into his mouth. He was thirsty for her and drank deep, stopping only to pleasure her electrified clit with his relentless rhythmic tongue. When the crushing climax washed over her, she arched her back and lost herself in the vibrations of the universe, becoming one with them and riding their ripples to the edge of every galaxy, and back.

Simultaneously, Mina turned the tables and found herself unexpectedly on top of Mayax now. It happened so fast, both were taken off guard, but it didn't take Mayax long to realize he loved being overpowered and dominated by her. It was an immensely pleasurable reversal of routine for him, since he was always the one taking control. Copunocture was often a fight, whereas this was...teamwork. Mina breathed in his intoxicating pheromones, his every desire revealed thanks to her acute feline senses. She was high on his scent; the sensation igniting a fire within her she never knew possible. Unable to wait any longer, she put his manhood inside her mouth and relished the taste of him. Her Pentavi yaggowar senses allowed her to enjoy every facet of lovemaking with heightened awareness. Every smell, taste and sensation titillated her and kept her on the edge.

There was no way for Mayax to describe it, but he knew at that moment he had met his true mate. Mina devoured him while running her hands over his tingling body, intermittently going from hot to cold in order to keep his nerve endings alert and receptive. She brought him straight to the edge of climax and admired his control. Hungry to have him inside her, she prowled her way seductively—almost predatory—up the length of his ripped, muscular body, and teased the end of his cock with her wet warmth. When she thought neither of them could take it any longer, she sank every inch of him inside her, sending shock wave after shock wave of intense pleasure throughout her body. The two lovers knew this coupling was special and poignant; not just from the incredible sexual intensity, but from the emotional and spiritual connection. They were meant to be.

She, born of fire and ice; he, born of blood. Together, they felt they might bring unity to the realms, as well as peace, love and prosperity. They could change everything, and everyone by showing them that division and hatred is a manipulation; strings created by puppeteers looking to segregate, subjugate, and enslave all souls. Our masters were perched on our shoulders from birth to death, capitalizing and feeding off the spilled blood of endless conflict, but no more.

If the two of them could break down barriers and see the truth like Mina's parents had, maybe there was indeed hope, and a worth in what they were doing beyond revenge. This revelation coupled with the intense physical sensation of Mayax deep inside her, pushed Mina closer to orgasm and a feeling of joy that was so alien to her. As she rode Mayax rhythmically to the sound of his pounding heart in her keen ears, she could also make out his promises to her of pleasures beyond anything she could fathom, in the inaudible utterings of his breathless whispers. Then, like the withdrawal of the tide before a tsunami, Mina's breath caught in her throat and she succumbed to her body's orgasmic, electrical overload. She called out loudly into the void of space, daring the cosmos to silence her. She dragged her nails down Mayax's heaving chest, and across his washboard stomach to tickle herself while she was at the height of sensitivity. Mayax put his huge, right hand in the small of her back, and rolled her over in one smooth motion. Now he was on top and ready to ride her through the approaching, undulating space cloud of colorful dust and gasses.

He tenderly, but forcefully, intuited her cadence and matched her cries with his actions. The barbarian was driven and focused, on the verge of sensory overload, when the two came together simultaneously; her breathing out, and him breathing in; then vice versa. They crumpled to their knees, still entwined in an embrace, and connected below. They reveled and marinated in the glow of their heated exchange, as the light of a hundred stars lit their way.

"Just to be clear," Mina said, "that was *not* Copunocture."

"No, it definitely was not," Mayax confirmed. "But it was...pretty spectacular."

"Agreed. But don't go falling in love with me just yet, please. Shit's complicated and at this point, you're still in rebound territory," Mina tried to lie.

Mayax laughed, "Well aren't you the presumptuous one? Not to worry, I'm not the clingy type."

They both shared a laugh and suddenly realized they didn't have any clothes. Mina, "You've got to show me how to conjure clothes...and cars, I just never bothered. I've always been a t-shirt and jeans kinda gal."

"Fair enough," he said, chuckling. "But I bet you look ravishing poured into an elegant dress."

"Naturally," she confirmed.

"It would be my pleasure. How about I show you when we get back, and in the meantime..." Mayax blinked his eyes and had Mina back in her, "It's the Bitches That'll Gitches" tight fitting baseball shirt, with black jeans and boots. "I sense this outfit is your favorite."

"You sensed right," Mina confirmed.

Mayax conjured himself another black, oversized SWAT suit, with a red rune on the front this time, symbolizing his name. "Now, how the hell do we get out of this place?" Mayax asked, looking around like a lost tourist.

"Allow me," Mina said, and opened a portal back to Bee and Auri's house.

When Mina and Mayax stepped through the portal into the sitting room, everyone was sitting there waiting with judging eyes.

Auri was first to speak, "There they are. I'm sure they've come back with everything all worked out and a master plan put together that's going to knock our socks off. Right?"

"How come you guys are all beat up," Avery asked suspiciously.

"Don't worry about it," Mina reprimanded. "We've decided to try to hunt down the Steplescar soldier that Rake...absentmindedly discarded in Reclon. Hopefully, we can get some intel and figure out how to beat these things. That is of course, unless Rake here decides he wants to let us in on the kill switch."

"I would if I could," Rake assured everyone. "Sincerely, the Master Elder and the others never discussed it openly. It was always in some code I couldn't make sense of."

"Great," Mayax grumbled. "So, I guess we're going to have to track it down in Reclon." Everyone sighed in unison because they knew what a colossal cluster fuck that was going to be.

Auri grabbed Mina by the hand and led her quickly out of the room, "Gonna get her cleaned up and changed, we'll be right back." Now in Mina's ear, "You better tell me everything, slut."

"Oh. My. God. How did you know?" Mina was beyond embarrassed.

"C'mon, who are you talking to? Besides, I'm your best friend; I know everything related to your life." Auri led Mina into her bedroom and slammed the door. "Also, you both smell like a damn whorehouse mattress—just sayin'."

"Jesus, Auri." Mina was deeply red-faced at this point. "Just point me in the direction of a shower."

"Can do, just don't look in a mirror." Auri urged her.

"Um, why not," Mina asked, anxiety rising.

"Because you slept in your makeup last night and haven't had a chance to fix it. Not to mention, I'm pretty sure the barbarian sex you just had didn't help much." Auri began to laugh.

"Oh fuck, I just had barbarian sex and my makeup was a damn mess. Christ, I'm trying not to be embarrassed here," Mina acknowledged.

"Don't fret girl, I got you." Auri reassured her. "You can wear my favorite Bulgari black spaghetti strap dress."

"I'm going to hunt a renegade soldier in the Reclon war realm with a bunch of savage and salty outlaws; somehow I don't think that dress would be à propos."

"Style is always à propos, but I see your point. I think Bee has just the outfit for you, anyway. She wore it when she fought in the Bone Wars of Bastiel during the Underworld uprising. Fair warning though, it's sewn from the poisonous silk of a black widow titan, which has been known to drive the person wearing it quite mad. It took me three weeks to finally get Bee to take it off. Mad, you know. Fucking gorgeous armor though, and comfortable...Let me tell you."

"Crazy hot outfit that might make me crazy—got it. Thank you, honey. I love you and Bee so much." Mina felt like such a charity case. "I hate to be here, unannounced, jamming up your whole world with my drama."

"Girl, the minute I saw Roland with his tongue down that bimbo's throat, I knew the shit was going down. I just didn't know it would be this big of a shit. Anyway, no worries, we got this." Auri kissed her on the lips and held her face in her hands. "Bee and I love you; you'll never be an imposition to us. Now, dish, bitch. I want to know every sordid detail." Mina groaned loudly, spurning Auri on. "Oh girl, he's like a Goddamn Brawny commercial, tangled up with some Sons of Anarchy shit, a splash of hot Viking Shemar Moore, and a side of UM, UM, UMMM UMMM, UM." Auri slapped Mina's leg and laughed hysterically.

"First of all...sho you right." Mina began laughing alongside Auri. "He's like having sex with one of those burly, Greek statues of men carved out of stone; and that Dee, girl it was the size of Rolands left arm."

"EWWWWWW, you're awful." Auri continued slapping Mina's leg over and over. "Sooooo nasty."

"Oh, you love it." Mina told her. "Now, I better go get cleaned up to get dirty again."

"Yes ma'am. Oh, and I'll be coming with you; something tells me having Hell's most renowned interrogator and executioner will be of great aid to you on your quest to find the chink in your enemy's armor."

"Really? Thank you, Auri. That means so much to me." Mina was truly grateful. "I didn't want to ask you, but I really appreciate it."

"Think nothing of it. I have the perfect outfit too." Auri said, smiling slyly.

"Oh God, I can only imagine."

"Haha, no you can't." Auri teased.

Mayax had everyone but Mina and Auri huddled up on the rear, stone patio, adjacent to the massive pool and outdoor kitchen, to get prepared for the hunt. The Blood Red Roses were still suited up in their Ceridome wraps and magical armor; Mayax, Rake and Zone had also chosen to remain in the black, flak vests and swat outfits; the only difference being they no longer carried the DHS stencil. Rake also chose a red rune symbolizing his name to wear as a front decal. "Where's Mina and Auri," Mayax asked Avery, who shrugged his shoulders dismissively.

"Man, I can't believe you're making me stay behind with Satan, which isn't nearly as cool as it sounds," Avery lamented. "She reminds me of my Aunt Ruth in California for crying out loud."

"Ugh, he's precious," Bee lied, while standing there in her silk, black robe with a martini in hand. "The girls are coming, they just need a little entrance music." Bee informed everyone as she played "In the Land of Gods and Monsters" by Lana Del Rey on her cell phone.

As if on cue, the french doors to the patio swung open like a gala, revealing Mina and Auri dressed in their warrior women outfits. Mina emerged, wearing the form-fitting, full body black battle suit woven from the poisonous silk webbing of a black widow titan, with her Ceridome wraps underneath to provide protection from the toxic fabric. Resembling the finest leather, the flexible and breathable material was as hard as Pentavi granite, but as sleek as Spandex. Additionally, she was strapped with an AR-15 rifle that boasted all the goodies, a .45 caliber pistol side-arm, a sheath for Beauty, and extra ammo. She was dressed to kill. "I know I look good, but damn, I feel baaaaaaad." Everyone began clapping while hooting and hollering at her. She gestured with her hands and Auri followed gracefully behind her.

Auri was wearing her best Lara Croft outfit, consisting of tight, black girl's boy-shorts, and a utility belt that would rival Batman's. She wore a black tank top and padded vest, with two holsters strapped across and underneath each shoulder. Within them were twin Walther PPK's, James Bond's handgun of choice. She had a samurai sword sheathed on her back and wore her executioner's hood like a cowl; she pulled the hood off to reveal her ruby red hair, flush Irish cheeks, and scarlet smiling lips. Her right naked leg had a boot knife the size of a tractor trailer buckled to it and her black, combat boots went all the way up to her knees. Bee stomped the ground and cat-called at her like a construction worker. "That's my lady right there. You all better recognize."

Rake seemed disenchanted, "I want guns. Can we have guns too?"

Bee shrugged her shoulders, "Sorry buddy, we're fresh out."

"Well, that's disappointing," Rake groaned. "Mayax, can't you conjure us some firepower from the armory?"

Mayax put his hands together, and his head down, then opened two portals on either side of him. In a flash, two metal armament racks came rolling out like trains from the station. They contained a myriad of guns and weaponry, as well as ammo and tactical gear. "Researching mankind's modern weaponry is kind of a hobby of mine; they have an amazing talent for war."

Avery threw his hands up in frustration, "This is bullshit. Man, I want a gun. Maybe I could fly a drone in and scout ahead?"

Mina hugged the little fella tightly, "No kiddo. I'm sorry, but I wouldn't be able to forgive myself if something happened to you. You hang out here with Bee, and don't give her any trouble, or you can kiss Prom goodbye."

"Whatever," the teenager huffed before thrusting his hands in his pockets.

Bee leaned in and whispered in his ear, "Don't sweat it, kid. I've got some beer and some hot girlfriends I can invite over."

"Really?" Avery asked hopefully.

"No. Of course not. Now, go in there and play on the VR like a good lad. You can have ONE beer."

"I guess this is still the coolest shit I've ever been a part of. Two beers?" Avery pushed.

"Christ Bee, give the kid two beers; he'll probably pass out and fall asleep before midnight." Mina winked at Avery.

"Okay, if were all done here, sure wouldn't mind getting a fucking move on," Viss Vascene barked from the end of the line. "Seems to me a lot of what we are doing is time sensitive."

Rake turned to look at her, "Why, Miss Viss, I forgot you were there. With me?" He joked, holding out his arm like a southern gentleman for her to grab.

"Fuck you, asshole." She spit at him.

"Indeed, ma'am." He proclaimed.

Mina stepped forward, slapped Beauty on her hip, and conjured a portal to Reclon behind everyone. "Alright y'all, let's get down in the mud and find ourselves a fight."

Rake, "Y'all? A country rose you are not."

"Fuck you, asshole," Mina said nonchalantly.

"Been getting a lot of that lately," Rake admitted. He turned to Zone and smacked him on the back, "But not from you, buddy. You a'ight."

CHAPTER 8
CHICKENSAUR

The regiment of nine oddball hunters stepped into the murky waters of Reclon's most dangerous and notorious swamp, ready for anything. Mayax led the way, with Mina closely behind. "I figured we'd start in the worst part, then work our way out," Mina said to Mayax in a whisper.

"Is there any other part than the worst?" Mayax asked. "Rake, can you come up with some kind of way to track that thing?" he inquired, keeping his head on a swivel.

Rake began vamping out monstrously in preparation for the hunt, "It has occurred to me that we share the same dark magic DNA, so theoretically, I should be able to craft a location spell based on my own genetic makeup." Rake seemed confident in his assertions.

"Excellent, do it," Mayax commanded.

"Sure thing, sarge," Rake grumbled through sharp teeth. "Bossy fucker, ain't cha?"

"The more you pick up and employ the colorful local language, the more I wish you were created with no mouth like your Steplescar brethren," Mayax quipped.

"Sorry, not sorry," Rake responded curtly before putting his hands together and chanting. After a moment, his left hand began to glow a sickly green, which he then pressed to the forehead of Zone. The greenish glow seemed to leave his hand and go inside Zone, turning his eye's that same sickly green glow. Zone hovered there for a moment, his new green eyes searching the landscape, then began floating forward. "It's the best I can do," Rake lamented. "I have no idea how long we have to follow him before we find the soldier; the fucking thing could be clear on the other side of the realm."

Mayax didn't panic, and Mina asked, "Is there a way for you to know where you dropped him initially, then we can start our search there?"

Rake pondered this for a minute, "Maybe—hold on a second..." He conjured a portal out of thin air. "This should be close to where I initially sent him," he reassured them.

"Excellent, you first." Mayax pushed Rake roughly through the portal, but he came splashing down close by a second later from high above.

"I guess we're close," Rake said, angrily pulling himself from the bog and spitting out marsh water.

"Sorry, not sorry," Mayax replied, stony faced.

"I see what you mean about the local lingo," Rake jabbed.

"Um, guys, Zone is floating away from us," Mina pointed out. "Best we keep him close."

"Agreed," Mayax said. "Follow Zone." They all got into position and moved quickly to intercept Zone. When they were about fifty feet from him, a gigantic, slimy, tarry leech-looking creature shot up out of the dark depths of the swamp and gobbled up the floating zombie in one bite. "Holy shit," Mayax screamed. "Don't let it get away."

The Blood Red Roses were the first to act and leapt into the air with their Ceridome wraps unfurled. They used the enchanted straps as harpoons, harnesses and reins to keep the beast tethered and above ground, but it fought them tenaciously. Mayax, Mina, and Rake charged in recklessly on the writhing, squirming monstrosity while it was still pinned down. Mina was quickly out with Beauty, and ran the length of the beast's belly, disemboweling it grotesquely. Massive ropes of intestines began to spill out while the ladies kept it wrangled. Mayax was next to move in and grabbed what looked like the beast's stomach and esophagus, then ripped it mercilessly out of the gash in its long belly. There appeared to be a large lump, most likely Zone, right at the precipice of the monster's stomach. Rake slashed the gigantic organ with Somhaine, his Blade of Black, splitting it like a sausage. Zone came rolling out, but he had both hands on something inside. Mina and Rake grabbed Zone's legs and dragged him out of the dying worms' insides. To their surprise and elation, Zone had his hands on the ankles of the Steplescar soldier and dragged him out along with him. "Well, that's lucky," Mina proclaimed.

Unfortunately, that's when an even larger winged predator, covered in huge feathers and scales, located the activity from high above and zeroed in on them with five bulging eyes. The sheer size of the flying titan alone was hard to comprehend; it was at least ten times the size of the slithering behemoth they were currently tangling with. "Heads up," Auri yelled as everyone tried to leap out of the way of its monstrous beak that came crashing down all around them. Mayax, Rake and the Blood Red Roses were all able to dive out of the way in time, but Mina, Auri, Zone, and the Steplescar soldier were caught up in its deadly circumference. The cross between a dragon and five-eyed rooster scooped them up, along with the worm, before trying to take off. Fortunately, the beastly leech's distal end was still miles underground and kept the scaly phoenix tethered to the earth. Mayax reacted fast and charged in screaming with Velocet. He used the jagged ax blade to climb the coarse leg of the beast and began making his way towards the belly underneath. Mina suddenly called from down below, having escaped the titan by conjuring a portal, "I got Zone and the soldier, but Auri is still in there." Mayax nodded and continued to hack and slash his way towards the titan's underside. Thinking fast, he conjured a portal inside its stomach to the outside of its stomach, and all its miles and miles of steaming intestines began pouring out of the portal and coiling on the ground beneath it.

"Do you see her?" Mayax screamed at Mina.

"No. Keep looking." Mina was frantic now.

The chickensaur thrashed around disastrously, making everyone below fight to avoid being crushed, as its head began dumbly lolling around on its long neck. In an instant, the five bulging beastial eyes began filling with blood, and Auri exploded out of its massive forehead like a bullet. The titian went completely limp and collapsed hazardously sideways, like a demolished building. The ground shook thunderously as the titan impacted, dead as a doornail. Regrettably, this was like ringing the dinner bell in Reclon, and a million different creatures of varying size took notice. Covered in blood and bone, Auri called out to everyone, "I'm fine, Mina and Zone have the soldier, let's get the fuck outta here."

Everyone who could conjure a portal did so, and everyone who couldn't made sure they were behind someone who could.

Three portals suddenly opened up on Auri's rear patio, startling the fuck out of Bee and Avery, who were sitting in elegant black silk bathrobes in patio chairs, while enjoying a beer by the fire pit. All nine warriors, and the Steplescar soldier, came tumbling out of the three portals, gore-covered and hysterical.

Bee and Avery let slip a little high-pitched yelp as the warriors dog piled on the soldier to keep him from escaping. "Well now, that wasn't such a chore," Rake called out sarcastically while returning to normal size.

"Holy fuck, you guys were only gone for like ten minutes," Avery hollered.

Bee quickly threw open the top of a huge cooler full of beer, "Grab a beer, we have smores too. How did it go, honey?"

Mayax looked unbelievably at Mina and they began to laugh loudly. Viss Vascene and her soldier sisters were already on their feet, cleaning themselves off. Auri looked to Bee, "Christ on a crutch, that could have gone a lot better and it could have gone a lot worse."

"Looks like you saw a little action there, sugar pie," Bee observed. "You'll have to tell mama all about it later tonight between the sheets. But first, get a drink."

"The kids right, we were only gone for like ten minutes, and you're already drunk?" Auri scolded Bee.

"Don't judge me. Love me," Bee demanded, eliciting a smile and chuckle from Auri.

Rake, still much larger than the Steplescar soldier even in his normal form, held up the mindless fighter by its armor. "They ain't so bad once you get one alone. Kinda cute, really."

"Give me a break, Rake," Mina huffed as she strolled up to get a good look at the soldier, who dangled there like a limp rag. However, when she got too close, the soldier sprang into action and tried to grab hold of her. She didn't flinch an inch though, rather, she stared deeply into its red, beady eyes. "Alright, Mayax, Auri, and Viss Vascene, you guys are with me. Rake, you too, and bring your pet. Let's get this fucker down to Auri's interrogation room and see if we can figure it out."

"Guess I'll just sit here and do nothing," Avery moaned.

"What're you talking about, Avery?" Bee called out drunkenly. "You were giving me ideas on how to get rid of Bob at the office. Now, what's this about a website where you can mail gorilla shit anonymously?"

Deep down in Auri's secret torture dungeon, the five generals of the new resistance chained down their enemy in a steel chair for a fact finding mission. Zone hovered coldly in the corner like a voyeuristic floating statue in the shadows. The Steplescar soldier represented their best chance at figuring out how to bring the Master Elder's indestructible army to its knees. "Last chance, Rake. Any information you can give us about these creatures and that kill switch would be extremely valuable," Mayax reminded his on-again-off-again-on-again comrade.

This elicited a great sigh of frustration from Rake. "You think I would have followed your dumb asses all the way to that piss hole to hunt this fucking freak down if I already knew how the kill switch worked?" Rake seemed genuinely ill-tempered with the ongoing accusation. "I already know how I'm going to build my army," He said, tapping his pointed canine teeth. "I can't control these things, so they are of no use to me. You can all rest easy for now, we are still allied in figuring these things out. Now pretty please, with sugar on top, can we take this fucking creature apart to see what makes it tick?"

Mina slapped Rake on the back. "You know what? This Dracula motherfucker is starting to grow on me."

"Oh well, pinch me I must be dreaming," Rake sang sarcastically.

Mayax pushed through the four of them and kneeled into the face of the soldier, studying it intently. The warrior didn't react, knowing it could do nothing chained down. "Mina, can you burn off its right arm?"

Mina lit a cigar with her right finger. "Is a pig's pecker pork?" Now her entire right hand was on fire. She traced her one finger down the soldier's left arm, reducing it completely to ash. The soldier maintained no reaction as the others looked on eagerly. After a few seconds, the ash began to crawl together and reconstitute. "Well, fuck," Mina sighed as the ash continued to form the soldier's arm out of thin air, like they were all watching a film in reverse.

"There's our answer surrounding incineration," Mayax said, defeated. "Any other ideas?"

Viss Vascene came forward now and slowly pulled out her dagger. She placed it against the soldier's left temple and promptly cut its face off. Naturally, there was still no reaction from the Steplescar. She pulled the grizzly skin mask from its head and set it aside curiously on the floor. Sure enough, the soldier's face grew back, but more importantly, the face on the floor seemed to be growing into a soldier. "Better get another chair and some more chains," she advised. Osha and Amira volunteered to go and obtain the items before the face on the floor became a problem.

"These things are like starfish herpes," Mina pointed out colloquially while pacing. "This could be a real problem for us. Maybe we just go after the Elders? Once they're out of the picture, maybe these things will...deactivate or some damn thing."

"Not likely," Rake added. "It's my understanding that without the Elders to control them, they will devolve into a pack of wild dogs; attacking anything that comes near them. I say we take out the Elders and dump the army in Reclon. It's possible we can extract the kill switch from the Master Elder if we can get him alone, but that's a few pretty big ifs."

"Reclon is too close for comfort," Mayax stated. "I prefer we discover how to wipe them out completely, but in the meantime, perhaps we can sequester them in a realm somewhere less accessible to the Elders, maybe somewhere in the in between? What do you think, Mina?"

Mina puffed her stogie and thought about it. "I don't see why not. There's plenty of unused real estate out there. As long as they can't conjure, we should be okay. Or...what if..." Mina thought long and hard while everyone hung anxiously on her last word. "What if we could somehow turn them against the Master Elder? Then he would be forced to throw the kill switch."

"I like it," Viss Vascene agreed. "Surely there is a way."

"We can't enchant them, and they aren't susceptible to hex magic. Rake, you got any suggestions? You have commonality with them," Mayax pointed out.

Rake raised his eyebrows in thought, "Thank you for reminding me...Maybe."

Osha and Amira returned with another steel chair and some chains. They gathered up the new, wriggling, sinewy, and cartilaginous soldier that was still coming together on the floor, and chained it to the chair. Mayax scratched his beard roughly and put his long hair back into a bun. Mina promptly walked over and took the bun out of his hair. "Nope, no, no..."

"What?" Mayax argued. "It's practical."

"I'm sorry, but the man-bun is a bridge too far," Mina said through a cloud of cigar smoke.

Rake chimed back in, "She's right about the bun, bro. Anyway, It's possible I could arrange consort with Athan Asios, my true father and architect of the Steplescar army. At the very least, I could learn more about the arrangement he has with the Master Elder. Perhaps there is a weakness there we can exploit. However, summoning him from the Dark Realm is extremely dangerous. He has nothing but contempt for this realm, and all the others. If we unleash him, it could be worse than what we are dealing with now."

"I know one realm Athan Asios favors..." Auri added, suddenly joining the conversation. "He is brother to my significant other, The Queen of Darkness herself - Bee." Turning to Rake, "I guess that makes you two related. Gross. Anyway, we could summon him from the Hell realm and be assured he wouldn't make trouble. He adores and respects Bee."

"Very clever," Rake praised Auri.

Mina turned to Rake, "You do realize that makes Bee your...Aunt Bee," Mina pointed out to Rake before laughing hysterically. No one joined her in laughter since none one else got her reference. "You know, from Andy Griffith...Nevermind."

Rake turned back to Auri. "You think you could get Bee to help us?"

"I think I can get Bee to help *me*." Auri said, delicately tapping Rake on the end of his nose with her finger. "Boop."

"I'll take it," Mayax said enthusiastically. "Auri, respectfully, can you take Bee, Rake and Zone to Hell to try to summon Athan Asios? Find out anything you can, try not to get killed, and report back to us as soon as possible."

Auri responded purposely, "Absolutely. Anything we can do to help."

"You really were made for giving orders and discipline," Rake jeered, smacking his scarred lips. "I'll do this, but not for you. I do nothing for your satisfaction unless it serves me - just so we're clear."

Mayax rubbed his eyes tiredly. "Rake...I only found out yesterday that you were not my brother, but it makes no difference to me. Despite our complicated relationship, we are more than allies of convenience, or adversaries for that matter; we are Nevuscar, which means we are indeed brothers. No matter what you say, I know that means something to you. Consider not making a full-time enemy of me."

Rake nodded dramatically and feigned sincerity with his huge, jagged smile. "Well...bye," he said dismissively and walked towards the door, motioning for Zone to levitate over and follow him out. Looking at Auri, "You coming?"

"Yep. This'll be a *hoot*," Auri said sarcastically. "Be sure to keep your fangs to yourself, pal."

"Don't worry, I'm in no hurry to make an enemy of my aunt," Rake said sincerely.

"Of that I am certain," Auri mumbled under her breath.

"Thank you for everything, Auri. We are humbled." Mayax offered as she began to escort Rake out of the interrogation room. "Contact us when you have information."

Rake stopped short of going up the stairs. "What do you and the girl gang plan to do?"

Mayax looked to Rake, then to Mina. "We're going to go get Vasser and Layluna. We will need their help when we are ready to launch an offensive."

Rake shook his head in disbelief. "I hate that idea."

A hush fell over the room as Mina sincerely thanked Mayax with her eyes; then the doorbell up above rang throughout the house.

Up on the rear patio, Bee and Avery continued to drink beers and discuss ways to fuck with Bob at Bee's work. "That sonofabitch has it out for me." Bee explained to Avery, who was pacing himself on drinks better than she was.

"But you're CEO; doesn't that make you the boss?" Avery asked while eating some Door Dash chicken wings.

"Yes, and no. See, I'm the head of the company, but Bob is the head of the board of directors. He represents all the investors and shareholders from the other realms, including this one. He's really pressuring me to change the business model and get into bed with more corporatists and politicians from Earth. Needless to say, I've had plenty of dealings with those types over the years and I can't say I like them much. Fucking greedy, pushy idiots with no clue on how things really work."

"So, what's your plan to get rid of him?" Avery asked through a mouthful of chicken wings.

"Past the gorilla shit? I got nothing," Bee admitted.

Avery considered this for a minute, "Hold on, I've got it. All you need to do is—" But then the doorbell rang inside.

"Who in the hell could that be." Bee asked out loud. "You order more food?"

"No," Avery confirmed.

"Hold that thought, kid; I am actually interested in hearing your ideas about getting rid of Bob. Excuse me for a moment, while I get that."

"Don't you have like a maid or butler or something?" Avery wondered. "It's weird you're so rich, but have no servants."

"Never believed in them. Anything they can do, I can do my damn self." The doorbell rang again, "Excuse me..." Bee staggered to her feet and went inside. She met Auri, Rake and Zone in the kitchen, then they all shared a worried look.

"I'm guessing whoever that is, isn't Amazon," Auri said quietly to Bee.

"Agreed." Bee replied as Mayax and Mina came barreling up the stairs behind Auri, Rake and Zone.

"Who the fuck is that?" Mina asked urgently.

"Hold on..." Auri checked the Ring doorbell video on her cell phone, "Um, it looks like the *ENTIRE* Sinteverete and Steplescar army," Auri whimpered, holding up her phone for everyone to see. "How the fuck did they know you guys were here?"

They all shared a bewildered look. "I have no idea," Mayax divulged as he shrugged his shoulders. "I've had a cloaking spell over this entire area since we got here."

"Me too," Mina said.

"Me three," Rake added.

"Me four," Bee finished.

"Well, what the fuck? There's no way they could have tracked us here," Mina said to Bee. "None of those pricks even knows I know you."

Acting fast, Mayax turned to Rake and Auri as the doorbell rang yet again. "Bee, I don't mean to order you around in your own house, but can you go with Auri, Rake and Zone right now?"

Bee looked down at her bathrobe, "Yeah, I guess I can change later."

Auri quickly opened a portal to Hell, and the four of them practically leaped through it. Mayax and Mina shared a fraught look as

Sistell, Osha, and Amira scuttled into the kitchen. Mina, "Weapons out ladies." The three Blood Red Roses unslung their rifles from their shoulders and prepared for war.

Sistell hollered down the stairs at Viss Vascene, who was still guarding the two Steplescar soldiers, "Weapons out."

Mayax went to answer the door as Mina rushed out to grab Avery.

CHAPTER 9
CAPPUCCINO AND WAR

T he moment they arrived in the courtyard of Hell's corporate headquarters, Auri, Bee, and Rake hit the sulfur running, with Zone levitating closely behind. All manner of demons, deities, and demigods rushed around in the busy streets outside the spikey wrought-iron gates that encircled the vast, smoldering magma that flowed within the courtyard. An enormous, showy, pretentious fountain made of black and red marble was the centerpiece, and spit hot magma up into the air like a volcano. The towering skyscraper of glass and steel, set in the epicenter of a bustling city on fire, stretched up for miles towards the burning red and orange sky that churned like a lava lamp high above. The massive monument sign on the face of the skyscraper read simply, "Hell." "Follow me," Auri instructed urgently as she blasted through the elegant doors to the infamous establishment. They ran past the demon security guards, then past the Starbucks to the elevators, and Auri frantically tapped the button to call the lift. "I figure we'll use your conference room, Bee."

"That's fine, should still be ready from yesterday," Bee assured her. The elevator dinged loudly and the four non-friends jumped inside. The muzak version of "I'm All Out of Love" by Air Supply played mellowly over the elevator speakers as they rode upward toward the top floor.

"I like this song." Rake mentioned casually, grinning that grin. "It always brought a smile to my face..."

Bee rolled her eyes at him "Try saying that after listening to it every single day for the past thirty-three years. It has played on an endless loop since the song launched in the 80s. Welcome to Hell."

Upon arriving at the top floor, the elevator dinged again and the doors slowly rolled open. Auri, Bee, and Rake walked briskly, as Zone continued to float ghoulishly behind them. The four made their way down an impressive black and red marbled hallway with classy light fixtures, then flung open the huge double doors to the conference room at the end and entered. The room had to be 5000 square feet if it was a foot, with huge paintings depicting all manner of sins and gory debauchery adorning the high reaching walls. The conference table inside was truly awe-inspiring. It was roughly a hundred feet long, thirty feet wide, and made of the most beautiful wormwood ever seen. The surface was stained a deep rich red, and each chair surrounding it was a luxurious throne. "Alright, Dark One, call ya daddy," Auri encouraged Rake in a condescending tone.

Looking annoyed with her, "You ain't the boss of me. Now, in all honesty, this will be the first time I've ever tried to contact the Dark Realm, or Athan Asios for that matter. I have absolutely no idea how he will react."

Zone found a nice, darkened corner to levitate in, off to the side.

Conjuring herself a very nice, elegant, professional and polished look, Bee responded to Rake, "If I know my brother, he will be aggravated that we dared bother him, but he and I have always had a pretty good relationship, so we have that going for us."

"Why don't you summon him then," Rake pushed.

"Better I remain in his good graces when we start asking him for shit," Bee pointed out. "Besides, it's a lot easier for you than it is for me."

"Okay, I guess I can play the estranged, needy son card." Rake raised his eyebrows and rubbed his hands together in preparation, "Here goes nothing…"

The son of dark magic closed his one red eye, focused, and began chanting. Auri realizing she was still wearing her blood-covered battle outfit, quickly conjured herself an appropriate and professional business ensemble, with stylish hair to match. After a few moments, thick black liquid began to bubble up and ooze out of the center of the table, before spreading out sickly in all directions. A fetid stench suddenly permeated the air and the glass windows went completely dark as a huge, clawed hand of midnight black shot up out of the ooze and grabbed hold of the edge of the desk. The appendage was connected to something far too large to pull itself completely out of the portal, but it raised the top of its unholy head out enough so its twin red eyes could look garishly around. Once the Lord of Faltous Estuche—the Dark Realm—was satisfied with the surroundings, he shrank into a much smaller form, composed entirely of dark shadow, with only the red eyes and a sharp, toothy smile set within. He levitated out of the portal, stepped across the desk to the head of the conference table and took a seat. "This is an unexpected amusement," the Dark Lord said in an imposing, thunderous tone. "To what do I owe the pleasure of this…unscheduled family reunion?"

Rake looked at Bee urging her with his eye, to which she sighed and responded, "Good evening, dear brother. It has been a long time." Bee was careful to bow her head in honor of his Lord.

"Indeed, it has, sister," he replied, returning the gesture. "I have missed you." Looking at Auri now, "Auri, my little Irish firecracker; you are as gorgeous as ever." Auri bowed her head honorably as well. "And look here; my son. I'm pleased our reunion has proffered such a broad smile from you." He said, winking. "I trust you are serving the Master Elder well per his and my agreement."

"About that," Rake began, "I have determined that he no longer has my—*our*—best interests at heart."

"What," Athan Asios screamed deafeningly, shattering every window in the conference room, allowing the poisonous atmosphere of Hell to spill in. The noxious red and orange clouds swirled inside, adding a nightmarish milieu to the meeting. "I gave the Master Elder my one and only son—YOU—along with my word, as part of a contract that you have now broken. How dare you shame me."

Rake stood tall and unwavering in the wake of his absent father's apparent wrath. "It was not my intent to shame you, father. Rather, I have decided *I* would serve as a far better master to the realms, instead of that impish twerp. All in your name, of course."

Athan Asios relaxed, "Excellent. Not even a hint of fear or apprehension when I reprimanded you. You are a worthy successor to my treacherous nature, son. You are fulfilling your true path and I am proud of you." He bowed his head to Rake, who quickly returned the gesture in penance. "I will help you in your destiny, but know this, the Hell realm is off limits." Athan Asios smiled at Bee, who graciously smiled back, knowing the promise meant nothing. If Rake was going to seize control of the Hell realm in his father's name, Athan Asios would do nothing to stop it. She, above anyone else, knew him to be entirely untrustworthy. He never failed to honor his contracts, but he always had a loophole baked in with enough legalese that no one would be able to slither out from underneath him.

"Understood, father." Rake said with a wink.

"Now, why have you contacted me?" He asked, feigning disinterest. "I can only assume you all need something? So, out with it."

Rake, now confident, addressed his father and Lord, "I wish to take command of the Steplescar army to aid in removing the Master Elder and his six cohorts, and the other three Pentavi Elders; as well as anyone else who would stand in the way of my taking control of the realms in your illustrious name," he added, looking pointedly at Bee and Auri.

The two wives both looked at Rake with accusing eyes, but held their tongues. Afterall, he had been straightforward about his intentions since the beginning, and they would cross that bridge when they came to it.

The Dark Lord melodramatically pondered Rake's query for a long time, knowing everyone was anxious and eager for his response. "While I'm perfectly comfortable with *you* breaking my word, I am not comfortable doing it myself. Besides, I have already provided you with the means necessary to create your own army when the time comes," he said, motioning to Zone floating over in the corner. "You'll have to earn some things in this life, boy, despite my being your father. That said, there are ways I can help without breaking my contract to the Master Elder."

"Please my Lord, enlighten me," Rake begged.

"First of all, enough with the 'my Lord' shit," he demanded. "Now, here's what I'm prepared to do for you all," he said, rubbing his shadowy hands together. "Rake, the Steplescar army is not mine to destroy or turn over to you, per my agreement with the Master Elder and his associates, so I'm afraid that's off the table." Rake was clearly disappointed. "However, Auri, I am prepared to offer you the same deal I offered the Master Elder, in exchange for the information you seek. If you provide me with the Alma from your dear friend Mina, the Yasmani Ro born of fire and ice," he said shivering with titillation, "it would enable me to nullify my contract with the Master Elder per a freelance contractor clause I have included. You wouldn't even have to do the ritual; just bring her to me, and I'll do the rest. Whattya say…?"

"I truly appreciate the consideration, Athan Asios; you are a benevolent, generous Lord," Auri prefaced her refusal with a little sweet-talk. "Unfortunately, as you most likely know, that price is too steep."

"The hell you say—" Rake began to protest.

Auri stared daggers through Rake, shutting him up instantly. "I don't want to seem ungrateful, Lord, but I should like to exhaust every possible option before betraying my best friend and condemning her to an eternity of servitude."

"Fair, 'nuff,'" Athan Asios replied. "I would have been remiss had I not offered. Besides, it's more interesting if I don't have permission." Turning his attention back to Rake, "Don't be so quick to take the easy way out, Prince. However, since you all are family, I can offer you this…" he began, pausing for dramatic effect, "You don't need to kill, confine or control the Steplescar army in order to defeat them; simple as that. Now, who in hell calls an urgent conference between such lofty offices without providing any fucking coffee?"

Auri quickly conjured a cappuccino of the finest quality, with a little heart design and devil horns in the foam. Athan Asios raised the cup to Auri, "Nice touch," then took a big sip. "I appreciate being remembered."

"You are family, after all." Auri said with a pleasant smile.

"You all are going to spoil me. Well, if that's it...I've got to be off now; much to do..."

Rake, Bee, and Auri all looked worried to one another with side eyes. It was Bee who finally found her spine and spoke up, "Brother, perhaps you could be a little more...direct in your assistance with the Steplescar army?"

"Ingrates," Athan Asios bellowed, suddenly transforming into a huge, terrifying and shadowy beast of biblical proportions. The three salty warriors couldn't help but shrink in the intimidating presence of such a powerful entity. He quickly shrank back again, chuckling, "I'm kidding, I'm kidding. The look on your faces...*priceless*," he laughed, slapping his knee. "Of course, dear sister. The answer is so elegant in its simplicity and obvious in its location, but as I've told my son, you have to earn some things in this life. I promise once you figure it out, if you figure it out, you'll appreciate the message and where I am coming from. Furthermore, if you are unable to figure it out, I'll be sorely disappointed, and you will forfeit my respect."

Still totally confused, but not wanting to press the Dark Lord any further, Rake, Bee, and Auri all bowed their heads and bid Athan Asios farewell. The Lord of Faltous Estuche bowed his shadowy head in return and vanished through his black, sludgy portal. Upon disappearing, the black sludge remained. "Goddammit," Bee huffed, looking at the huge mess. She moved over to the phone hanging on the wall and called housekeeping. "I'll need a conference room prep and clean on six thousand and seventy-three, please." She hung up the phone and looked at Rake. "What now?"

Rake sighed and bowed his head, "Well, that was a bust, unless..." Rake looked pleadingly at Auri.

"Absolutely not," Auri told Rake flatly.

"Okay, well then, as much as it pains me dearly to suggest this, and I know I'm going to fucking regret it in a profound way..."

"Out with it, Rake." Auri was losing her patience with the Undying one.

"Alright, alright, UGH, we'll need to liberate Mina's parents. Vasser and Layluna are the only ones who have personally witnessed the Elder's confession, and their memory can serve as irrefutable evidence of the Sinteverete and Pentavi Elder cabal. Not only can they aid us, but they can help us convince the two clans to unite against the Elders. It's no Steplescar army kill switch, but it's something."

"Agreed. Do you know where they are being held?" Auri asked anxiously.

Rake conjured a portal into the Sinteverete temple's trophy room, directly in front of the slab of white Pentavi granite that served as a prison cell for the two legendary fighters. "Let's do this before I change my fucking mind..."

Meanwhile, behind the facade of the innocent looking millionaire's mansion in New Jersey, war was brewing. Mayax opened the front door to Auri and Bee's palace, and put his eyes on the entire Sinteverete army, the regiment of Pentavi slave warriors, and the easily three hundred thousand Steplescar soldiers, who were all waiting patiently in the courtyard, and miles beyond. "I see the puppets, but where are the puppeteers?" Mayax chided, hoping the jeer would call out the Master Elder and the other six.

Sure enough, the Master Elder and the other six Elders rose up out of the epicenter of the unnatural army to face him. The Master Elder did all the talking, per usual. "There's my wilful, former number two. Slumming it with the other nouveau riche, I see."

"Pretty ballsy showing up here in full force; the Masters of this realm might take this as a declaration of war. Especially with their military so close by. Mankind is formidable, *Master Elder*," he said sarcastically, "and you would do well not to minimize their insatiable hunger for conflict. Not only will you be dealing with me and mine, but you'll have to take on them as well; are you ready for that?"

The gleeful little imp began spinning horizontally around in circles, laughing and clapping his little hands in mid-air. "Ready? I'm counting on it."

"Pride cometh before the fall. In any case, how did you find us, if I may be so bold?" Mayax queried.

"You really do underestimate me, you arrogant, oversized twat." The Master Elder flashed his gremlin style smile, but there was something false about it. "Do you really think I wouldn't order my undefeatable, immortal army without all the bells and whistles?" Having the upper hand, he snickered like a third grader, "Not only do my soldiers come complete with a lifetime warranty, they also come equipped with GPS tracking."

Mayax nodded his head, acknowledging their oversight. "I should have known."

"You should have known," the tiny, evil emperor confirmed. "I've been watching you through the eyes of the one you dragged out of Reclon. It was a precocious plan you all had, testing my soldier, then trying to elicit the kill switch from Athan Asios, but I assure you, he would never breach our ironclad contract. You are out of avenues and options, my friend." Gloating now, "No more scurrying around, causing me trouble; there is nothing left for you and the others to do at this point, but admit defeat. I have you in a hopeless situation strategically—you're lost. You should just admit your failure; there is more honor in it."

"You lecturing me about honor is laughable," Mayax retorted. "Additionally, I'm done bending the knee to a worthless, infantile little turd like you, his six cucks, and the three treacherous Pentavi Elder sellouts. So do your worst; we are ready for war."

"Then war you shall have..." the Master Elder replied.

Mina, still dressed in her silk, black widow titan armor, ran outside and found Avery where she left him, lounging by the firepit, with a beer and some more snacks. He brightened, "Hey, just you and me at last. So, I was wondering—"

"You have to move, right now," Mina yelled frantically. "Quick, through this portal," she ordered, while casting a portal to his parent's house. "Get your family and get them the fuck out of Jersey."

"They won't know who the fuck I am," he argued. "Plus, they're about 15 miles away, won't that be far enough?"

"No, no, it won't if this goes the distance, and I suspect it will. Now round up your family and convince them to get as far away from this area as possible."

"Okay, okay, I will." Avery got up and moved towards the portal before Mina all but shoved him through.

"I'll see you for prom." She promised, before closing the portal.

"You better," Avery managed before losing sight of her.

As the gateway vanished, Ashen, Bael, and the other two Nevuscar stepped up from behind. "There's my favorite little outlaw," Bael beckoned. "You didn't think you were gonna get away, did you?"

"I'm not trying to get away, dumbass, and I've had just about all I'm going to take out of you four clowns. I'm ready to go to the mattresses, y'all."

"Ewwwww, promises, promises," Bael said in a suggestive tone. "Are you finally warming to the idea of Copunocture?" He asked in a mock southern accent.

"Nope, I'm not here to fuck you, pal, I'm here to fuck you up," Mina said, slinging her AR rifle for emphasis. Without waiting another moment, she perforated Bael's tortured flesh with hot lead, forcing him backwards. She turned her barrel towards Ashen, who simply held up his hand to block the onslaught of bullets with a protection spell. "Cheater, cheater, pumpkin eater," she goaded him, tossing the rifle aside and unsheathing Beauty. "Let's see that body wine, blondie."

"I am Ashen the Abhorrent, and I can't wait for you to try," he announced, before simply gesturing for her to bring it.

And bring it, she did. She rushed in and instantly transported a microsecond before she collided with him, then reappeared unexpectedly behind an unsuspecting Bael. Mina reached in through his coarse back and pulled out his spine and ribs. He doubled over in crippled shock, so she planted her heel on his ass and shoved him out of the way, tearing free his vertebrae. "That should keep you on the bench for a minute," she cackled. The other two identical twin Nevuscar warriors, who still had yet to offer their names, or speak for that matter, rushed her with violent intent. Without hesitation, Mina brought up her left hand, which was radiating unforgiving levels of glacial cold, and cast them into an impossibly thick block of near indestructible ice—literally freezing them in their tracks. Now she focused on Ashen. "Are you idiots seriously still buying the whole facade that audacious, baby-faced freak is selling you? Wake up, man, we are not your enemies."

Ashen was solemn, "I was bred right before the Great Divide and the dissolution of Zol; allegiance to the Master Elder is all I've ever known. There is no hope for change within me, so your poignant words are futile." Ashen seemed almost regretful his beliefs were so galvanized. "I fought by your father's side while fighting your mother, and then I fought them while they were fighting side-by-side. I like to think I know them very well. Your father was born long before me but was my mentor and trainer. We were inseparable for more years than I can count. We fought together, we hunted together, and we trained together. Then..." Ashen seemed on the verge of actual tears, "he traded me and the entire Sinteverete clan, everything we fought for and believed in for so long, because of a Pentavi *woman*. The shame is inescapable."

"I believe you knew my father well," Mina began, "so tell me this: would he betray all that so lightly? Would he upend everything he has ever known, all the brothers he held so dear, all his ingrained beliefs, if it wasn't for a goddamn good reason? Would he throw it all away If he had not come across some kind of irrefutable proof, that transcends even the potent pull of true love? Clear the shit from your eyes and see, Ashen."

He bowed his head and unsheathed Acheron, his cursed Blade of Black, "I cannot."

"You can, and YOU WILL," Mina screamed, and rushed him.

The newly promoted Nevuscar lead crossed Acheron with Beauty and a knock-down, drag-out slash and stab struggle ensued. Ashen was a deeply dangerous, skilled and meticulous fighter, with a million years of hard-fought training under his belt, but he was still no match for Mina at full strength. She began toying with him, matching his best moves with one hand behind her back.

"You arrogant bitch, don't you dare condescend to hold back on me," Ashen demanded.

"As you wish," Mina warned, and promptly beat the absolute fuck out of him like a 70s kung fu movie, until he was dangling dazed and disoriented from her tight hold around his throat. "Any other demands?" she asked rhetorically.

Things seemed to be kicking off around the front of the house as Mayax and the Blood Red Roses engaged the Steplescar army. Mina maintained her hold on Ashen and dragged him dangling through the air, over the house and down to the main event.

Mayax single-handedly stared down the seven Elders, along with the entire Sinteverete and Steplescar army, and the Pentavi Slave soldier regiment, before Viss Vascene, Sistell, and the Savvoy twins came from behind and took his back. "We are the Blood Red Roses," Viss Vascene cried out loudly in her almost robotic voice, "and we stand with Mayax, former leader of the Nevuscar, sworn enemy of the Pentavi, and murderer of our sisters. We stand together in defiance of *YOU*," she screamed, pointing her long finger at the Master Elder.

To this, the Master Elder and his council of six laughed shrewdly over the heads of their undefeatable army. Mayax whispered to Viss Vascene, "Let's get them."

"There's the thorn we've been waiting for," Viss Vascene whispered back in his ear. "Attack Roses." The four Blood Red Roses charged the Sinteverete Elders with steel and stone, tooth and claw. Viss Vascene and Sistell unloaded their fully automatic AR rifles directly at the Elder's smug and smiling faces, forcing frowns upon their grins. Unfortunately, the bullets ricocheted off their auras of protection, but managed to provoke a retreat out of them. Osha quickly shifted to a gorgeous, mid-sized, black and orange spotted yaggowar, then leapt bravely into the mobilizing Steplescar army with her fangs leading the way. Amira, ready with her mace, unfurled her Ceridome wraps and used them like tentacles to carry her high above the faceless freaks frantically reaching for her down below. Looking like Doctor Octopus, she made her way fearlessly towards the Elders with lethal intent. Viss Vascene and Sistell continued to pin the Elders down with suppressing fire, and did their damndest to provide Amira with an opening. Unfortunately, the Steplescar soldiers began to pull her down into their churning ocean of weapons, grabbing hands and red eyes, using her enchanted Ceridome wraps as leverage. Amira began spinning the Ceridome wraps around her like a razor sharp gyroscope, shredding the immortal beings within her range indiscriminately.

Mayax was next to join the fight by leaping high into the air and changing his black flak SWAT suit back to his usual terrifying, thorny armor, minus the helmet. He brought Velocet down in a deadly arc and connected explosively with the ground like Thor's mighty hammer. The contact and subsequent discharge of rock and debris sent the first regiment of Steplescar soldiers tumbling to their backs. Then it was an all out hack and slash fest. Mayax buried Velocet in any head he could find, penetrating their armor and crushing their helmets with tremendous force. He squashed them underfoot and mercilessly pulled their heads off with his bare hands, but they just kept coming.

Viss Vascene and Sistell followed Mayax into the mosh pit and the three of them joined back up with Amira, still clubbing heads with her mace and slicing her way through the horde with her Ceridome wraps, and dagger of stone. Osha was a few hundred yards to the left, mauling and mutilating Steplescar soldiers in yaggowar form with unrestrained violence. The five of them were like a giant, multi-bladed blender, reducing the Steplescar army to a drippy, pulpy ruin. However, it was a brief reprieve, and the fearsome five knew it wouldn't last long. Unfortunately, no matter how much they turned the surging front-line into bloody, gooey pudding, there was no end to them. The five warriors easily remembered from their first encounter that a head on approach was a fool's game, but it had been foisted upon them so they had little choice. The small Sinteverete army of warlocks, numbering only in the thousands, and the slave Pentavi warriors, numbering even less, maintained a protective barrier around the Elders in the rear, while the Steplescar soldiers kept taking the punishment from Mayax and the Blood Red Roses right on the chin.

The ground beneath the five warriors' boots was now three-feet-deep with blood, cartilage, muscle and bone. They trudged through it pointlessly, trying to destroy their way towards the Elders, but the slurry underfoot began to gel unnaturally and clump together on a much larger scale than they thought possible. Instead of each soldier reconstituting individually, they were coming together unexpectedly as one big, nasty, fleshy fuck-tangle of broken bodies and shattered armor. The abomination quickly grew in size, with three flailing arms, a large misshapen, screaming head, then a smaller, equally nauseating head sprouted from its right shoulder. The giant carbuncle seemed to pull itself up out of the chummy remains on the battlefield until it was several stories high. Mayax and the ladies of war looked on with unbelieving eyes. "You've got to fucking be kidding me," Viss Vascene cried out. The bestial behemoth continued to coalesce grotesquely until it was a hundred feet high and churning like a meaty thing of prehistoric origins. It didn't look good for the five of them, and their hearts began to fill with doubt.

Out of the blue came the thundering sound of trumpets, and Lindria came screaming out of the air like an Apache warrior woman, her hair aflame and flailing dangerously with knives. She landed squarely between the creeping flesh of the kaiju and the determined regiment of the formidable five. She was followed by the other fourteen Roses with Thorns who stood like mirror images of the Blood Red Roses. Lindria looked deep into Mayax's eyes and announced her allegiance. "I am Lindria, General of the Roses with Thorns, and we will stand with you."

Mayax couldn't hide the smile beneath his black eyes. "Your help is greatly appreciated, General. You and your warrior women of the Roses with Thorns, meet the Blood Red Roses."

Lindria and her Roses with Thorns sounded off along with the Blood Red Roses in unison, "HU-RAH!"

The monstrous thing responded angrily behind them by pounding the ground with its cannonball hands, dispersing everyone as though it were the epicenter of a massive earthquake. Lindria, her hair still a halo of fire, and Viss Vascene united their bouquet of Roses and attacked the giant Steplescar abomination like ants on a wasp. Lindria let loose her battle cry, "We are the Bouquet of Roses, and we will make war with you."

Mayax used the hysteria as a diversion and teleported right to the edge of the seven Sinteverete Elder's sphere of protection. The first line of Sinteverete sorcerers responded immediately with Blades of Black and hex spells at the ready. Mayax grabbed the first Sinteverete warlock closest to him and tore his arms off at the shoulders. The screaming mage fell out of the air like a stone as Mayax drank deep the still flowing blood from the tattered stumps in loud, throaty gulps. When finished, he tossed them away and wiped his mouth on the sleeve of his armor, spreading the body wine across his lips like war paint. He beckoned the other Sinteverete sorcerers, who had roaring yaggowars on lightning leashes, with his bloody hand, before raucously shouting, "That's first blood, my Sinteverete brothers. Last warning; stand with me or die screaming; the choice is yours."

A quintet of five Sinteverete spell casters were suddenly in his face, the captain replying to Mayax, "Why should we abandon millions of years of dedication to our clan and cause on the word of a bastard Nevuscar traitor, barely a hundred years old, who stinks of Pentavi pussy?"

Mina suddenly joined Mayax's side with Ashen still swinging despondently by the throat, his hands clawing at her wrist. "No pussy like Pentavi pussy," she quipped. The captain and his four Sinteverete soldiers held back dubiously, startled at the sight of her carrying Ashen, the new lead Nevuscar, helplessly and quite literally in the palm of her hand.

The Master Elder screamed loudly in a tantrum, while the other six Elders levitated around him with heads bowed and hands together, urgently preparing to conjure an escape portal. Mayax knew he had only seconds to act, and whisper chanted a powerful binding hex that wouldn't allow the seven elitists to make good their escape right away. However, it wouldn't take them long to break it, so he eagerly plucked two Elders out of midair by their necks like ripe fruit. He held them both weak and whimpering close to his bloody, bearded face, "You are deceivers, Liars. All because you want everything for yourselves. Greedy and selfish, it's fitting you are led by a childish adolescent; forever in pursuit of new toys, and things to own...people to own. Die now." All Mayax had to do was slowly close his fists, and the two Elder's heads came off at the neck like wine corks in his hands. Their limp, rag-doll bodies fell to the trampled, well landscaped grass far below with a thud. As Mayax attached the two Elder's heads to his belt, the Second Elder blinked his eyes and an entire regiment of Steplescar

warriors was suddenly levitating into the air and encircling Mina and
Mayax at a distance.

Below, the Roses with Thorns and the Blood Red Roses combined
their strength to wrangle the flailing freak show that lumbered around
the battlefield like some low budget horror movie monster. Steplescar
soldiers began climbing the beast in an attempt to engage the Bouquet
of Roses, still fighting for their lives atop the monstrous tumor. The
ladies of war began steering the unearthly beast towards the house,
using their Ceridome wraps, hoping to shake off some of the soldiers.
The behemoth crashed explosively through the stately manor, casting
off many of the clinging Steplescar fighters who were struggling to
hang on. This bought them a few more minutes, but they wouldn't
be able to hold on much longer.

As Mayax dispatched the two Elders, Mina reeled Ashen in close,
her emerald eyes smoldering with fire and ice. They reflected in
Ashen's fading gray eyes as she kept him on the edge of unconscious-
ness so he could hear her, but not fight her. "I'm done brawling with
you, frustrating pricks." Mina was charged and ready to blow. "You
do realize I could teleport your dumbass to the core of a star right
now and let you spend the next two million years as a formless swirling
cloud of ash; praying in your purgatory for the star to explode so it can
spread your insignificant ashes across the universe, before ultimately
allowing them to ride the solar winds back together again, over the
course of a trillion years, just so you can float around ugly, naked and
aimlessly through the vacuum of space for all eternity like a weightless
meatball."

"You'll get nowhere using logic with this one," Vasser suddenly announced from behind.

Mina spun her head around and stared into the old familiar red eyes of her beloved father. Layluna was there with her arms around him, smiling ear to ear, and her emerald eyes welcomed Mina back into her heart. "Hello, bunny. I have missed you so much, but I knew you would persevere." Auri and Bee flew through the portal in their best battle gear, with Rake and Zone close behind. They all were within the circumference of the encroaching Steplescar regiment that continued to coalesce around them in mid-air. The soldiers were still being controlled by the one Elder, desperately trying to ensure their safety while the others worked feverishly to break Mayax's binding hex.

Tears left Mina's eyes in an explosion, and she released Ashen like a forgotten love note. Rake was quickly there to grab the semi-conscious Nevuscar out of the air and pull him into the shadows like a spider. Immediately, he sank his long canines deep into Ashen's neck, between his segmented armor, and turned some of that pretty blonde hair red. The former, and third lead Nevuscar in as many days, succumbed to Rake's poisonous bite and joined his ghastly growing clique of ravenous, toothy floating zombies.

"I don't believe it," Mina proclaimed with a mixture of amazement and joy. "You're free. How?"

Layluna cupped her head in her hands. "It's not important now; what is important is that we show the Sinteverete and Pentavi soldiers here today, what's left of them anyway, the truth. You are the Yasmani Ro born of fire and ice; you must unite the clans and fulfill your destiny. You can use your father's and I's memories of the Master Elder's confession. Use the spell I taught you—the undeniable truth."

The Captain and his four Sinteverete men continued to watch everything from a safe distance with growing interest. "The spell of undeniable truth, you say?" The Captain shouted above the loud, blowing wind. "We demand you show us."

Mina didn't waste another second, and planted both her hands firmly on her mother's and father's foreheads. Her hair began to glow and turn white once again, matching the glow now emanating from her parents' eyes. The four beams of light suddenly projected her parent's memories of that fateful day when they took on the Sinteverete and Pentavi Elders single handedly. The drama played out on the converging storm clouds high above, with the Master Elder and his four remaining consorts glued to the projected memory, complete with booming audio.

The Master Elder screamed loudly while flailing his clenched fists and levitated over top of Mayax and the others. "NOOOOOOOOOOOOOO," he cried, trying in vain to block the repeating projection, which commanded the eyes of not only the Elders, but everyone in the fight; even the Steplescar soldiers, and the mountain of mixed flesh lumbering below them, couldn't look away.

So there it was finally laid out for all the Sinteverete and Pentavi warriors to see with their own unlying eyes. The horrible, ugly, unde-niable truth. After about the fifth replay, all eyes began to turn slowly towards the Sinteverete Elders, more specifically, the Master Elder. The four Sinteverete Elders, now exposed and vulnerable, shrank away in fear.

Mina released her parents, who hung onto each other in utter ex-haustion, and addressed the battle in a booming voice. "The Elders of BOTH clans have now been laid bare." Mina called out, relishing the revelation. "Brother's AND sisters, let us unite as in the old times, and oust these greedy, cheating, lying, scandalous, conspiratory oligarchs that have pulled our strings for so long. We shall show them what comeuppance looks like." That said, Mina transported above and grabbed the Master Elder by the throat in her right hand and forced him to look into the face of every single fighter on both sides for the first time ever. "This. This is the cantankerous little worm that has been controlling and subjugating us for so long. An Elder with the mind of a broken child. Look into his face for the first and last time. Tonight, he dies, along with these other Elder scoundrels, and would be schemers."

For the first time ever, the Sinteverete and Pentavi fighters both got to see what the Master Elder and his consorts' fear looked like. As mutiny began to spread amidst the two clans, the Second Elder quickly closed the noose of circling Steplescar soldiers around the insurgents. Five of the immortal soldiers broke off with swords and axes at the ready, then went straight for Mina, who was still holding their master like a mischievous puppy.

Unbelievably, it was the Captain of the Sinteverete regiment that came to her aid; his Blade of Black stopping a Steplescar's axe and hammer in mid-swing. Unfortunately, the other four slipped by him and jumped Mina in an effort to free their master. Mayax saw the undying soldiers ganging up on her, but before he could teleport up to help, she incinerated them and cast their ash into large falling stones, imprisoning them within. She maintained her hold of the Master Elder as Mayax conjured a mage cage around him, canceling his magic. Mina looked down at Mayax. "Got room on your belt for this whelp?"

"Sure do, right here next to his pals," Mayax said, pointing to an open slot on his trophy belt.

"Excellent, here." Mina roughly tossed the cage containing the Master Elder end-over-end down to Mayax, who promptly grabbed it and attached it to his belt, right next to the severed heads of his two former cohorts. The grizzly, dead faces stared back at the Master Elder with eyes frozen forever in fear, and he began to scream in abject terror. Immediately, the Steplescar noose tightened around everyone, and the aerial battle was on. Mina zeroed in and targeted the Second Elder, who was still controlling the Stepelscar soldiers and levitating them up into the air. She flashed over to him like a white haint and had Beauty pressed to his neck within microseconds.

The Second Elder whimpered and begged for his life, "Please, you must understand—"

"I understand this..." Mina barked and peeled his head from his shoulders with violent precision. She stowed the head on her hip using her Ceridome wraps and looked for more prey.

With the Second Elder dead, the Third Elder stepped in to keep the Steplescar army levitating and in the fight, but quickly saw Mina targeting him. He begged the remaining two Elders to hasten breaking the binding hex so they could transport the hell out of there, but Mina and Mayax were both suddenly in his face.

The ground war was a cacophony of heaving bodies below, as though it was a lifeform all its own. In its center, the Bouquet of Roses continued to try to ride the raging Stepelscar monstrosity to pasture. Naturally, the barnacled behemoth would not go down without a fight; even with all eighteen Roses hacking and slashing away at it to little effect. Suddenly, a most peculiar thing happened; the Sinteverete sorcerers and their former Pentavi Slaves came side-by-side to their assistance. The Pentavi warrior women joined the Bouquet of Roses and helped them force the freakish Steplescar golem face-down on the ground, while the Sinteverete sorcerers cast powerful hexs to chain the giant in place. Their victory was short-lived as a massive regiment of Steplescar soldiers washed over them in a merciless wave. Not only were the faceless aberrations crossing sword and axe with them, they were trying to free the sequestered behemoth as well. The influx of Sinteverete and Pentavi warriors was vital in holding back the immortal army, but even with their assistance, it would not be enough.

As if sent by providence, Vasser and Layluna joined the fight down below, while Rake and his two Nevuscar zombies joined Auri, and Bee in the aerial fight unfolding perilously above. The fiery conflict was sure to draw the US military at any moment, adding another wild card variable to the volatile battle.

Vasser started casting Steplescar soldiers into pillars of salt, but the magic made him violently ill since he wasn't a trained practitioner of dark magic like Rake and Mayax. He began to vomit salt uncontrollably from his mouth and nose. He would have to be clever since most of the imprisonment spells he knew were dark magic, and he didn't have access to large quantities of Pentavi granite, or did he?

Thinking fast, Vasser created a mammoth portal inside the miles-high mountain of common gray Pentavi granite back in the mines of Val Tebrae, and prepared to transport a massive slab of the ashen stone to the sky above the battlefield. He amplified his voice magically and yelled to the Bouquet or Roses and the other Sinteverete and Pentavi warriors fighting alongside them to "MAKE WAY." They all quickly acknowledged Vasser and fled the area post haste. Some of the Roses and other warriors were tangled up in Stepelscar soldiers, so several Sinteverete sorcerers had to teleport them to safety. When all friendly's were out of the area Vasser dropped the enormous wedge of rock from the sky, roughly the size of eight stacked end-to-end football fields, directly on the head of the sequestered Steplescar golem and a thousand of its comrades at arms. The impact was absolutely apocalyptic, crushing everything in its path, and collapsing most of Auri and Bee's house as well. Vasser shot an apologetic glance to Auri and Bee above, who, while in the midst of fierce battle, still found the opportunity to flash him a prickly look of irritation. Vasser shrugged his shoulders apologetically and began casting Stepelscar soldiers into the gray stone as if he were adding beef to a stew. He also began to whisper chant and turned the rocky monolith into a Stepelscar magnet, which began to draw the soldiers to it, absorbing and trapping them within.

Layluna had armed herself with an enormous Stepelscar war-hammer, and was pounding the unnatural soldiers deep into the ground like coffin nails, one right after the other. It was working well enough, but it wouldn't take them long to claw their way back to the surface.

Within the storm clouds above, Rake - a true prince of dark magic - began turning Stepelscar soldiers into pillars of salt by the hundreds. Lightning cracked, and thunder boomed as the pillars of salt fell from the skies or shot up out of the ground like tombstones; regrettably, it barely made a dent. Zone and Ashen were working well together in their own right, ripping and tearing through the army, but the immortals were reconstituting almost as fast as they could tear them apart.

Elsewhere, Auri and Bee were having to get creative. Auri cast a large roving, two-sided portal, and Bee cast a portal behind it to a third portal that looped back to the second portal, creating an infinite transport loop similar to images in two facing mirrors. The ingenious portal vacuum sucked in Stepelscar soldiers by the droves and juggled them between worlds, keeping them from joining the fight.

However, despite everyone's best efforts, the undying army continued to swarm up with infinite numbers and threaten to overwhelm everyone.

Mina and Mayax were eagerly trying to dispatch the last three Elders before they could escape, but they were playing hard to get by casting illusion, confusion, and blocking spells. Eventually, the three Elders were able to break Mayax's binding spell, blocked any possible others, and prepared to flee immediately. M and M fought off the levitating swarm of Steplescar soldiers, knowing if they didn't act fast the trio of con artists would escape, and it would be near impossible to hunt them down. The greedy three already had a portal open and were quick to step through when two U.S. F-15 Eagles streaked by and fired off a twin set of missiles each. The four rockets exploded right in the Elders' faces, dispersing them in a flash of fire. Mayax had two Stepelscar soldiers still clinging relentlessly to him by fingernail and dagger, but decided to take them along for the ride. He instantly teleported to grab up one of the flailing Elders, and Mina, free of any hitchhikers, teleported to grab up the other. The third Elder fell smoking and smoldering to the ground like a meteor and impacted just as dramatically. Mayax desperately tried to get a death grip on the Elder, clenched precariously in his left hand, but the two soldiers were holding his right arm back with all their strength. Mayax gritted his teeth in absolute frustration because he was so close to another head.

In a sudden flash of blurry motion, the previously frozen Nevuscar twins arrived just in the nick of time to rip the freakish Stepelscar fighters from his back. Mayax was shocked to see them back on his side. "Thank you for standing with me, brothers." They never spoke, but nodded their bald heads in solidarity before tangling with the two soldiers and the fifty others behind them. Mayax, now free, quickly plowed his right fist through the sternum of the Elder, grabbed his spine from the front, and ripped it out of the gaping, gory hole. Upon pulling the vertebrae out, the Elder's skull came attached and his head deflated like a blown basketball. Mayax discarded the body, and quickly attached the spine and skull to his trophy belt. Within seconds, another wave of levitating Steplescar was crowding in on him. The Master Elder, helpless, could only cry and cower in his cage, surrounded by the heads of his decapitated congress.

Meanwhile, Mina used Beauty viciously to peel the face off of the screaming Elder she managed to catch in her claws. The Elder howled in anguish like a captured coyote, but Mina showed him no mercy. Once she had the face pelt locked into her Ceridome wraps alongside the other head, she got to within inches of his skinless, shrieking rictus, "I'll see you in Hell." Upon considering it a moment, "Seriously, I'll come see you suffer in Hell; I know the boss." As Mina drew Beauty raggedly across his neck and bathed in his body wine, she reminded him, "It's the bitches that'll gitches, motherfucker." The two F-15's suddenly charged around for another pass, and unloaded their chain guns right at Mina. The bullets shredded the Elder's lifeless body, but she dodged them like a Matrix Agent. However, her incredible speed was not enough and a few rounds grazed her flesh. "Assholes," she bellowed angrily, and threw a spinning rune hex at the twin jets. The hex, resembling a massive circular saw, managed to connect with one of them and split it like a log of wood. The pilot ejected as the plane crashed dramatically into the center of the Steplescar hoard. Unfortunately, the pilot was parachuting down into the violent epicenter of the undying army. "Sucks to be you," Mina noted.

The third Elder snapped back to consciousness on the ground, but was horribly burned and battered. He was encircled by Stepelscar soldiers who were protecting him against all comers, but it quickly dawned on him that he was the last Elder standing. He was the only one left to direct the endless army, and without him, they would simply go feral and destroy everything in their path. The final Elder contemplated and weighed the possibilities: stay and direct the army, or flee and hide. Naturally, he chose to flee and hide.

Conjuring a portal to anywhere, he launched himself through it, but a rough and ugly hand suddenly snatched him out of mid-air. It was Bael, "And where do you think you're going, little fella?" The scarred and savage Nevuscar warrior asked his former master. The walking wound of a man had unbelievably teleported into the circle of protective Steplescar in order to prevent the Elder's escape. "I have seen the undeniable truth, and it's not looking good for you." The Elder quickly commanded the undying swarm to swallow Bael in their sea of featureless faces and grabbing hands, but before he could be engulfed entirely, Vasser and Layluna led a pack of raging yaggowar to his rescue.

The soldiers immediately began to wrench the Elder from Bael's powerful grasp, but Vasser pulled Sepultura from its sheath for the first time since being imprisoned and hacked off their hungry hands.

Layluna swiftly transformed into the largest yaggowar known to the clans, and along with her new pride, launched a bloody revolt against the Stepelscar swarm. They batted the immortals around like lions with mice and gave them unmerciful hell. Several regiments of Sinteverete sorcerers also joined the skirmish and fought alongside the Pentavi for the first time ever. Their onslaught proffered Bael and Vasser the opportunity they needed to finally dispatch the last Elder standing - once and for all. Bael hoisted the Elder upside down by his ankle and let Vasser stare him deeply in the eyes. "I told you I would collect your head," he reminded him. The Elder's only response was a craven mewling. Vasser laughed shrewdly. "It's fitting that your final words be a whimper."

"You wanna do the honors?" Bael asked respectfully.

Vasser simply nodded a single time thankfully to his former friend and nemesis, before returning his focus to the Elder. "Enjoy eternity trapped within my Blade of Black, you selfish, disgusting, weak and wanton simp." That said, he lopped the Elder's head clean off above the lower jaw, and fed the remains to Layluna and the other yaggowars waiting anxiously for their elegant meal. They proceeded to tear him apart at the seams and devour the bloody remains in an instant. "It is done," Vasser announced to the battlefield as he held up the top half of the Elder's head for all to see. After everyone got a good gander, he attached the gruesome trophy to his belt and prepared to rejoin the fight. "Time to put an end to this invasion."

A massive explosion suddenly rocked the ruckus and announced the arrival of U.S. ground forces. "Great, these assholes are just going to get in our fucking way," Bael groaned.

A regiment of Steplescar soldiers finally had Zone and Ashen beaten and restrained, but they were encountering the same problem with them that everyone else was having with the Stepelscar army: they couldn't kill them. Fortunately for the Steplescar, there were enough of them to hold the vampiric fighters down indefinitely.

Taking a page from Vasser's playbook, Rake also dropped two mountains of gray Pentavi granite on the battlefield alongside the first one, in an attempt to crush and capture Stepelscar soldiers. Additionally, it was to create a barrier to hold the military forces at bay who were swiftly organizing around them in force. Rake blinked his eyes, and the twin monoliths joined Vasser in sucking Stepelscar soldiers into the liquified rock. Disappointingly, the massive slab that Vasser conjured first finally reached its limit and could cage no more soldiers. Rake could no longer portal any more gray granite in because they had used the entire mountain. Still, the immortal army came at them.

"Fuck all this shit," Rake conceded, and gave in to the simple solution. "I don't care if these fuckers are a problem five billion years from now..." He opened a traveling portal to the Earth's sun and began scooping up the incalculable army and transporting them directly to the core of the star."

Auri and Bee had Stepelscar fighters all over them who were attacking them from all angles; not to mention their clever portal loop had reached its limit as well. "Damn right," Bee said, bruised and beaten. "Let's send these fuckers into the light."

"Fuckin' A," Auri agreed. So the lovely ladies of Hell transported their portal loop to the sun's center and created another portal similar to Rakes to teleport as many soldiers as they could to the sun's surface.

The Bouquet of Roses went from battling the Stepelscar behemoth to crowd control with the military. They moved in quick between the massive columns of common Pentavi granite to keep the humans out of the way. Sistell called to Viss Vascene, "This'll be a fucking cake walk compared to scrapping with those fucking things."

"Truer words never spoken," Viss Vascene acknowledged in her strangely robotic voice. "Guns out, ladies, it's time to remember how good it feels to kill something."

"HU-RAH," they all responded in unison.

The minute the ladies of war were visible, the military soldiers opened fire with everything they had. Amidst a barrage of explosions and gunfire, Lindria ordered nine of her ladies to bring Vasser's slab of prison granite down on their heads. Viss Vascene suggested the rest of them take out the soldiers and prepare for the next regiment of fighter jets that were most likely on the way. Lindria agreed, and they went to work.

Nine Roses headed straight for the towering stone column and unfurled their Ceridome wraps, which they used to harpoon into the hard surface of the stone. Once attached, they used them as pull cables, and dug in fiercely to bring the huge slab down. Five quintettes of Sinteverete warlocks also joined the Roses and used their best magic to push the enormous column from the other side.

Lindria and Viss Vascene, along with the other seven Roses, mobilized to provide cover for the warriors trying to topple the monolith. They surrounded themselves with their swirling Ceridome wraps that acted as a bullet shield and charged in with grim purpose. The fierce ladies of the Roses had their guns at the ready, and fired enchanted bullets between the oscillating Ceridome wraps, perforating the human soldiers with targeted death. The sound of four jet fighters suddenly boomed from above as they streaked overhead, threatening their entire position.

Viss Vascene positioned herself to use her Ceridome wraps like a makeshift slingshot and propelled herself at a hundred miles an hour into the path of the incoming F-15s. They zipped past her at 1,600 mph, but she was able to grab hold of the rear jet with her wraps and carefully maneuvered to the area above the cockpit. "I love a little wind in my hair," she yelled enthusiastically into the mach two winds without even batting an eyelash. The pilot caught sight of her and immediately ejected, providing her easy access to the control panel. The salty old gal penetrated the flight controls with two strips of her enchanted Ceridome wraps, grabbed hold of them like reins, and began to steer the aircraft like a giant chariot. With a sinister smile on her seasoned face, and her gray dreadlocks flapping behind her, Viss Vascene drew down on the other three jets. She made short work of the first fighter because the pilot never anticipated the attack. The other two caught on quick and rapidly started evasive maneuvers to try to out fly her. The effort would ultimately prove futile, but the two pilots put up quite an impressive defense. The lead jet hit the brakes and instantly went nose up into the toiling black clouds above, while the other zig zagged and spiraled elusively. Viss Vascene, using her enchanted wraps, opened fire with the chain gun on the front jet, and peppered its rear thrusters with thousands of bullets. The pilot frantically went into a nosedive, followed by a swift jerk of the aircraft to the left, but Viss Vascene was right on him. She let fly two missiles, which the pilot tried to intercept with mid-air anti-missile charges, but was only able to catch one. The other missile slipped through and impacted the right quarter undercarriage of the jet, blowing its wing completely off. The fighter spiraled out of control, but the pilot ejected before it crashed explosively into the battlefield. "Two down, one to go..." Viss Vascene screamed into the bleak night as lightning cracked loudly around her.

Rain started pouring down in sheets and the warrior Rose welcomed its cruel reprieve. In an instant, the lead jet reemerged from above and let slip two sidewinder missiles that parted the rain like diamonds and headed straight for her. The deadly rockets were right on top of her in seconds, but using her wraps, she slapped one out of the way and sent the other cartwheeling right back at the F-15. The fighter jet had little chance of avoiding the out-of-control missile and collided with it explosively. A massive fireball erupted before propelling shrapnel and wreckage in all directions. Sadly, there was no escaping this calamity for the pilot, and he was instantly incinerated.

Viss Vascene then steered her jet through the torrid storm, back towards the main event, and the massive rock column they were attempting to drop on the remainder of the military. She saw her target dead ahead and raced towards it like a suicidal psychopath. Moments before the jet impacted the back side of the gargantuan slab, she fired off all remaining missiles at the vehicles and soldiers below, then bailed and let the aircraft slam into the slab at full speed. The missiles rained unholy hellfire down on the military below, scattering them like ants. Meanwhile, the explosive impact from Viss Vascene's jet was just enough to give the Roses, now all shifted into yaggowars and pulling their wraps like mules, that extra nudge they needed to haul the titanic tombstone forward. When they were certain the slab was going to fall, they forced the Stepelscar swarm apart, and fled at top speed. The military soldiers gawked in utter disbelief as they were cast into the elongating, growing shadow of the monumental megalith that began its catastrophic descent directly over their heads.

The Stepelscar army was now out of control with no one to direct them, and they began to spread out in all directions, destroying everything in their path. Even in the torrential rain, they began attacking the U.S. soldiers without so much as a molecule of concern for the looming 6,480-foot-tall doom slab pitching forward overtop of them like a death shroud.

Viss Vascene used her Ceridome wraps as a parachute, but still crashed to the ground at break-neck speeds underneath the canopy of falling gray granite. Before she could even pull herself from the mud, the Steplescar soldiers were there, stabbing, slashing, and pummeling her violently.

Things were getting complicated for Mina up in the troposphere as she crossed stone with Stepelscar steel. Beauty shattered their common metal weapons effortlessly, but still left them dangerously jagged and broken. She pulled out all the stops now, using her arctic left hand to cast the immortal warriors into blocks of unbreakable ice, then using her burning right hand to cremate the rest. Mina was quick to cast as much of the falling ash into stone as she could, but the rain carried much of it down to mix with the mud below where it began to reform into chunks of flesh, thus creating more Stepelscar soldiers.

Amidst her onslaught of fire and ice, Mina caught sight of Viss Vascene's perilous situation down below. "Back in a minute, Mayax," she informed her bloody beau.

"Copy that," he acknowledged from within a writhing cocoon of mangled Stepelscar soldiers. "It's all good; I got this."

Mina had her doubts, but knew Viss Vascene needed her help immediately, and teleported down to her position. She was joined by the other three Blood Red Roses and the twin Nevuscar. They all worked together doggedly in an effort to drag her out of the Stepelscar swarm, while simultaneously trying to keep themselves from being overrun by the encroaching horde. Things were looking grim as wave after wave of wild, rouge Stepelscar savages piled on them relentlessly. There was a silver lining, though; the immortal army was keeping the military occupied and out of their way.

Mina had several Stepelscar soldiers on each arm, so she was unable to clap her hands together and create the powerful shockwave necessary to buy them some much needed respite. However, she had to act fast because the swarm was only moments away from hacking them to pieces. Out of options, she used her right hand of fire to blast a vast incendiary path through a couple hundred of the ungoverned soldiers, allowing the team to break free and collect everyone for that split-second escape. Regrettably, Mina's attack unintentionally unleashed a poisonous ash cloud that blew right at them. Mina screamed a warning to everyone, "Don't breathe in the ashes." Meanwhile, the cinders swirled amidst the fighters' faces on the dry winds blowing underneath the umbrella of stone above, now a mere two hundred feet from crushing them all.

One of the Nevuscar twins, along with Viss Vascene, were hit square in the face with the toxic ash cloud and inadvertently sucked the deadly material deep into their lungs. The Savvoy Twins and Sistell all quickly wrapped their faces with the Ceridome wraps, and the other Nevuscar twin cast a protection sphere around himself with only seconds to spare. Mina just held her fucking breath. "Oh shit," Viss Vascene managed, knowing it was over for her. "Go on, get the fuck outta here, I'm done for." Osha, Amira and Sistell all reacted to the news at the same time with shocked gasps. "Seriously, GO."

Sistell screamed in anguish, "NOOOOOOOO." But she barely spoke the word before a Stepelscar soldier tackled her roughly into the mud.

"Jesus Christ," Mina bellowed, and used her Ceridome wraps to snare Sistell, Osha and Amira; before dragging them all abruptly out from under the miles-high collapsing column of granite with her own bare hands. There were literally only millimeters to spare. Twin number one grabbed twin number two, who was violently vomiting blood and gristle by the handfuls now and teleported far away from the danger zone.

Viss Vascene was also projectile vomiting flesh and blood at this point as the Stepelscar ashes in her lungs began to reconstitute like a cancerous growth. Her eyes filled with solemn acceptance as the colossal slab of rocky granite finally connected apocalyptically with the Earth, obliterating her, and crushing everything beneath it to atoms. The multitude of military personnel, presently still running around willy-nilly, were all flattened alongside the Stepelscar soldiers currently hacking them to pieces.

The impact was entirely biblical and devastated miles and miles of the once lush, wooded area. Debris, mud, water, buildings, body parts, rubble—all exploded outward like a nuclear detonation and leveled a huge part of the landscape in seconds. The rain began to subside, and the fires began spreading throughout the acreage of woods surrounding the area.

Mayax was suddenly there, distraught and ripping Mina from the wet wreckage. "Please tell me you are alive."

"Five more minutes, ma..." she joked beneath five inches of blood and mud.

"Fuck's sake, you got balls bigger than a barbarian," Mayax announced.

"The others—" Mina began searching for Sistell and the twins.

"We're here," the twins said roughly in unison.

"I'm here," Sistell began, "But I've got company."

Everyone snapped around to see that Mina had not only saved Sistell, but the Stepelscar soldier as well. "FUCK," Mina barked, "Everyone back away." Everyone did exactly that, but the Steplescar soldier, oddly enough, didn't seem like he was going to attack. Everyone was poised and ready for it to run wild, but it never did; it just stood there dumbly looking at Mina like she was special. After a moment it examined its hands, then the rest of its body, and finally it went back to looking into Mina's eyes. "Someone want to tell me why the fuck that thing is staring at me like I'm its mother."

"Shhhh," Sistell instructed, "Wait a minute." They all hung on pins and needles as the Stepelscar soldier continued to look sheepishly at Mina. The battle was on pause while the dust settled from the cataclysmic event they had all just narrowly escaped, but it wouldn't last long. Vasser and Layluna were suddenly there and ready to pummel the soldier, but Mina quickly gestured for them to wait. The Bouquet of Roses, along with Auri, and Bee were next to arrive, but read the room and hung back anxiously.

Then there was Bael, who came charging in, bellowing his battle cry, but stopped short when he saw everyone staring at the Stepelscar soldier. "What did I miss?"

Sistell again, "Shhhh."

Auri came to Mina's side, and whispered very quietly into her ear, "What the Hell happened?"

Mina marinated on the thought for a moment before answering simply, "I don't fuckin' know. I uh...I...accidentally saved the fucking thing."

"You saved it? Why?" Auri whisper-shouted in her ear.

"Well, I didn't do it on purpose, goddammit; I was helping Sistell." Mina huffed under her breath.

"Interesting," Auri pondered. "So...you saved it, and now it seems...benign, docile even? I mean, hell, he looks like he wants you to fucking hug it."

"I'm not hugging that fucking thing," Mina said flatly.

"Why not?" Auri responded with a breathy chuckle. "I mean, based on the insights Athan Asios gave us...and...I mean, the guy loooooooves satire, irony, and meta; not to mention his temper is matched only by his sense of humor. I'm serious, go fucking hug that thing. Or shake its hand or something."

Mina looked at Auri unbelievably. "You're totally fucking with me right now, aren't you? Admit it. I know it."

"No, seriously. Look—I'll go hug the goddamn thing," Auri said, gesturing with her hand at the soldier and raising her voice.

"Uh, I think we missed that train," Mina stated matter-of-factly while pointing to the Savvoy twins hugging the Stepelscar soldier like he was a beloved Shih Tzu. "No fucking shame, those two."

"Awww, you're just jealous we got to hug one first," Amira sang mockingly. "We're gonna call him Soul Destroyer."

Mina looked at Auri and burst out laughing. The two collapsed into each other's arms with uncontrollable giggles. "I can't fucking believe my life. So, I absolutely can't wait to meet this Athan Asios guy."

"Yeah, 'bout that, he totally wants to kill you and extract your Alma," Auri stated blandly like she was talking to customer service. "He's the reason the Master Elder and his band of douche canoes were after you all this time. Something about you being Yasmani Ro, born of fire and ice, blah, blah, blah."

Mina blew the hair out of her eye. "That's a lot to unpack. 'Sides, it's time for the fat lady."

"Say what now?" Auri asked, befuddled.

"The fat lady. The end. The song. A cigar—you get it." Mina assured her, while conjuring a cigar between her lips and lighting it off of burning wreckage. "At least it quit raining, for fuck's sake." Mina drank deep the cigar smoke and was transported to her happy place.

Rake finally teleported to the party, frantic and bloody. He was covered in daggers and broken swords that were sticking out of his back and belly, with severed hands still clinging ghoulishly to them. "Holy fuck. Those fucking bastards have Zone and Ashen trapped and were fucking piling up on me like—like...Um, why are Osha and

Amira hugging that Stepelscar soldier? Why aren't you all stomping that Stepelscar soldier's guts out? I mean, I was only gone for like fifteen minutes." Rake began pulling the weapons painfully from his body and dropping them forgotten to the ground with a clank.

Mayax pushed past Rake and marched his bruised, bloody, and battle torn ass right up to the Stepelscar soldier and extended his hand to shake. The puzzled soldier amazingly put its hand in his and allowed Mayax to shake it vigorously while laughing heartily.

The sweet moment of realization, elation, and levity was quickly replaced with terror as the horde of not-so-friendly Stepelscar soldiers suddenly discovered them. They were perched high above on the ridgeline of the toppled monolith and quickly zeroed in on them. They began leaping down in droves like falling snow, ready for endless battle, but they would no longer find war waiting for them.

The band of impossible allies—every single one of them—(even Rake, but only after everyone else) laid down their weapons simultaneously and bowed. This profoundly confused the rowdy regiment of Stepelscar soldiers, who were all looking for a fight. Mayax and Mina both walked right up to the frontline, hands raised peacefully, before extending them politely for a shake. The gathering group of perplexed immortal soldiers all looked to one another, mystified. After a moment, two of the Stepelscar soldiers stepped forward and shook their hands.

"Unbelievable," Rake chuckled to himself. "That's my pop."

Vasser and Layluna were next to stroll up confidently and extend their hands. Like before, two Stepelscar soldiers cautiously walked up and shook their hands.

Without warning, the Master Elder began to scream from his cage on Mayax's belt. "What are you doing? Attack them. Kill them. Obey me." But they didn't seem to notice him anymore. Auri and Bee,

Lindria, and the Bouquet of Roses all walked up to the converging multitude of curious Stepelscar and extended their hands; some even hugged them straight away. The Pentavi and Sinteverete alike were kindly interacting with them, while embracing the joyous feeling of freedom and unity. The formerly blood-thirsty army of deadly, immortal fighters seemed to absolutely love the attention. It was contagious too; as other Stepelscar soldiers arrived, they were infected with curiosity, then struck down with kindness. It was absurd, but magnificent.

Rake, still in full vamp mode, actually picked up two or three Stepelscar soldiers in his muscular arms and began hugging them, before placing them lovingly back down on the ground like puppies. "I told ya, they're kinda cute." It was all quite a scene. Rake shrank back to normal and tried to avoid Mayax, knowing the big speech was coming.

The Master Elder flailed hopelessly in the close-fitting cage on Mayax's belt, "Why? Why? Why?" The impish puck screamed over and over again. Mayax plucked him, cage and all, from his belt and set him on the devastated landscape. He kneeled down like a giant would to a worm and stared at his bowed head. "Face me." Slowly but surely, the Master Elder raised his eyes to him. "I would not want to be you right now."

"Things are not as they seem, barbarian..." The Master Elder lied and cried. "You think you are in control of this army now? You're mistaken..." With that, the Master Elder whispered a word to himself, so quiet that no one could hear it, and the entire Stepelscar army dropped dead where they stood. Moments later, they began to dissolve into a quivering stew of fetid flesh.

Everyone was shocked and appalled having just made friends with their enemies. It is a rare thing for armies to lay down their arms and appreciate the joy of unity. The moment was poignant and impactful, despite being spoiled by the insufferable Master Elder.

"Aw man, I was just warming up to them," Rake said disappointedly. Almost as if answering his lonesome call, Zone and Ashen floated creepily down from over the massive prison slab. They joined his side, "There they are," Rake said, entirely cheered up.

Mayax scowled into the Master Elder's defiant eyes. "Petty," he chastised him scornfully. "I suppose the question now is, what are we going to do with you?"

Mina stepped up, her mother and father close behind, and offered her solution. "I say we gut this fucker's head off and hang it from a belt."

Everyone sounded off in agreement and started chanting, "Off with his head. Off with his head." Over and over again.

"Yeah, I think that'll work just fine," Mina said, spitting the words into the face of the Master Elder, who was still smirking and scrappy. "Mom, father, what say you?"

In chorus, "We say, off with his head."

Everyone on the battlefield who was still standing hollered in celebration.

"Excellent. Anyone else, if you have something to say, now's the time," Mina proclaimed fiercely.

"I'm sorry, I'll have something to say about that," a dark, mysterious voice suddenly declared out of thin air. "You see…" after a moment, a dark shadowy figure began to take shape as black sludge bubbled up from the ground, "I have a contract with this little guy." Athan Asios stated, finally materializing into his tall, lanky, shadowy form. His red eyes and toothy mouth spoke volumes and commanded respect. Any mortal that dared look into those eyes, or that featureless form of darkness, would surely go mad. He was pure evil.

"Athan Asios, I presume," Mina said respectfully. "Your reputation precedes you."

"Ahhhhh, Mina. *Same*, I can assure you." He smiled brightly from the darkness of his face. "Now, about this pickle. Clearly this *whittle wascal* needs a spankin', and I am one hundred percent in support of that; there's just the little issue of my compensation per his breach of my contract. You see, this little tadpole failed to deliver his end of the agreement and now owes me in a pretty significant way. I'm afraid I'll need to extract my payment from him before you divorce his head from those narrow shoulders."

Bee and Auri both arrived at Mina's side to back her up, no matter what. Athan Asios absolutely loved that about them. Mina knew the game though, pure and simple. She reignited the cold half cigar, still held between those luscious red lips that somehow looked more beautiful smeared with blood, and chose her words carefully. Puffing, "Respectfully, Lord Athan Asios, may I inquire as to whether or not your payment will interfere with us collecting ours? Our payment being this scoundrel's head still attached to his living body."

"Very specific, but I can assure you there will be no conflict," he said smoothly, before strolling over to her, and leaving that tarry, black sludge behind him with every step. Everyone stood by breathlessly in anticipation of how the drama would play out, and were captivated by the suspense. One thing was certain, and everyone knew it, you didn't fuck with Athan Asios. Mina stood her ground with her soldier sisters and extended her hand of ice toward the caged gremlin. "It's agreed then. Please, have him," Mina graciously offered.

Athan Asios took her glacial hand in his, her cold meeting his empty, and pecked it gracefully on the back. To Mina, it felt like a kiss from the void. "Mmmmmm, that ice is spicy," He let slip. Mayax stiffened, but maintained his respectful posture. Athan Asios cast him a genuine smile. "Mayax. At last we meet. I appreciate your doing all the heavy lifting with this one," he said, patting the Master Elder's cage. "Let's say I owe you one."

"An invaluable gift, my Lord," Mayax said, bowing his head penitently.

"Oh, stop it; you'll embarrass me. I've always enjoyed the chemistry you have with my son. Talk about spicy," he proclaimed, laughing and looking around at everyone's reaction, especially Rake's. "I can't wait for the next episode."

"Indeed," Mayax grumbled light-heartedly, while Rake rolled his eyes.

Athan Asios, like a smokey wraith, moved over between Mina and Auri. He placed his hands on their shoulders appropriately, "I am so proud of you both for figuring out my little caveat. It was so thrilling to watch. I never for a second doubted the two of you, and I hope you appreciated the theme of unity, Mina."

"I found it to be quite refreshing," she said sweetly, smiling and nodding her head.

"Fantastic. Okay then, I must be off now. You know, busy, busy..." Everyone kept waiting for him to collect the cage and take it with him, but he did not. The God of evil merely walked to the front of the cage, kneeled down and tapped the little scamp on his forehead through the iron bars with the first finger of his black right hand. The Master Elder screamed bloody murder and collapsed. Athan Asios stood up. "Alright then. That's my payment collected. I'm sure you'll find him to be alive and ready for execution after a due rest. Don't expect him to be...quite the same happy-go-lucky chap he used to be, but enough of him remains—I've seen to that."

Bee leaned in close to Auri, Mina, and Athan Asios, then whispered so only they could hear, "I'm curious brother, what did he owe you?"

"Bee, you're diabolical," he whispered back. "You know I don't usually talk about work on off hours; it's impolite." He feigned offense. "Well, if you must know, he owed me 480,723, 622 days of his ageless life in clerical servitude. Yes, I said clerical. It's all done through something called dimensional time and quantum parallel realm manipulation, or some damn thing. It's all very boring, but in short, I'm able to take him for that time, make him do whatever I want, in his case that was paperwork. and then return him right back to the second I took him. All like, no time has passed for any of us."

Mina shook her head approvingly. "I like your style, even if you want to kill me."

"Oh, my dear, I hope Auri didn't give you the impression that I wanted to kill you. I just need your Alma. In any case, I don't expect you to understand, or willingly offer it up, but it will be interesting to see where our journey takes us."

"Indeed, Lord," Mina said, bowing her head again.

"Mina, I'm looking forward to seeing you again...real soon," this statement followed by a wink. "Mayax, it's been my pleasure to finally meet you."

"Lord," Mayax replied, bowing his head as well.

"Rake, you stay out of trouble, you crazy kid. And I'll see you, Aunt Bee, and Auri next month for Indian food. Don't you reschedule on me again, Bee."

"Of course not. Work, you get it." Bee was already dreading having to return to her job on Monday.

"I do, I do," Athan Asios confirmed. "I do hope you'll join us, Mina...and Mayax, of course."

"I would actually enjoy that," Mina admitted. Mayax reluctantly nodded.

"Oh, before I go, I just wanted to point out that I noticed a certain three Pentavi Elders were ostensibly absent from the shenanigans here today. Better move fast, they will disappear and you will never ever be able to find them—without my help, of course." This earned another wink. "You know, it's almost as though they were the ones always pulling the strings on our little Master Elder puppet. Perhaps they held some kind of swagger over him." The Dark Lord insinuated, rubbing his nonexistent chin in mock consideration. "Anywho, something to consider. Alright then, Mina, Mayax, I hope to see you at dinner. Good luck to you all, and let me know if you need any assistance with those pesky Pentavi Elders."

Mina smiled wide. "Oh, we will. Shouldn't be too much trouble for us to rustle them up, though. We're all pretty eager to have them lined up next to this little cherub," she said, kicking the cage.

"Wonderful. Adieu, ladies and gentlemen." With that, Athan Asios sank into the bubbling black sludge and back to his realm.

"That is one cool motherfucker," Bael said out of nowhere. "Where the hell are the twins?"

"Right here," the Savvoy twins proclaimed.

"Not you two; the Nevuscar twins." The girls huffed as Bael looked around. After a moment, he saw two far off silhouettes coming around the end of the massive stone barrier about five hundred yards away. "There they are." Turning to Rake, "and we're gonna have a little chat at some point about what you did to Zone and Ashen."

"Anytime you like...*friend*." Rake promised, smiling that ghoulish smile while tapping his teeth.

Vasser and Layluna made their way over to Mina and Mayax. Layluna wrapped her arms around Mina and held her tight. "We better get everyone out of here before the military regroups and comes back looking for trouble."

"Absolutely. We can all go to Val Tebrae. We'll get everyone settled and organized, then try to hold council."

"Spoken like a true leader," Mayax pointed out.

"Don't you start with me," Mina demanded, slapping his arm.

Vasser spoke up now, "He's right, Mina. You are a natural born leader. We will all be looking for someone to guide us, and who better than you?"

"Have you met me?" Mina asked seriously. "I don't know; let's not get ahead of ourselves. We'll figure everything out."

Lindria approached from behind, her hair extinguished and her eyes somber, "We better get everyone the Hell out of here before we're balls deep in human soldiers again. And I don't know about you, but I'm pretty fucking ready to call it a day."

"I couldn't agree more." Mina said. "Mayax, want to take us home?"

"It would be my honor...Home; I like the sound of that." Mayax noted softly before conjuring a massive portal back to Val Tebrae. Everyone, for the first time in millions of years, made their way back to their motherland—united.

Chapter 10
Cigars and the "Unofficial Prom"

Things were coming together well in Val Tebrae only a few days after the unified clans arrived. The Pentavi and Sinteverete were bruised, cut, hurt and exhausted, but not broken. They now carried with them a profound sense of understanding and perspective. Their scars, physical and emotional, were potent reminders of the incredible lesson they learned, and the lofty price they paid to learn it. They had all chosen to cut the puppet strings and put the past in the past so the healing could begin. It was going to be a long, grinding road, but they all possessed the warrior's heart, and the wisdom to walk it.

Mina stood with Layluna as Vasser and Mayax labored underneath the morning's twin rising suns. Huge mountains with their vast forests surrounded the valley on all sides, and you could hear the waterfalls cascading majestically throughout. The animals were returning now that they no longer sensed the darkness pulling strength in the Sinteverete Temple. The wicked monument to dark magic now stood empty and alone within the center of the vast, barren salt flats. A decaying, but critical reminder of their dark past.

Vasser and Mayax were busy building an ancient Zol style domicile for Vasser and Layluna to live in, deep within a lush, green valley on the Eastern side of Val Tebrae. The location was not random; it was where Vasser and Layluna's journey began, so many years ago. A circular den was carved deep into the ground, with a round wooden framework extending several stories above. Long, thin sheets of rich, burgundy wood from the Quader Tree, along with sturdy canvas wraps, were used as walls. They were elegant, practical and sturdy, not to mention easy to maintain, replace and repair. "Will you live here with us?" Layluna asked, threatening to release the floodgates to her millions of questions.

Mina was certain of her answer. "I have decided to live here in Val Tebrae, but I still have a lot going on in the Earth realm, so I'll be back and forth." Sighing, "Ugh, I'm going to have to adjust my age when I'm there for a while since my picture is all over the place, but things will eventually cool down. They always do. Besides, I like the idea of spending my time here, helping the clans grow together and watching them find their way. It's a very exciting time, as I'm sure you and father can appreciate."

"I have to say, I never thought I'd see the day when Sinteverete and Pentavi were working together in order to rebuild a community for them both to live in. You were able to achieve what your father and I could not. You unified the clans and beat the Elders. My dear daughter, born of fire and ice." Layluna beamed with pride so brightly Mina thought she could feel the warmth.

"I helped finish what you two started, but I haven't beaten anyone yet. There are still three Pentavi Elders out there hoping to escape punishment, but I will find them. And when I do, we'll execute them alongside the Master Elder, and place all their heads in that trophy stone." Mina proclaimed, looking at the large slab of rare, white Pentavi granite that rose naturally out of the ground, not two hundred yards away. It was where Vasser and Layluna first placed the three heads of the Pentavi Elders, and now it contained eleven. The same simple rune Vasser and Layluna had carved into its surface all those years ago was still there, reminding them of their mission.

Layluna hugged Mina, "There is no path more worthy than revenge. Have your life, love your people, but never forget. Forgiveness is for the clans, execution is for the Elders."

"I knew an old samurai once who would agree with you completely," Mina said, fondly remembering her old friend and teacher.

"And Mayax?" Layluna probed further.

Mina smiled, "I've really missed having you to talk to, mother. We have so much to catch up on, and so much more life ahead of us. Eternity, if we're smart."

"I've missed you too, bunny. Now, stop dodging the question," Layluna said, chuckling.

A sigh escaped Mina. "I have strong feelings for him. Do I love him? I haven't known him long enough."

"You've known him for over a hundred years." Layluna pointed out before snickering and letting her off the hook. "But, you've only known his heart briefly. I get it. It was so easy for your father and I. My first mate, Maysiff..." A tear threatened at the edge of her eye as she remembered her. "She was the first one to give Vasser a chance and trust him; she helped remove my doubt and gave me the strength to love him."

"You've told me everything about Maysiff and your relationship, but you never told me that. That's lovely." Mina was touched.

"Take your time with Mayax; you deserve to savor it. He reminds me so much of your father it's uncanny." Layluna said, lovingly. "Your being drawn to him is no surprise. I guess the apple truly does not fall far from the tree, as the humans say."

"He reminds me of father as well." Mina admitted. "Strong, relentless, focused...accidentally funny." They both shared a laugh at that. "I was so fortunate to grow up with you two. You both prepared me for everything; made me strong, relentless, and focused. I'm funny on purpose, though." Mina reminded her mother, while conjuring a Havana cigar between her lips. "As mornings go, we could do a lot worse," she said, looking out at the beautiful landscape, and their two men sweating and working hard to provide.

Layluna looked scornfully at Mina and the cigar. "Um, were you going to offer me one?"

"Oh. Of course, I'm sorry." Mina conjured another one into her hand and passed it to her mother. When she was ready, Mina lit it with her finger. "Now tell me that doesn't treat you right."

Layluna inhaled deeply, and exhaled as though she were daydreaming. "I feel like I've been working my whole life, and I just took a break. The flavor is outstanding."

Mina nodded her head vigorously, "Riiiiiiight."

Mayax looked up and called out to them, "Careful Layluna, she got me hooked on those things too. They're magnificent, aren't they?"

"These are absolutely fantastic. I thought I was free before, but this—" she took another drag, "this is freedom." Layluna savored the cigar, lost in its warm embrace. Mayax conjured one for himself and Vasser and suggested they take a break.

Vasser smelled the Havana and nodded his approval. "The aroma is rich, and rather spicy." Mayax lit it for him and he took in a large drag, then exhaled. "Oh, my...I haven't been alive my entire life until now."

Mina smiled wide, pleased she had introduced them to something they could enjoy with her. "Oh, just be careful about where you smoke these in the Earth realm; some incredibly stupid people get pretty offended by them."

"Nonsense," Vasser declared, while taking another puff. "This is the only thing of worth the humans have ever created." Vasser was dumbfounded.

"Apparently they eventually kill humans," Mina said.

"I would die for these," Layluna admitted, as she blew on the tip to get it cherry. "I would die a thousand times," she added lovingly.

Mina wrinkled her brow as she puffed the stogie. "I'm told they can be extremely addictive, but I haven't had that experience."

"They can't kill us, so I don't see the problem," Vasser said, staring affectionately at his cigar. "I'm not even done with this one and I can't wait to have another. Is that normal?"

"It's fine. No downside," Mina reassured them.

Mina, back to her trademark T-shirt and jeans, accompanied Mayax, looking like a new man with his new duds, on a pleasant walk through the woods. "You like the clothes?" Mina asked, while checking him out.

"I love them," he bellowed enthusiastically. "I can't believe I was hauling all that heavy ass armor around for so damn long; I had no idea what I was missing." Mayax spread out his arms and legs, demonstrating the tight, form-fitting black jeans, conjured to fit just right, and a thin, burgundy, half-sleeved fashionably distressed cotton Henley shirt, four buttons to the collar, with the sleeves rolled up. "It's so comfortable."

"I wouldn't steer you wrong," Mina assured him with a wink. "Cigar?"

"Yes, please," Mayax said, but suddenly noticed something high on the ridgeline of the nearby mountain. "Hey, look there." He pointed past the tall trees to a cave hundreds of feet above on the upper rock face. "Look, it's facing the setting suns. You'll have that to see at the end of every day."

Mina seemed encouraged. "I love where your head's at. It even overlooks the valley."

"Let's go check it out," he suggested.

He began to levitate up into the air, but Mina stopped him. "I think we've done enough floating around; let's hike up there. It's not that far, for crying out loud."

"Hike?" Mayax asked, coming back down to Earth.

"Yeah, let's walk there, ya big lug." She rolled her eyes and began pulling him up the slope. "That's why I gave you the hiking boots."

Mayax looked down at his new, black, burly hiking boots. "Ahhh. I have to say, I'm loving these too."

"Okay then, let's put some miles on 'em." Mina pulled his arm again, and he finally followed her up the path.

When they arrived at the entrance, Mina marveled at how large and open it was. It was set deep within the top of the mountain, but was dry, with a nice little stream that flowed through the center. The opening may as well have been a huge picturesque window looking out onto the beautiful countryside of Val Tebrae. "This will do nicely," Mina said confidently in the fading light. The second sun was just about beneath the horizon now and night was upon them. Mina conjured a fire in the center of the floor that illuminated the cave mysteriously with warm light and dancing shadows. "Thank you for helping me find it."

Mayax put his hands on her shoulders from behind. "This cave is so you."

Mina put her right hand over Mayax's left hand. "You can stay tonight if you like," she said, conjuring a massive bed full of warm furs and soft pillows by the fire.

A warm smile crept across the barbarian's face. "I can think of no place else I'd rather spend the night." After some thought, "If I am clumsy and awkward with...*things*, I apologize. I've always been a soldier with a mission, never a lover with passions. It's all very new to me; but I am anxious to see what the future holds for us."

A warm breeze blew in and gently ruffled Mina's hair, putting it slightly in her face. "I have yet to meet a man who isn't clumsy and awkward with *everything*, so try not to worry yourself too much about that," Mina advised, while adorably blowing the hair out of her face. "Now, genuine, first-time lover's passion? Mmm, that is quite an attribute—among many—that you bring to the table, barbarian. I know you've never been in a relationship, but I've been in A LOT, so just do what I tell you and we'll be disco."

"I don't know what 'disco' is, but I have no problem deferring to your expertise on relationships." Mayax shrugged his shoulders. "Has that been a problem for you in the past?"

"Honey, you have no idea." Mina dribbled off her clothes and stood naked for a moment, letting the warm breeze caress her skin. She walked over to a good-sized collecting pool of water, down the stream a bit, and towards the back of the cave. She splashed water on herself to cool down and clean off the day's sweat.

Mayax made his way over to the pool and disrobed, showing his multitude of new scars. "Looks like I have a lot more skin stories to tell. Glad my rank doesn't depend on how flawless I am anymore."

"Flawlessness is a farce. Besides, I think you look very handsome; I like a man with a little mileage.." Mina said, coaxing him closer with her eyes.

Mayax obliged, and kneeled next to her, before washing himself as well. They both stood and embraced, skin-to-skin, for a long moment; Mina tracing his scars with her finger.

The twin suns rose on the other side of the mountain, proffering the cave cool, dark shadow in the morning. Mina and Mayax stirred with the sound of chirping birds and held each other, reveling in the moment. Mayax pointed to the far side of the cave. "You can put your coffee machine right there. You won't even need a humidor for your cigars; you can store them in the far back rear of the cave. It's perfect."

"You get me," she said. "In the meantime..." She conjured them both a cigar and a nice cup of Joe.

"And you get me," Mayax said, chuckling. "Black, just the way I like it. Look at you."

She winked. "Sooooo, Mayax, I know we're getting all whatever about each other, even though I'm fresh on the heels of a failed engagement, but I was wondering if you'd mind if I..." sighing, "took Avery to prom."

"That kid is something else. He risked his life for you, and has just as much heart as any of us. Also, if I hadn't heard him talk for like an hour straight about prom, I would have no idea what prom even was. However, since I'm in the know, I have absolutely no problem with it as long as you kids are home by one - and there is no alcohol."

"Pffffffft," Mina huffed. "That's such bullshit."

"No compromises here, young lady."

"Oh, you're hilarious," Mina lamented. "I'm going to need a very big glass of wine before I even think about stepping one foot on a dance floor in front of a bunch of teenagers."

"I think I would be more afraid of that than the shit we just went through. I don't envy you, my beauty." Mayax was completely serious.

Hugging him tight, Mina gave him a little kiss on the cheek, "I appreciate your being so cool about it. I really like the kid; besides, I promised him I'd take him since he found out his girlfriend was a cheatin' hoe."

"I'm actually quite fond of the kid as well," Mayax admitted. "Real swagger. He thanked me for saving his life, then told me to watch my step with you in the same breath. Priceless."

"Yeah, he's a sweet kid," she said, nuzzling into his shoulder. "—Oh fuck," Mina proclaimed loudly.

"What?" Mayax asked, ready for anything.

"I forgot to un-wipe his family's memories. Christ, it's been three days." Mina jumped up, conjured herself washed and dressed, and dialed her age down to 19. "Tell my folks I'll be back later."

"No alcohol," Mayax joked.

In the bright light of morning, Mina teleported to Avery's backyard and began assessing the situation. Fortunately, the house was still standing after the epic battle from a couple of nights ago, but it looked abandoned; much like the rest of the neighborhood. "Where did you go, kid?" Mina let herself in through the back door and into the kitchen. She began looking around for signs of life, but found no one there. Upon searching, she came across a very obvious note in the living room that simply had an address on it. "That's my boy." Mina fished out her iPhone and plugged the address into her GPS, then used it to teleport right to the spot.

It was some run-down log cabin in the woods, on top of a mountain in rural Pennsylvania, but it was in the middle of nowhere and safe. Without warning, the front door flew open and there was Avery's dad with a shotgun pointed at her. "Where did you come from, little missy."

"Hey, I'm Mina, a friend of Avery's. He, uh...told me to meet him here because of...all the trouble in Jersey." Mina improvised pretty well, but kicked herself—AGAIN—for not thinking of having a better story ready. Next time, she promised herself.

"You mean that kid that keeps insisting I'm his dad and that he was sent from the future to help us survive armageddon? *That* Avery?" His dad racked a shell into the shotgun as emphasis.

"Yeeeeaaaahhhh, that kid." Mina said sheepishly. "He uh...here?"

Avery came flying out of the cabin, "Dad. Hey, that's Mina. Stand down, stand down."

Avery's dad lowered his gun, seeming to give them all the benefit of the doubt. "I don't know about future sons, or whatever, but he was right about all the shit going down in our town. I figured, better to err on the side of safety. You from the future, too?"

Mina snickered, "Noooooo, no, but the kid is def on the level. May I come inside? I can help fill in a lot of the gaps, and I promise I'm not hiding any weapons in these capris." She offered a sweet, funny little smile.

Avery's dad considered it for a minute, before finally relenting. "Sure, why not. I've had to suspend a lot of my common beliefs over the last three days, anyway. I'll warn you tho, any funny business and I start shootin'."

"Fair 'nuff.'" Mina offered. "I have irrefutable proof that will clear everything up if you can give me two minutes."

"Alright, fuck it. This I gotta see. Come on in. My names Chuck, but you can call me Mr. Burlington."

"Thanks, Mr. Burlington. I really appreciate it."

Once inside, Mina searched the room eagerly for the rest of Avery's family. Mom was there, but looked frazzled and terrified. She held Lilly, Avery's little sister, who looked oblivious to everything. Jefferson was also there and had the exact same reaction to her this time that he did last time. Naturally, he was first to speak, "Hello there. I'm Jefferson—"

Mina curtly interrupted the twenty-something, seeing as though everyone was there, "Yeah, I know who you are." She immediately went to whisper chanting so she could wipe certain things from their memories, and restore everything else that was related to Avery.

Avery began frantically talking to her while she was trying to concentrate, "Ohmigawd, I thought you were dead and they would never remember who I was - which didn't bother me as much as it should have. But, dude, trying to convince them to come out here with me was fucking brutal. I told them I was from the future and all this other shit, but couldn't get them out the door until the shit started going down at Auri and Bee's place—"

Mina curtly interrupted him now, "Do you mind? I'm trying to unscramble their friggin' heads here."

"Oh, yeah, sure. Sorry. You're still going to take me to prom tomorrow, right?" Avery asked desperately.

Mina gave him a very annoyed look, "Yes, dammit. Frankly, I'm surprised they're still having it after everything that's happened."

"Well, *officially*, prom was canceled, but everyone took to Facebook and put together an...*Unofficial* Prom group, so we could organize one for tomorrow night at a friend's beach house, down the shore. Their parents are out of town."

"I guess this generation is full of latchkey kids," Mina observed. "Okay, they're all set; let's get them back to their kitchen in Jersey ASAP." Mina conjured a portal right there in the cabin, then put Mr. Burlington's shotgun on the kitchen counter. She grabbed him under his arms and began dragging him to the portal. "I got him; you get your mother. We have five minutes..." Avery quickly ran over, put his little sister on the dusty couch, and started dragging his mother towards the portal as well.

Once they had everyone through, and positioned at the dining room table, Mina cast one more portal in the driveway so she could drive their Suburban SUV directly into the garage. With seconds to spare, everyone started coming around as Mina entered the kitchen through the garage door. Mrs. Burlington was the first to snap out of it and zeroed in on Mina. "Well, Mina, back again I see. Just in time for breakfast, too. Dinner wasn't enough," she joked pointedly.

"Can't get enough of that home cookin'," she proclaimed melo-dramatically. "I can't stay for breakfast, though; I was just coming by to firm everything up about prom with Avery."

"I'm surprised it hasn't been canceled with everything that's been going on. Frankly, I'm not sure I want Avery fooling around out there with all the violence that's been happening."

Mina thought fast, "Well, I'm on the committee and we have arranged to relocate the dance down the shore. That should be more than far enough away from everything to be safe. That means it'll be over night though. Will that be okay?"

Avery's mother furrowed her brow. "I don't think I'm comfortable with this..."

Avery rolled his eyes." Oh, for crying out loud, mom. I'll be eighteen in a few months, we'll be fine. Everyone's going."

"Well, I just don't like the idea of you going down there, overnight, after a national crisis in OUR TOWN." Mom was getting ornery.

"Okay, okay, what if one of you came along to chaperone?" Mina suggested. Avery's mom seemed to brighten exponentially at this prospect. "There will be other chaperones, but we could always use more."

There was an almost audible pop as Avery blew his top, "WHAT? Hell no. COME ON."

Mina yanked Avery close to her and whispered in his ear, "Shut up, kid. I can zap them to sleep and we'll leave 'em in the car. Besides, you ain't getting out of here without one of them tagging along."

"Ahhhhh, gotcha." Avery whispered. "Ugh, okay, whatever; can we just get this together? I already have a suit and everything."

Mister and Mrs. Burlington talked it over for a minute amongst themselves, and finally Mrs. Burlington announced that Mr. Burlington would be accompanying them.

Mr. Burlington seemed less than thrilled about the idea of having to go with them, but knew better than to try to simultaneously take on his son and wife in a serious debate.

Avery clapped his hands together. "Sweet."

Mr. Burlington accepted his fate. "Ugh, fine. I'll tell you right now, I'm not putting up with any BS. Got it?"

Avery and Mina both nodded their heads enthusiastically and assured him together that, "Everything will be fine."

After tying up some loose ends in the Earth realm, Mina was back at Avery's house roughly eighteen hours later to pick him up for prom. His mother was visibly excited, and his father visibly wasn't. Mina had conjured herself a stunningly beautiful red dress and four-inch heels to match. Her hair was piled high, and her emerald eyes were piercing.

Mrs. Burlington herself couldn't get over how amazing she looked. "You look just beautiful, Mina. It's nice to see you all dressed up and not all...gothy."

"Thanks?" Mina replied to the backhanded compliment.

After a few awkward moments, Avery came down the stairs in his dapper suit. It was a dark, shimmery material that really complimented him, with a matching tie and cumberbund that were perfect. He also had slick, iridescent shoes that tied everything together.

"Wow, you clean up good, kid." Mina said, authentically impressed. "I mean, Avery."

Avery stopped dead in his tracks a few steps from the bottom; he was in total awe. "You...look absolutely...unbelievable."

Mina blushed a bit and looked away. "Oh, this old thing..." Mina said bashfully. "I've had it lying around forever."

"Don't be so modest, Mina. You look positively gorgeous." Mrs. Burlington fawned over the both of them like a doting mother is wont to do. "Okay, pictures. Pictures."

Jefferson slapped his younger brother on the back. "Looking good, partner. And you'll have to tell me later just how you managed to land a date like her for prom."

Avery patted his brother's back slyly. "Brother, you wouldn't believe me if I told you."

Mrs. Burlington positioned Mina and Avery for about sixteen thousand pictures before reluctantly letting them move towards the door to go. "CHUCK!" She screamed.

"What," Mr. Burlington replied from right behind her.

"Oh." She was delightfully flummoxed. "The kids are ready to go."

"Yay," he grumbled. He was wearing an old, ugly suit that barely fit, and would definitely embarrass any teenager in public.

Jefferson positioned himself between Avery and Mina, "What's your angle? You gonna drug dad or something? I think we all know there's no way in hell any of us would be seen with him in public looking like that."

The prom couple stole a look between them, then Avery said, "It'll be fine. We'll stick him in the back somewhere with a beer."

"Ummm, hmmmm. I know that prom was canceled and you guys are going down the shore to your friend's house for the 'Unofficial Prom.' I do have access to Facebook, you know. So seriously, how are you going to handle the dad factor?"

Mina, finally reaching her limit, turned and zapped Jefferson with an enchantment. "Thanks Jefferson, we will have a great time."

Jefferson fluttered his eyes, lost. "Yeah...sure. Have fun."

Avery elbowed Mina lightly in the ribs. "Good one."

"Thanks, now let's get the hell out of here."

"Totally." They threw open the door and rushed out, with Avery's dad reluctantly plodding along behind them.

Upon getting into the back seat of Mina's conjured 2022 blood-red Chevy Camaro, Avery's dad scoffed. "How the hell can you afford a car like this, little lady."

Mina sighed, "Here, let me show you—" She snapped her fingers and Avery's dad went to sleep.

"I think I love you," Avery said sincerely.

"Now look, I can't have you going and falling in love with me, okay kid. I am very fond of you, but my life is...complicated."

Avery rolled his eyes, "I know, I know. You and Mayax. He seems...nice for a caveman, but I already had the talk with him about treating you right, so..."

Mina turned her head to Avery, "That's pretty sweet of you, and if you were like...40ish, you would have a shot, but I'm over two hundred years old and looking to settle down. Besides, you have your whole life ahead of you, so take your time; don't rush into anything. You're a great looking young man with a lot to offer a girl. You'll be fine, I promise."

Avery smiled, "I know. I do appreciate you going to prom with me, though. Especially looking like that—BOOM. And driving this—BOOM." He emphasized both statements by pointing at her, then the car. "E'rbody gonna' be talkin' 'bout it."

"Especially that Kendra girl," Mina promised him. "She's going to eat her fucking heart out."

"Oh, most definitely," Avery confirmed, beaming.

Mina diligently filled Avery in on everything that had happened over the last four days during the two-hour car ride. She talked about the big battle, losing Viss Vascene, uniting the clans, killing the Elders, and jailing the Master Elder. Avery was completely blown away and speechless; even though he had only known them all for a few days, he had become a part of the team in a strange way. Auri and Bee absolutely loved him, Mayax was quite fond of him, and Rake, well Rake probably still didn't feel too bad about almost killing him.

Avery's father continued to sleep soundly, snoring loud enough that they could hear it over the radio. After a quick stop for gas and road sodas, they arrived at the shore house for the "Unofficial Prom." It had been slow going, with checkpoints and police everywhere, but they made it. Looked like about two hundred horny, raucous, and randy kids had made it as well.

Perking up, Avery began looking all around. "Oh man, this is gonna be fucking EPIC. Hey, pull right up to the front; they're supposed to have valet parking with a red carpet and everything."

"Are you fucking kidding me?" Mina was shocked, but secretly impressed. "Fucking rich kids, I swear."

"I'm not about to complain," Avery stated. "There," he shouted, pointing. "Haha, they got Richard and Stacey doing valet, classic." He was so excited, and Mina couldn't help but revel in the moment with him. I mean, how many kids get to pull up to their prom in a brand new, blood-red Camaro with a hot date like her? She was feeling very holier-than-thou, but figured she'd earned it.

Mina pulled the muscle car around, the engine thundering and the dark tinted windows promising a Hollywood reveal. "You ready, kid?"

He threw on some shades, "I've never been more ready for anything in my life. Also, I'm really glad you didn't die. Not just because of this, but because...you're my good friend."

Mina amazingly fully blushed this time. "Stop, you'll flush my cheeks."

Laughing now, "I didn't think anything could make you blush. I have arrived, ladies and gentlemen."

"Let's light this fire." Richard and Stacey came around to each side and opened their doors, then gasped in disbelief as Mina exited the hotrod, looking ten times hotter than the car itself. Now that she was 19 again, she was only six-feet-tall, but the heels gave her another four inches. "Thanks, dollface," she said to Richard, before putting a hundred-dollar bill in his top pocket and slapping it like a boss.

"Wow, thanks," Richard exclaimed.

"That's for babysitting papa here," she said in her best smoldering sexpot voice, while hooking a thumb to the backseat where Avery's father was fast asleep.

"I promise I'll take good care of him," Richard assured her. Now looking at Avery, "Dude. Legendary. Fucking legendary."

Avery saluted his buddy. "Don't make a big deal out of it."

Mina demurred, "But honey, you are a big deal." Richard and Stacey both threatened to faint on the spot, but the future Unofficial Prom King and Queen walked away and left them wanting. They sashayed up the red carpet like a couple of celebrities. Everyone on both sides of the carpet were snapping pictures, cheering, hooting and hollering as though it were opening night for some huge movie. Mina took Avery's arm at the door, and he led her inside.

"Can we get some pics?" Avery asked. There was a picture stand, with a professional photographer no less, to the left as you walked in the front door and through the entryway. The words over the apocalypse themed booth read: "Welcome to the Unofficial Prom Post Apocalypse Party."

Mina laughed, "That's appropriate. Yes, let's definitely take some pics."

As soon as the incendiary couple stepped further inside and headed for the photo stand, everyone within the sprawling grand room, including the people on the stairwell balcony above, went dead silent. Even the DJ scratched the proverbial record as he drank them in and choked on the hotness. He instantly got on the mic and gave them a shout out, "This next song is dedicated to Avery, the fucking man Burlington, and his insanely hot date. I smell a king and queen y'all.

BOOM." Then he dropped the remixed track of "Prom Song (Gone Wrong)" by Lana Del Rey.

The grand room disco floor, also decorated in a post apocalyptic theme, erupted with thunderous dancing, as Mina gave the DJ a resounding thumbs up. He blew her a kiss and saluted Avery. Mina smiled then elegantly smooched Avery right on the lips. "I love Lana Del Rey," she whispered in his ear as everyone in the grand room went completely nuts.

Avery jerked his suit collar flat and put his arm around Mina's waist like a pimp; he felt a hundred feet-tall at the moment. Playing the role to a tee, Mina grabbed his butt and gave it a firm squeeze, which blew the party up even more.

They hit the photo stand like a wrecking ball, every pose a fashion magazine cover, and walked away like "WHAT." The photographer even gave Mina his card, which she promptly tore up and threw into the air like confetti. This garnered raucous applause from the multitude of ladies standing around, waiting for drinks.

"Would you like a drink?" Avery asked politely.

"A white wine would hit the spot," she said in her best sexy woman's voice. Avery went to go fetch it, but she grabbed his arm. "Let's go together; I don't want to be away from you that long." The girls waiting for drinks melodramatically fanned themselves, swooned and grabbed their pearls.

Avery looked at them. "She deserves the best of me," and extended his arm. Mina took it tenderly and accompanied him to the party room. Everyone parted like the red sea as they walked up to the bar, no waiting.

The bartender was a very handsome guy, with bulging muscles, a tight shirt, and a suspiciously large pants bulge. He immediately stared slack-jawed at Mina, "Hey there, beautiful. What can I get you?"

Mina squinted her eyes at him. "First of all, you can get your damn eyeballs off me and then you can get *us* whatever my lover here orders for us." Mina gave the corner of Avery's mouth a million little kisses.

The bartender held up his hands in surrender. "So-rry."

Responding like a James Bond villain, "No worries, guy; if a woman this put together chooses to be with a guy like me, you know she's comparing every other man on Earth that isn't me—to me. And let's be honest...Honey?"

"There is no comparison," Mina finished for him.

"You guys win the fucking prom," the bartender relented, bowing his head.

"Too right," Avery said like it was nothing. "Now, I would love any beer you have on tap that isn't an IPA, and for the lady, I think a glass of the 1811 Chateu d'Yquem might be worthy of her."

The bartender raised his eyebrows. "You're my hero, kid."

"Quite," Avery said dismissively, before laying a dollar bill on the bar that Mina promptly conjured into a hundred-dollar bill.

As they got their drinks and walked away, Mina leaned into Avery's ear, "I would be lying if I said I wasn't absolutely enjoying every damn minute of this. You're such a slick operator."

"Don't go falling in love with me," he chided with a wink.

"And just when I thought you couldn't be any smoother..." she said laughing.

After they had their drinks, Mina suggested they hit the dance floor. "Let's get out there and show these kids how it's done," she yelled, grabbing his arm.

A look of desperation crept into Avery's eyes and he held back, "I uh, don't know how to dance, like at all. Seriously, if you electrocuted a cat sewed to a six-legged chicken, it would be less embarrassing than watching me dance."

"Have you such little faith in me, young man?" She asked in a hushed voice. "I got you." She placed her right index finger on his forehead and whisper chanted for a hot second. "There, now you can dance. And not just dance, but *fucking* dance."

"I know you told me not to fall in love with you, but if loving you is wrong, I don't wanna be right," Avery proclaimed as he grabbed her hand and led her to the dance floor.

The DJ saw them arrive and blasted the sickest hip hop jams he could muster. The two started out conservatively at first, but as the music escalated, and the beats hit their crescendo, Mina started b-girling in high heels like a fucking Don, before she dipped and got low as fuck. Avery did a kick up just as she went down and began popping and locking as though he'd been doing it his whole life.

Everyone on the dance floor quickly shrank away, forming a circle around them, and started clapping while they went at it hard. At one point, the music went old school rap, and Avery began to break dance with incredible skill. Mina broke loose like a Fly Girl and unbelievably tore shit up with her four-inch heels on. The DJ decided to try to test the dancing duo and threw on some swing dance music mixed with dubstep, his own creation, but the two hammered it with sick swing moves that no one had ever seen before. They quickly became the talk of the Unofficial Prom.

After an epic run on the dance floor, Mina and Avery took a break on the veranda so Mina could have a much needed cigar. She puffed the Havannah enthusiastically, "And that, my dear boy, is how you do an Unofficial Prom."

Avery's face hurt from smiling so much. "I really can't thank you enough for being so fucking cool about everything. I mean, not three days ago you were fighting the forces of oppression against an unstoppable army, but you still kept your word and took me to prom. Not only that, you made it the best night of my entire life. I can never repay you for that. Thank you, Mina."

"It's my pleasure, kid. Listen, I think you know me well enough by now to know that I've had just as much fun tonight as you did. Honestly, I really needed this after the fucking week I've had." Mina said sincerely. "I don't have a lot of friends and I'm honored that you're one of them. Seriously, you've been such a cool customer since day one. I mean, you didn't even really get all that boogered when you noticed me at the cafe and the shit went down. You even risked your life to come back for me and almost got yourself killed. Trust me when I say this is the least I could do. Frankly, I should be thanking you. We fucking lit this shit up like Kodak Black."

"Sho you right," Avery proclaimed. After a moment, he began to laugh, "You know...I saw Kendra and Allan in there fucking hating us so hard."

"Oh, yeah. Shit, why didn't you point her out to me, I would have really poured it on thick."

Still laughing, Avery assured her, "I think you poured it on just right. I've never seen anyone so red faced; It was like Christmas morning."

"Oh, shit, heads up. Speak of the Devil..." Mina said, drawing Avery's eyes to the french doors with her own.

Gasping, Avery stood up and prepared himself for the impending onslaught of drama about to go down. "I'm going to apologize in advance for everything that's about to happen," Avery said.

Chuckling, Mina waved him off. "Don't sweat it, kid. If I can handle fighting the forces of evil, I think I can handle a jealous 17-year-old girl. Actually, on second thought, I think I'd rather deal with the forces of evil..."

Kendra exploded out of the twin doors, looking and acting like a Real Housewife of Orange County. "Avery. What. The. Actual. Fuck? I can't believe you would hire a hooker to take you to prom. It's so desperate and in amazingly poor taste." Allan was behind her with two of his football buddies, trying to look tough and failing miserably.

Mina stood up calmly before cooly responding, "I find it interesting that you would call me a hooker with your face slathered in five inches of whore paint; and I'm sorry, but that cheap, old-ass, hand-me-down dress is begging to be retired, so why don't you upgrade to a potato sack and burry that fucking train wreck in the yard," She said, blowing a thick cloud of cigar smoke in her face. "Not to mention, last time I checked, it was you who took this magnificent, brilliant young man for granted when you banged this twerpy twat over here." Mina casually pointed out while nodding her head at Allan.

"What'd you call me, fucking cun—" Allan called out.

Avery was immediately in his face. "You finish that sentence and it's going to be you and me, right here, right now."

"Oh what, am I supposed to be scared of *you*?" He and his two buddies began guffawing like a trio of apes. "Dude, I shit bigger turds than you."

Mina turned from Kendra to Allan. "First of all, gross." Allan betrayed a look of embarrassment. "Second of all, you might want to watch your mouth around a mixed martial arts, two-time state champion. Just sayin'."

"What, this clown?" Allan slapped his buddies back, "I don't know what he's been posting on his Tinder account, but this pussy couldn't beat his own meat."

Now it was Mina's turn to laugh, "I don't know; I've seen his matches, and he's a very compelling fighter." Mina winked at Avery, letting him know he now knew kung fu.

"I went out with him for like five months and he never said *ANY-THING* to me about martial arts or some shit like that." Kendra said loudly, while pulling hair out of her face with her huge pinky nail.

"And I bet you didn't know he could dance either," Mina pointed out. This gave Kendra pause. "Yeah, that's what I figured. If you pulled your head out of your ass for two minutes and thought about someone other than yourself, you might just learn something about them."

"Who the fuck are you to judge me?" Kendra demanded.

"I am your superior in every way," Mina said factually. "If you care to test that, feel free at any time, but I wouldn't suggest it." Kendra backed off. "Better."

On the other hand, Allan got to within an inch of Avery's face. "I don't believe for one second that this little dip shit is anything other than a wimp and a loser."

Avery snickered, "Look man, you guys were fucking around behind my back, so I don't know why you're sour grapes now; other than being jealous of how hard we're crushing it tonight."

Immediately, Allan tried to sucker punch Avery, but the new kung fu king effortlessly dodged the clumsy swing and grabbed his arm. After wrenching it around, he put his hand behind Allan's shoulder and completely immobilized him. Allan was in shock and at Avery's mercy as the two jocks rushed in cavalierly. Avery shoved Allan into the first guy and had the other guy on his ass in seconds. The skirmish lasted only a few moments but garnered a large group of onlookers from behind. Avery delivered the coup de gras by putting his shades back on and snapping his fingers in Kendra's face. "Bitches hate us, cause they ain't us." Everyone in the party lost it at that point and began cheering Avery and Mina on as Allan and his toadies looked on from the ground.

Avery extended his arm, which Mina took, before thumbing her cigar butt at Kendra. "See ya when I—*see ya.*" The uber couple walked off the veranda and through the doors to thunderous applause.

Approaching 2 A.M., the DJ announced the big drawing for the Unofficial Prom Post Apocalypse Party King and Queen. However, before they could pass out the ballots, the crowd surged and forced Avery and Mina up onto the stage. "It looks like the masses have spoken, y'all." The DJ announced before placing the crowns on both their heads. "Meet the Unofficial Prom's official King and Queen. Avery Burlington, and...miss..."

Mina snatched the mic out of his hand, "Miss Mina." Then handed it back to him. Everyone cheered and clapped as the two highschool royalty bowed and gave praise to their loyal subjects.

The DJ started spinning some more tunes and instructed the two to hit the dance floor for the King and Queen dance. Avery and Mina happily obliged and descended the stage down to the dance floor. The DJ quickly changed the music to a soft romantic tune so they could slow dance for a while. After a few minutes, the DJ switched it up and put on the Tango, to which Avery and Mina made the transition to effortlessly. Mina grabbed a rose off a nearby table and they set the dance floor on fire. A few moments later, the DJ changed things up again and everyone joined them on the dance floor for some get down.

Avery and Mina made their way off the dance floor and back out onto the veranda. "Whew, I think I'm about spent," Avery admitted. "It was those last three beers. Ugh, I'm beat."

"Yeah, me too. Maybe we should call it a night, huh?" Mina took off her high heels and moaned in relief. "Oh. My. God. That is just heaven." She conjured herself another cigar as well and quickly set fire to it. "The perfect end to the perfect night, am I right?"

Avery shook his head in agreement, "Amen. So, I guess we should drive back pretty soon."

Mina scoffed, "Ugh, na; I'll conjure a portal back for us."

"Oh yeah, why didn't we portal here in the first place?" Avery asked.

"Well, because I wanted to catch you up on everything, and get us in the right mindset for the evening. I like a nice drive to decompress once in a while; Collect myself, you know?" Mina puffed her stogie and pulled out the keys to the Camaro. "'Sides, we had to roll up to this shit in style."

"Haha, Hell yeah."

Mina handed the keys over to Avery. "Here you go, kid. Consider it my graduation present. All the paperwork is in the glove box."

"Are you serious?" Avery asked, shocked. "I couldn't."

"It's not like I paid for it or anything. Consider it an apology for disrupting your life." Mina rubbed his back lovingly.

Avery smiled, "You can disrupt my life anytime you like." After a moment's consideration, he asked solemnly, "Does this mean I'll never see you again?"

Mina laughed, "No way, kid. We're practically family now. I promise I won't disappear. I mean, you're my bestie and I wouldn't do you like that." She hugged him tightly, and they embraced for a very long time. "Here," she said, conjuring a cell phone into her hand and placing it in his. "Anytime you need me, just call, and I'll be there. I promise. Actually, text, I hate talking on the phone."

"Meeee tooo," Avery joked, and they shared a laugh.

"You're going to grow up so damn cool, I can't stand it," she observed. "And I'll make sure I'm there with you. Someone's got to make sure you don't fuck your life up." Mina put her arm around his shoulder and shook him lovingly.

She went to kiss him on the cheek, but Avery turned his head at the last minute and kissed her full on the lips. "Had to get one more in before you put me in the friend zone forever."

"Smooth, kid. Smooth." She chuckled, then gave him a real, long, deep kiss right on the lips. "Now, that's one to remember, pal." They burst out laughing together.

Unexpectedly, a portal suddenly opened up right there on the veranda, and Osha and Amira came running out. Mina and Avery immediately stood up and prepared themselves for the worst. "How did you find us? What is it?" Mina demanded.

Osha was quick to respond. "Rake found you; it's your parents and Mayax...they are missing."

"What the Hell? How do you know?" Mina was hanging precariously on the edge of panic.

"We went to your parents' domicile to see if they would help us with the construction of the new training temple, but they weren't there, and we saw signs of a struggle. We went looking for Mayax at the cave to see if they were with him, but he was gone as well." Amira was holding back something, Mina could tell.

"Okay, stay calm. What aren't you telling me?" Mina remained controlled, but her eyes called for answers.

Osha spoke up, "We did find...some blood in the cave - not a substantial amount, but it was there."

"Jesus Christ, can't have one good night out. Okay, okay, Osha you stay with Avery; Amira, you come with me." Mina handed the keys to the Camaro over to Avery. "Get home right now and be careful; we have no idea what this means, and it could mean trouble. Stay watchful."

"Of course, don't worry about me. Go and be careful." Avery was clearly more worried about Mina than himself.

"Alright kid, stay tuned and take care of each other." With that said, Mina and Amira darted through the portal and closed it behind them.

The two adolescents stood there dumbfounded. "Shit, what now?" Avery asked Osha.

She looked him up and down. "Nice crown."

"Oh, thanks." Avery couldn't hide his worry. "You think they'll be alright?"

She was quick to answer, "It's not them I'm worried about; they can handle themselves. It's the other three I'm concerned for. I mean, someone would have to be pretty fucking serious to tangle with Vasser and Layluna, much less Mayax. Whatever happened, it's not good."

Shaking his head. "No rest for the weary. I guess we should head back to my house. We can hunker down there until they come back and tell us what's up." Avery looked at Osha, really looked at her for the first time since he met her. She appeared to be about 19 or 20 in age, thin, tall, about five eleven, with short cropped red hair and beautiful gray eyes. She was wearing her battle gear and looked like an elven warrior. "You, uh, may want to conjure yourself some different clothes..."

She looked down at herself. "Oh, yeah, good idea." Without hesitation, she transformed her warrior's uniform into an elegant, tight, deep blue dress with black heels. "How's this?"

Drinking her in with big eyes, "Gorgeous," Avery said dreamily.

Osha raised her right eyebrow. "You really think so?"

"Uh, yeah, I really think so." Avery turned as red as a radish.

"You're cute." Osha studied him; seeing him now for the first time since she met him. "Actually, no." He blanched. "You're far more handsome than cute."

Avery threatened to fall all over himself. "Ha, uhhh, well—thank you." He managed, hopelessly trying to keep himself together.

"Maybe you'll take me dancing sometime?" She mentioned suggestively. "Maybe tonight...?"

The cool night air seemed to envelope the two as they discovered an undeniable attraction. "I would love to dance with you - tonight." Avery was no longer charmingly befuddled. Instead, he started to embrace his confidence and swagger. He extended his hand, and she took it softly. They began to dance right there on the veranda, everyone else around them forgotten.

Allan was lurking behind the french doors to the veranda, nursing his damaged ego with booze when he caught sight of Avery and Osha slow dancing and staring deeply into each other's eyes. He shook his head in total disbelief. "This fucking guy."

Epilogue

Tension and fear permeated the air back in Val Tebrae. Mina stood in the partially constructed domicile of her parents and studied the scene like a seasoned detective. Lindria, Sistell, and Auri were with her, combing over things as if they were a CSI team. "Anything?" Mina asked the ladies.

"Nothing," they all said together.

"Fuck." Mina was doing her best not to show anyone just how disturbed she was, but it was futile. "What the fuck does this mean?"

Moving carefully through the scene, Auri was quick to comfort her dear friend. "This has to be the Pentavi Elders. This is some kind of warning or retaliation."

"Maybe," Mina conceded, "but how could the three of them even hope to kill or kidnap my parents *and* Mayax? They can easily take all comers. It just doesn't make sense."

The air was so still and quiet it was unnerving, and the silence was deafening. Lindria spoke up from a few feet away. "I have something..." They all rushed over and took a look.

"What is it?" Mina demanded.

"It looks like a rune, but it's like nothing I've ever seen before." Lindria said, while holding up a stone rune roughly the size of a fifty-cent piece, carved out of extremely rare black Pentavi granite.

"Black Pentavi granite." Mina stated matter-of-factly. "I've never even seen it before, but you can tell that's what it is from the subtle blue veins running through it. That rune, it's not Sinteverete or Pentavi. What the Hell does it mean?"

They all studied the stone intently, but it was Sistell who finally spoke. "I can't be certain, but it looks similar to a tattoo I once saw. It was only in passing, but it was at a market bazaar in one of the outer realms, back when I was freelancing as a bounty hunter. A real nasty place. It was so long ago, though, well before the last war in Reclon." Turning the stone over and over in her hand, Sistell searched her memories. "I just can't say for sure, but the symbol struck a chord."

"Considering it's the only lead we have, I say we run with it," Mina suggested, perplexed. "Seems like some sort of a calling card to me; especially because it's a symbol unknown to the clans, and is carved out the rarest Pentavi granite there is. I'm not even aware of anything, magic or otherwise, that can carve it."

"Indeed," Auri added, lost in thought. Suddenly, as if a lightbulb went off in her head, she had an idea. "Let's show it to the imp. Maybe it's some kind of connection to the Pentavi Elders."

Electricity seemed to crackle between the four of them as they came together with a plan. "I like it," Mina said. "I'm glad we haven't chopped his shitty little head off yet."

"Agreed," Lindria added.

"Let's search the cave first," Mina suggested.

The four new gumshoes arrived at the cave and searched Mina's new home diligently for clues. Aside from a small pool of blood, it didn't take them long to find another identical rune, carved from the same ultra-rare black Pentavi granite, slightly hidden. "Whoever this fucker is, they want us to find them," Mina observed with a clenched fist. "They better hope we find my parents and Mayax—alive."

Sensing Mina was holding it all together to put on a strong front for everyone, Auri pulled her best friend aside. "Don't worry, honey, we'll find them. Mayax and Vasser are immortal, and Layluna is too damn tough to die. Someone is just trying to get our attention and use them as leverage. If they do something to them, their leverage is gone."

Mina took hold of Auri's hand, "Thank you for that; that makes sense. I feel sorry for anyone foolish enough to pick a fight with me and my family, though." Mina kept her voice down, but the intensity was palpable. "I will rain unholy fucking pain down on their miserable heads in a torrential onslaught - the likes of which no one has ever seen. This will be blood-for-blood and by the gallons."

"We'll find them and make whoever is responsible pay," Auri promised her.

Lindria and Sistell joined them, with Lindria offering a few words of barbed wire comfort, "Hold on to your fury and anger, Mina. When you finally have them under your blade, it will all have been worth it. Revenge is as integral to us as the air we breathe. It is in our genetic code; it's been who we are for so long we will forever be in search of bloody retribution."

Mina hugged her trio of girl friends firmly, then lamented, "It's true. I was starting to feel something for Mayax, and having my parents back in my life was truly remarkable." Mina darkened now. "I should have known the buildup was just to tear me down. Only when I feel peace do I soon have to prepare for war."

After searching the cave, Lindria and Sistell stayed behind to continue their investigation, while Mina and Auri made their way to the makeshift stockade within the main village. Pentavi women and Sinteverete men were awkwardly working together in a multitude of tasks, trying to make the settlement look more like a home. There was, however, an underlying sense of trepidation now after the recent disappearance of their three strongest warriors. Currently, there was only one prison cell in the stockade, with one prisoner, the Master Elder.

Auri hung back as Mina approached the iron cage, squatted down and called him out. "Hey, imp. Wake up." The imp stirred on his bed of stone, his back to them. "We know you can hear us; quit fucking around."

The imp rolled over and faced them with a gaunt face and thinning hair. Absent now was the arrogant smirk, or the imperious eyes - Athan Asios had seen to that. There were no more tantrums left in him; only quit acquiescence. He was to be pitied now. "Is it finally time for my execution?"

"No such luck," Mina happily informed him. "What can you tell us about the three remaining Pentavi Elders?" Mina wasn't just probing him for answers, she was also watching him for any physical tells.

Amazingly, the imp began to smile; if the ghoulish, smarmy slit could even be called a smile. "Those three Elder cunts sure got the best of me." He was weakly giggling now. "You've no idea. You're fucking clueless." He tried to laugh, but broke down whimpering instead. "The three of them have been controlling me, the other Elders, the clans—*everything*—this whole time. Not only have they been the true governing force since day one, they knew about Mayax and used him as a means by which to control me. I have to hand it to them, their calculating and cunning hearts are bottomless. They were the ones that made the deal with Athan Asios for the Steplescar army and left me holding the bill. I knew it, but there was no recourse for me other than to try to win the war for them. What else could I do? What is it you always say? It's the bitches that'll gitches."

"Words of wisdom," Mina was shocked to say the least, but held up the two runes carved in black Pentavi granite. "What can you tell me about these?" Immediately the imp betrayed a fearful but subtle look of recognition, and Mina's acute feline senses caught it right away. "Tell me."

"I'll tell you, under one condition..." the imp wasn't smiling now, he was begging with his eyes. "Execute me. Don't make me wait and don't line me up with those rotten whores. Do it tonight, no, do it right now. No production, no ceremony, just...fucking kill me."

Mina stood straight up. "Deal. Now spill it."

The imp sat upright on the stone slab and looked her dead in the eyes, "It's no accident Layluna and Maysiff killed the first three Pentavi Elders; it was orchestrated. You see, they were trying to organize a revolt themselves. The final three Pentavi Elders were also behind..." unbelievably, tears began to well up in his eyes, "the execution of my love, Jendrell - one of your Pentavi Elders...Mayax's mother." He wept now. "I never had her executed - they did, but I was able to pull the baby from her belly, bloody and crying. The only reason they let me put him in charge of the Nevuscar was so they could lord it over me. You only got part of the story, my dear. I was the one who conspired with Jendrell to make Mayax Nevuscar to ensure his survival. Rake's bugs only knew fragments of truth and manufactured knowledge; certainly only the parts the three Shadow Elders wanted him to know."

Mina was blown away. "Shadow Elders?"

"That's right. A sinister breed you never even knew existed, but was there the whole time...like a parasite in your gut. They feed off conflict and cruelty; they are pure darkness, old as time itself. I spoke earlier of their calculating and cunning hearts, but that doesn't begin to illustrate just how vicious and malevolent they truly are. I'll put it to you this way; they're the only ones I've ever seen push Athan Asios around, if that gives you any idea. The runes you have there...That's the calling card of their most deadly, feared assassin and bounty hunter Zyberiz Olig. How did you come across them?"

"They were left after my parents and your son were abducted last night." Mina revealed, skating the knife's edge between rage and anguish.

"Well then, I can tell you this: they are still alive, but only as long as it takes Zyberiz to lead you into his web. The Shadow Elders want you for something. I know Athan Asios was consumed with obtaining your Alma; perhaps there is a connection there? Where were you last night, if not with your family or lover?"

"I was at prom." Mina stated, her mind a cacophony of thoughts. "So, you think Zyberiz was coming for me last night?"

"I know he was," the imp said with certainty. "I haven't put all the pieces of the puzzle together, and I accept that I never will, but somehow, you are always at the center of everything. The Yasmani Ro born of fire and ice." The imp put his head in his hands, "I realize I have no place to ask favors from you, but...when you find my son, and I believe you will, please let him know I cared for him a great deal."

"I believe that, but I also believe you cared for yourself more." Mina was harsh with her words and they cut him.

"You are right. I...I was a blight on the realms and my selfish needs always came first. It was rightfully my undoing. In any case, the time for reform is long past, and I wish to lie down and die now. If you don't have any other questions for me..."

Mina conjured open the cell and stood tall before the imp. "You've had this coming for a long time. My only regret is that you now want it." She unsheathed Beauty, the polished surface reflecting sunlight from the high, barred windows into the imp's eyes.

"It's beautiful..." the imp conveyed with admiration.

Mina unceremoniously chopped the imps head off without a moment's pause. "Beauty is a blade."

ABOUT AUTHOR

Justin lives in North Carolina with his beautiful wife and lovely step-daughter. He works as a CT tech during the day, but his true love is art. He is an artist and writer at heart. He enjoys bringing his characters to life and challenging his writing skills by changing genres. His beautiful wife is the one who got him into romance. He loves living in the mountains and hiking but has lived all over the country and enjoys writing about all of these various locations.

You can find out more about him and his stories on his website.

https://www.justinbourneboring.com

Also By Justin Bourne Boring

Dark Fantasy Romance Series:

A Thousand Scars for You series, book 1: Beauty is a Blade

https://books2read.com/beautyisablade

A Thousand Scars for You series, book 2: Violence & Roses

https://www.books2read.com/ViolenceRoses

A Thousand Scars for You series, book 3: A Hell of No Hearts

https://www.books2read.com/Hellofnohearts

Standalone Contemporary Romance:

Beau-laid

https://www.books2read.com/Beau-laid